FRACTURED

DL GALLIE

Rookie racecar driver Marshall Kerr had the world at his feet until one accident fractured his dreams, and his body. Forced into rehab in the middle of nowhere, he's in a downward spiral of self-destruction.

Until he meets E.

Eloise Masters is living a lie. Terrified and on the run, she guards her identity as closely as her heart. Both of which Marshall is determined to conquer.

When the past catches up with Eloise, the pieces of her soul healed by Marshall begin to fracture once more. Only this time, she's not alone. She has Marshall by her side to give her the strength she needs to face her demons head-on.

Are they strong enough to survive this collision, or will they fracture on final impact?

For Stefanie,

Marshall is yours, you claimed pole position.
Thank you for being in my life, even if you did make me cry when you
did that thing with you know who in INPOY…and make me like
Lauren

WARNING

Fractured is a spicy contemporary romance intended for adult readers. Reader discretion is advised.

Fractured contains content that may be triggering for some, including a loss. For a full list of warnings, please visit my website.

Reading the list, may contain spoilers BUT your mental health matters. If you want to discuss any of the warning, my e-mail is always open, dana@dlgallieauthor.com

PROLOGUE

MARSHALL

The engine rumbles beneath me.

My heart races, threatening to burst through my chest.

Blood pumps through my veins faster, with each breath I take.

Adrenaline courses through me, causing every nerve ending in my body to come to life.

This is when I feel most alive.

This is what I was born to do.

This is what I love most in the world … until it all comes crashing down.

Leaving me broken.

My future uncertain.

From today, my life will be forever fractured.

MARSHALL

The ladies love me.

The fans adore me.

Hey, I love me, and who wouldn't?

I'm Marshall Kerr, rookie driver for Scofield Racing. My dream was to race for 777 Racing. I'd wanted to drive for 777 for as long as I can remember; Chance Daniels is my hero. I aspire to race like him. To be like him. The first time I saw him race, I knew that was what I wanted to do when I grew up. From that moment forward, I wanted to be a race car driver. With the support of my parents, my dreams have come true thanks to Linc and Scofield Racing. Their offer came in first and the offered contract was too good to turn down, so I signed with Linc and the rest is history.

Mom and Dad did everything in their power to make my dreams a reality. Keri and Ryan Kerr are my biggest supporters and my number one fans. Had I not received an offer, I'm sure they would have started a team just for me; they have that much faith in my ability to race and they love me unconditionally.

Luckily for me, and Mom and Dad's bank balance, Lincoln Scofield wanted me to race for him. With his support and guidance, I'm so close to winning that trophy in my rookie season.

With only two races to go this season, that number one spot is mine. As long as I don't fuck things up but because I'm the best racer out there, that won't happen—that trophy is mine.

I'm not being cocky—okay, well maybe I am a little—but I'm the best driver out there, my stats and multiple first-place positions back up my claims.

My life is racing. I live and breathe the racetrack and everything associated with being behind the wheel. Whenever I pull on my race suit, everything around me fades away and it's just me, my car, and my team. My team has my back and they're a major factor to my success. It might be me behind the wheel out there but without them in the garage, I would be nothing. This is a team effort and #TeamKerr is fucking amazing.

We're in Chicago for the second last race of the season and tonight I have to attend the gala that Scofield Racing hosts each year when we're in Chicago. As usual with these things, I fly solo. That way I can find a lucky lady to take home when the night ends.

With the next race in two days' time, tonight will be my last chance to get wild—code for down and dirty—before I start my prerace preparation.

I'm wearing an Armani suit and if you ask me, I look fucking incredible. I'm more of a jeans and T-shirt kinda guy but if I arrived at a function dressed casually like that, Linc would have a coronary, especially since he's hosting this one.

Stepping out of the elevator and into the foyer, I walk toward the exit and climb into the waiting car. It takes me directly to The Geraghty where tonight's gala is being held.

The car pulls up and when I climb out, I'm met with camera flashes from the waiting parasites, known as the paparazzi. They yell my name, commanding my attention. It's still so bizarre to hear people calling my name, wanting my pic or my autograph.

Ignoring the calls, I walk up the red carpet, smiling diligently and waving at the paps as I head inside. One reporter shouts, "Marshall, do you think the title will be yours?"

Looking over, I smile at her as I head in her direction to answer her question. "With only two races to go, I'm hoping so."

"That's quite a feat for a rookie," she states.

"What can I say, I have a great team behind me but it also helps that I'm the best." Winking at her, I turn and continue along the red carpet.

Back in the day, this was a paper mill but it looks nothing like that today. Inside is stunning. High ceilings. Extravagant light fixtures. Plush carpets and shiny marble flooring. High-top tables are scattered around the room and a bar is set up along the side wall. Tonight's event is a cocktail style function, not a sit-down dinner, and I thank Lincoln for that. I hate making small talk with those sitting beside me. This way, I can escape when I've had enough.

Heading straight to the bar, I order a beer and as I wait, I look around to find the lucky lady who I'll be taking back to the hotel with me later. My eyes land on my hero, Chance Daniels, and his music star wife, Darby Daniels, or DD—and we're not referring to her tits, I made the mistake of making that comment when I first met Chance. He slapped me up the side of the head and told me to 'stay away from his wife's tits, they are his and his alone' and to this day, I have never made a comment about her rack again. I have however looked because hello, tits.

With a beer in my hand, I make my way over to them. "Kerr," Chance offers in lieu of a general greeting.

"Chance," I return, offering my hand, "good to see you again." Turning to Darby, I smile. "You look gorgeous, as usual, Mrs. Daniels."

"Does that line really work on the ladies?" she teases when I lean in and kiss her on the cheek.

"Well, I learned all I know from your husband," I nonchalantly reply, shrugging my shoulders.

"I wasn't as arrogant as you are."

"You sure about that, Flyboy?" Darby questions him with raised eyebrows and a cheeky smirk for using his nickname. Chance, or 'Flyboy' was a legend on the track. It was said that Chance Daniels could fly around the track, hence his nickname.

"Touché my love, touché." He leans in and kisses her passionately.

The love radiating between these two is off the charts. I can't ever see myself settling down like Chance has but if I do, I want a woman like Darby. She's a phenomenal lady and Chance is a lucky, lucky man.

"You trying to poach my racer?" Lincoln teases as he walks over, joining us.

"I could click my fingers and your boy here would come running," Chance taunts back.

Hell yes, I think but I just laugh.

"I'd like to see you try," Linc replies. "DD, you look stunning as always."

"Thanks, Linc." A smile graces her face at his compliment. "And this is amazing. You've really outdone yourself this year."

"I can't take all the credit. The team here at The Geraghty deserve all the accolades. This year's event will be hard to beat."

"You say that every year and each year, you nail it," she reminds him.

"Thanks, DD, means a lot coming from you."

Lincoln is called away and he leaves me with Darby and Chance. It hits me that I'm standing at The Geraghty and my idol, Chance-freaking-Daniels is chatting to me like we're buddies. It's so surreal to be talking to my hero in a tux worth more than the rent on my first apartment.

"You nervous about the next race?" Chance asks, snapping me back to the present.

"Nah, it's in the bag," I cockily reply, taking a sip of my beer.

"And attitude like that is why you don't race for me. You need to pull your head in and focus."

"I'm focused," I snap, my tone high.

"There's focus, and then there's *being* focused. Once you can distinguish the two, that's when you'll be at the top of your game."

Nodding, I process his words, but right now, I'm focused on a sexy redhead in the corner behind Chance. She's been eye-fucking me, well I think it's me, the whole time I've been here chatting to the Daniels's.

"I'll keep that in mind," I reply. "It was great catching up with you both. Now, if you'll excuse me, I need another drink."

Leaving Chance and Darby, I make my way over to the woman who I'll be leaving here with tonight. Stopping in front of her, I stare into her eyes. Hers roam over my body and I give her the smile that landed me a toothpaste commercial. "Hi, I'm Marshall."

"Rayna." She offers me her hand.

Taking her hand, I bring it to my mouth and kiss her knuckles, my eyes locked on hers as I make her acquaintance. My lips linger longer than necessary, but it's long enough to seal the deal with her. She's not as gorgeous up close, but that's never stopped me before and it's not going to stop me tonight. Sure, that sounds arrogant and conceited but at the end of the day, pussy is pussy. Again, arrogant and conceited, but I'm always upfront with them. They know going in this is a one-night thing. I'm not cut out to be a one-woman-for-the-rest-of-my-life man. There's enough Marshall to be shared and I wouldn't want to deprive the ladies of the world me. It's a public service of sorts.

"Can I get you a drink, Rayna?" I emphasize her name and from the dreamy look she's giving me right now, I know she's already under my spell.

Bringing her glass to her mouth, she finishes her almost full champagne in one gulp. "I'd love one," she purrs, her voice dropping to that sexy, husky tone that reaffirms to me I've found my bedmate for the evening.

Once this shindig is over, she's definitely the one who'll be leaving with me.

Lacing my fingers with hers, I walk us toward the bar. I order her another champagne and a beer for myself. With our drinks in hand, I find us a quiet corner so we can get to know one another more, intimately. She cozies into my side, and before we've finished our drinks, I have my hand up her dress and I'm knuckles deep inside of her, fingering her in the middle of the event. When she climaxes, her moans garner the attention of those around us, Chance included. He shakes his head in disappointment and turns his attention back to his wife. That action hurts a little, because back in the day, he was in my shoes.

Removing my hand from between her thighs, she grips my wrist and brings my fingers to her mouth. She proceeds to lick her juices off, her gaze locked on me as she cleans them up. Normally that would turn me on but Chance's reaction just now, and his words from earlier, are playing over and over in my mind.

Maybe it's time I curb my wild ways and focus on winning. On winning the season and my future. When Rayna grabs my cock, squeezing and rubbing me through my dress pants THAT snaps my attention back to the now.

She's staring seductively at me, her gaze full of lust and hunger and I realize Chance is right. There IS a difference between focus and being focused, but that's for future Marshall to worry about. Current Marshall is going to focus on Rayna and bringing her unbridled pleasure.

Future Marshall will focus on winning the championship.

I'll prove to everyone, including Chance, that I'm not just a playboy. I'll prove to them all I'm a winner, on and off the racetrack.

ELOISE

Standing in our bathroom, I stare at my lingerie-clad reflection and my eyes well with tears. Not with happy tears, no, they're tears of despair and utter defeat. I don't recognize the woman staring back at me. I should be elated and living my best life but instead, I cower in corners. I live in fear, waiting for the next explosion.

I'm a shell of my former self. I live each and every day wondering what will set him off this time. Did I look at him the wrong way? Is my hair too long? Did I kiss him longer than allowed? Did I breathe too loudly?

You'd think coming from Trenton, the wrong side of town, would have made me strong. Given me the backbone I needed to survive, especially living across the tracks in Collinsville and in a mansion no less. The evil that lurked in Trenton is NOTHING compared to the hell I live in, and with now.

To everyone else, he's a saint. Revered businessman. Someone who can do no wrong, but that's so far from the truth. Duncan Montgomery is the epitome of evil, and behind closed doors I get to see just how evil, sadistic, and violent he really is. If you looked up the definition of sadistic in the dictionary, there would be an image of his smarmy, smiling face.

The day I met Duncan, I thought all my Christmases had come at once. That finally, I was going to get my happily ever after. Up until that point, my life hadn't been easy. We were poor, poorest of the poor. Mom, Dad, and I lived in a tiny apartment that reeked of mold, stale beer, and cigarette smoke. The paint was peeling. The carpet worn down to the plywood beneath. The water ran brown when you first turned the faucet on and if someone flushed while you were in the shower, the water temperature changed. My Dad died just before I turned sixteen and then Mom ran off with the first asshole who offered her money and freedom. That left me on my own, fending for myself but I survived…just.

Then I met Duncan.

Finally, life was looking up. And for a little while it was. For the first few months with Duncan, it was all sunshine and roses but as soon as he slid that ring on my left hand, his mask slipped, and before my eyes he slowly changed into the monster I now live with.

Behind closed doors, I get to see the real Duncan Montgomery and let me tell you, he's the asshole of all assholes. The sickest of the sick and twisted. His charming smile and three-piece suits fool everyone, me included. However, now that I'm living with him—no, now that I'm his live-in prisoner—I have front-row seats and get to see his vicious side each and every day, up close and personal.

My only reprieve is when he goes to work.

Those few hours he's not here are my salvation. They allow me to put myself back together and regroup for when he returns. To heal the fractures in my soul, and sometimes my body too.

Some days he's gone for hours, others it feels like only minutes. Those are the days that are the hardest because I haven't had time to mentally prepare for what's to come.

To those on the outside I'm the luckiest girl in the world. To them, Duncan is my knight in shining Armani, who swooped in and rescued the girl from the wrong side of the tracks. But in reality, he's the devil incarnate, disguised as a gentleman. Turns out, I'm nothing more than his prisoner.

I'd give it all back in a heartbeat if it meant I could be free, but as he always reminds me, "Eloise, I will always find you. You are mine, now and forever." That phrase 'now and forever' should be associated with love and eternal happiness but coming from him it's a life sentence … in hell.

Fairy tales are full of shit, no one gets a happily ever after … especially not the girl from the wrong side of the tracks.

A door down the hall slams with a bang, causing me to jump in fright. Today is one of the days where nothing I say or do is the right thing.

Silence is the wrong answer.

SLAP

Words are the wrong answer.

SLAP

Breathing is the wrong thing to do.

SLAP

Everything I do today is wrong. Wrong. Wrong.

SLAP

SLAP

SLAP

When he left for work, he was in a mood and when he returned, his mood had soured further. The monster of all monsters was in place. I haven't seen him like this in a few weeks, so I knew it was coming, but today, it's different. He's different. He didn't hold back with the hits. How I didn't lose consciousness is beyond me. I'm currently sporting a black eye, a bump on the back of my head and bruised ribs. I'm pretty sure he cracked one but I can't go to the doctor because they'll ask questions. So like usual, I tend to my injuries myself. He usually avoids my face as a beat-up face arouses suspicion, but today he didn't give a damn.

Looking over my body I see bruise upon bruise upon bruise. My skin is a constant kaleidoscope of purples, greens, and yellows. The first tear falls and I collapse to the floor. I don't have the strength to hold it in, today was the worst it's ever been.

I cry for the girl I used to be.

I cry for the girl I want to be.

I cry because that's all I can do. I'm too weak to leave because I know, as he promises, he will find me. And that's a lashing I never want to be on the receiving end of. It's safer to stay, so I do.

I take the hits.

I put on a fake smile and I play the doting fiancée.

Falling for Duncan was meant to be my get-out-of-jail-free card but instead, it opened the door and condemned me to hell.

The door to our bathroom flies open. He stands in the doorway, leering at my crumpled form on the tiles. Lifting my gaze to his, he stares down at me menacingly. "Why do you make me do this to you, Eloise? If you just behaved, I wouldn't have to punish you." He pauses. "We have the Robinson-Bailey fundraiser this evening, make sure this," he circles his finger around my face, "is hidden. You don't want me to get angry again, do you?"

Shaking my head, I swallow. "I'll be ready." My voice wavers and I hate that my fear is showing. He nods and turns on his heel, leaving me alone to get ready. Taking a deep breath, I stand up and do my makeup. I've become a pro at covering the bruises and tonight is no different.

Curling my hair, my dark locks hang over my shoulders. They are my curtain to hide behind, but they are also my downfall. My long locks are easy for him to grab; how he hasn't pulled every follicle on my head out surprises me.

Stepping into the bedroom, I see he's picked out a navy, one-shoulder, figure-hugging dress. Slipping it over my head, the silky material slides down my body. It fits me like a glove. Walking over to the dresser, I grab my diamond studs and put them on. No necklace is needed due to the neckline. I pick up my engagement ring and stare down at the jewel. It's big. It's gaudy. It's not my dream ring at all, but Duncan needs the biggest of everything. Hence the monstrosity of a house that we call home and the gigantic rock that sits on my finger.

His voice from behind startles me. "You really are a vision," he declares, his tone soft and nice, the complete opposite of how he was earlier. Jekyll and Hyde could learn a thing or three from Duncan.

Forcing a smile, I turn to face him. "And you look pretty good yourself, Mr. Montgomery." He really is a handsome man, it's a shame he's rotten to his core.

He steps over to me and cups my cheek. "I can't wait to fuck you when we get home."

My heart begins to race at his words, because he'll get drunk tonight, and when we get home he'll be rough. Forcing himself on me in ways that a man who loves a woman never would.

His hand rests on my hip and a sinister look appears in his eyes. The hairs on my neck stand on end. I don't like it. "Remove your panties, Eloise. I need you bare so if I want to fuck you while we're there, I can without anything in my way." *Not that it matters*, I internally mumble to myself. He slides his hand between my legs and cups my mound, "this is mine and I can do what I want with it whenever and wherever I want."

"We can't do that at the fundraiser, it's too public." As soon as the words leave my mouth, I know I've made a mistake.

"As I just said, I will fuck you whenever and wherever I want. Now, remove your fucking panties, Eloise. Don't make me ask you again." He stares down at me. "Now," he growls through clenched teeth, spittle forming at the edge of his mouth.

I'm shocked at his words, and clearly I don't move fast enough because he grabs me roughly by the throat, walks me back toward the bed, and throws me onto the mattress. He pushes my dress up my thighs and tears my panties off me. The material burning my skin before snapping and disintegrating in his fingers. He throws them in my face. "That wasn't so hard now, was it?"

Shaking my head, I swallow deeply and wait.

I wait for the slap.

And I wait.

It doesn't come, instead he stares down at me and fear begins to build when he flips open the button on his slacks, lowers the fly, and pulls out his cock. He drags me to the edge of the bed and pushes me down to my knees. He shoves his cock between my lips and begins to thrust his hips back and forth. Luckily for me, his dick is small, it barely reaches the back of my throat. Sooner than is acceptable for a grown man, he comes. He pulls his cock out and redresses himself. I wipe at the corner of my lips, thankful for lipstick that doesn't smudge. He cups my cheek and stares down at me. "Such a good little cocksucker. We leave in ten."

He spins around and leaves me on my knees. My eyes welling with tears again. Taking a deep breath, I compose myself, willing the tears not to fall. Feeling defiant, I walk into our closet and slip on a new pair of panties. I know it's a mistake, but I'm pushing him in the hopes that he'll just kill me. Death would be a holiday.

Looking in the mirror, I fix up my hair and step back into the room. Grabbing my clutch, I head downstairs to meet him.

"Miss Masters, you look beautiful," Miles, our driver, voices as I walk across the foyer toward the exit.

"Thank you, Miles."

"Shall we?" I say to Duncan with a sweet smile. He nods and silently the three of us walk to the car.

Miles pulls out of the driveway and we make the twenty-minute trip to the Robinson-Bailey estate. Miles opens my door and helps me out. From behind, I hear a growl. When he stands he leans down and hisses, "I told you no fucking panties, you'll pay for that."

Looking up at him, I hesitantly smile. "I thought it would be fun to discreetly remove them in front of everyone during dinner."

His eyes widen and a sinister grin appears on his face. "You're such a whore." I exhale with relief that my defiance has paid off, but there's a huge part of me that's disappointed I didn't piss him off enough for him to end me.

Linking my arm with his, I smile. "Shall we?"

He nods and we start walking inside.

My moment of peace is interrupted when he stops abruptly. Gripping my upper arms roughly, he spins me to face him. Leaning forward, he menacingly whispers, "You *will* pay for this, I make the rules. Remember that."

Swallowing deeply, I nod. He knows I won't react. He knows I won't make a scene because I never do. Even if internally I'm kneeing him in the balls so I can make my escape.

He slides his hand down my arm and squeezes my wrist. To anyone watching, it's a possessive, loving gesture but little do they know, his grip is like a boa constrictor, crushing the life out of its prey. I whimper and bite my tongue, knowing anything I say right now will antagonize him further.

Taking my hand in his, he pulls—well, drags—me toward the party as if he didn't just threaten me. We climb the stairs and at the entrance, we're met by the hosts, Fleur and Arnold Robinson-Bailey.

"Duncan. Eloise," Fleur greets us, her voice faker than her face. "So glad you could both make it." She smiles sweetly at Duncan but sends daggers my way. She's just as vapid as Duncan, but she's not as good at hiding her secrets as Duncan is.

"We wouldn't miss it," Duncan croons, kissing her on the cheek and shaking Arnold's hand. I awkwardly stand at Duncan's side and silently watch the three of them.

"That's very kind of you." She eyes my ring finger and smiles at us both. "So, when's the big day?"

Nonchalantly I shrug and internally I shout *never*. Duncan pulls me into his side and places a loving kiss on my temple. "This summer," he tells them. My eyes widen at this revelation because as soon as I officially become Mrs. Duncan Montgomery, I'll be trapped forever with no chance of escape.

"That's wonderful news," Fleur singsongs but her tone is anything but happy to hear the news.

"Thank you," I quietly reply.

Someone yells my name and when I turn my head, I see Faith, Arnold and Fleur's daughter. "Excuse me," I tell them and walk over to her. "Hi, Faith."

"Thank God someone my age is here," she admits. "Let's get a drink and you can tell me all about life with the stud who is Duncan Montgomery."

"You don't want to hear about my boring life."

"Please, he is, well was, the most eligible bachelor until you snagged him. Mother dearest was pissed when she heard about the engagement but she's holding out hopes that two aren't hitched yet, it'll all fall apart. Then she can hook he and I up." My eyes widen at her response and it explains the daggers from her mother just now. She leans into me and whispers, "Truthfully, I was relieved. He seems like such a stick in the mud."

"He's…" but I don't know how to answer that, "he's Duncan." I offer her with a smile that I hope looks sincere.

"I bet he's wild in the sack."

"Wild is one way to put it." *If only you knew how wild.*

"I knew it," she screeches.

"Knew what?" Duncan asks, joining us.

Her eyes widen at being caught but I save her from embarrassment. "Knew you were a complete sweetheart. Shall we get a drink?"

"Sure," he agrees, and I can tell he doesn't believe me. *That's strike two for tonight,* I think as I stare at my captor.

"It was great to see you again, Faith." Smiling at her, I take Duncan's hand and lead him toward the bar.

The evening drags by and as I predicted, Duncan gets drunk.

Tonight's drink of choice is scotch and when he drinks scotch, he becomes handsy and after feeling up the waitress for the millionth time, I manage to convince him to take me home.

As soon as we're seated in the car, he raises the partition. Miles looks in the rearview mirror and smiles sadly at me, he knows what's coming. Before we've even pulled onto the street, Duncan has me on my back and he's viciously fucking me. I'm drier than the Sahara Desert. It burns and I scream at the pain. My screams of pain, and not pleasure, piss him off. He begins to beat me as he fucks me.

His hands wrap around my throat, cutting off my airway. I scratch at his hands but he doesn't release his grip. I'm on the verge of losing consciousness when he comes with a guttural roar.

Once he comes, he loosens his grip on my neck, rolls off me, and promptly passes out.

Curling myself into a ball, I lay next to my passed-out monster of a fiancé and begin to cry. If I thought the beating slash fucking just now was bad, I was sorely mistaken. He shows me just how vicious he really is when I tell him some unexpected news in the coming weeks.

MARSHALL

Ever since the other night at The Geraghty, Chance's words keep playing over and over in my head. *"There's focus, and then there's being focused. Once you can distinguish the two, that's when you will be at the top of your game."* I should be focused on the race I'm about to begin but I'm not. Chance is correct, I'm not *focused*. If I'm going to continue to win, I need to BE focused.

Grayson Walker, one of my best friends and our lead race engineer, walks over. He taps me on the shoulder and nods to the other end of the garage. Turning my head, I see Saxon Nobel, our other best friend, casually leaning against the wall. His ankles crossed and his hands in his pockets. A smile graces my face, I didn't think he'd make it to Chicago. He recently left for Australia on a gap year—long story short, his parents are assholes and he wanted to get away so he went to the other side of the world to get away from them. The fact he's here in Chicago means a lot to me, especially since Australia is a billion-hour flight from here.

Grayson, Saxon, and I have been friends since we were kids. They're both older than me but the three of us gelled the first time we met. Unofficially we became the three amigos. There's not a story from my childhood that doesn't involve one, or both, of them.

They're my brothers from another mother.

My ride or die.

"You've got this," Saxon declares, pulling me in for a one-arm bro hug.

"Thanks, man. Glad you could make it. Means the world that you're here," I honestly tell him.

"Dude, I wouldn't be anywhere else. I needed to be here in the flesh for when you win the trophy in your rookie year. Did I not tell you this was gonna happen before I left for Oz?"

"You did, but I thought you were just full of shit. But seriously, I appreciate it, man, I really do but there's still a race to go after this one."

"Yes, but when you win this one, as long as you don't fuck up the last one, you're the season champion," Saxon states matter-of-factly.

"Let's hope you're right." One of the mechanics calls me over. It's GO time. "We'll catch up for drinks after the race."

"Sounds good." He fist bumps me and exits the garage, giving me a thumbs-up as he turns the corner and heads up to hang with Mom and Dad in the team box.

"Let's do this." Grayson slaps me on the back and we walk over to my car.

Like always, I run my hand over the shiny green exterior and before I climb in, I say an internal prayer. Grayson helps me buckle up and once I'm strapped in, he taps my helmet twice— our prerace ritual—and then walks over to the monitors, joining Linc and the rest of the team.

The team rolls me into the pole position, gripping the wheel, I stare down the straight but my mind keeps drifting to the other night and what Chance said about focus. I *should* be focusing on the race ahead, but instead I'm obsessing over my idol's words.

"Pull your head in, Kerr," I berate myself. I need to focus on this race and not Chance's words.

"Marshall," Linc shouts, his booming voice echoes through my headset, grabbing my attention and bringing my focus back to the task at hand, winning.

"What?" I snap.

"Get your head in the race," he growls.

Taking a deep breath, I nod and chant, "I've got this. We've got this."

"Don't go getting cocky," Linc utters, but I can totally tell he has a smirk on his face.

"Not cocky," I inform him, "confident. Confident that I'm gonna win today."

He laughs. "All right, Cocky McCockerson, get your head in the race so you *can* win this thing."

Now it's my turn to laugh.

Closing my eyes, I take a deep breath.

Everything around me fades away.

It's just me and my green machine on the track … finally my head is in the race. Opening my eyes again, I can hear the crowd cheering. Their cheers and excitement heighten the energy around me. My body buzzes the closer we get to the start of the race. The noise is deafening. The excitement and cheers increasing with each ticking second to the start of the race.

My excitement and adrenalin peak causing my heart to beat faster. Blood pumps furiously around my system, much like the fuel combusting in my car's engine.

"It's go time," Linc declares. "Good luck."

Gripping the wheel tightly, I inhale deeply and slowly let it out. My eyes locked and focused on the light panel ahead.

Four

Three

Two

One

Go.

Pushing my foot down, the car propels off the starting line and I speed down the straight and into the first corner. Everything around me fades away and it's just me and the track.

I'm in my happy place.

Lincoln speaks, telling me what I need to know, what's happening behind me and most importantly, what's up ahead.

Lap after lap, I maintain the lead.

Each pit stop is flawless because I have the best team and that's why I'm at the top of the leaderboard.

Pulling away from the team after the final pit stop, I'm stuck behind my rival, Marcus Randall. On the track, Marcus and I are fierce nemeses and off the track, we're fierce nemeses. Put it this way, if either one of us were on fire, neither one of us would piss on the other to help.

We both enter the track and he misses a gear. "Eat shit asshole," I mutter as I take the opportunity and I pull around him, taking the lead.

We're neck and neck for the final few laps.

"He's getting antsy," Linc vents, his tone laced with concern and worry about Marcus and his erratic driving. "Be careful, I don't trust that son of a bitch."

"I won't let him get past me. This race is mine."

We're on the final lap and I'm in the lead. Marcus tries to take me on the second to last corner and then all hell breaks loose. His wheel tags the edge of the track and he spins out. His back end clips my car and it sends me flying.

One minute I'm on the track. The next my car is flipping through the air.

Whereas Marcus's car crashes into the tire wall, my car becomes airborne and repeatedly flips, nose over tail, before I eventually land upright in the middle of the track.

I'm sitting here stunned when the sound of metal crunching against metal rips through my ears and I'm once again spinning.

The last thing I remember before darkness engulfs me is a searing pain tearing through my abdomen and lower body.

MARSHALL

An incessant beeping grates through my brain.

Everything hurts.

Never have I felt pain like this before. I groan and try to open my eyes but I can't, they're heavy and each time I open them, they drop shut again. Finally, they stay open. I blink a few times and the room comes into focus, I'm in a hospital bed. The annoying beeping comes from one of the many monitors beside me.

Turning my head to the side, Mom and Dad are standing in the corner with Lincoln. There's a dude in a white coat, I presume he's my doctor. They're softly speaking to each other and that's not a good sign.

"You're awake, Sleeping Beauty," Grayson playfully teases from the doorway.

All eyes turn to face me and when Mom sees me, she races over to my side. "Baby," Mom cries. She leans down and kisses my forehead. Pulling back, she takes my hand in hers and holds it tightly in her grasp. Her perfume permeates the air around me and I smile. Mom has worn True Love by Elizabeth Arden for as long as I can remember. "How are you? Are you in pain? Can I get you anything?" She rapid-fires the questions at me.

"Water," I croak out, my mouth and throat are drier than the Sahara Desert.

Mom fills a cup, pops in a straw, and holds it to my lips. I drink and the cool liquid feels like heaven on my throat.

All too soon, Mom pulls the cup away. "Not too much, you'll make yourself sick." Placing the cup down, she runs her hand across my forehead in her mom way, it's oddly soothing. "Now, how do you feel? Are you in pain? What else can I get you?"

I think about the first one, how do I feel? "I'm sore," I tell her, then I ask, "Wwwww … what happened?"

"What do you remember?" Mom asks, the usual protocol for a head injury. We've been in this scenario a few times over the years, but this time feels different.

I think back to the last thing I remember. "We were on the final lap. Marcus, the dick, tried to take me on a corner. He hit the gravel and clipped me. I went flying. Then there's nothing until I woke up." I pause. "How long have I been out?"

"Honey, you've been out for four days."

"Four days!" I shout. The sound of my voice pierces my brain and I squint. I try to sit up but a searing pain radiates through my lower half. I groan in agony. "Why does everything hurt?"

The doctor walks over to my bed. "Marshall, I'm Dr. Flynn Kelly. I treated you when you first arrived at Western General. You were unconscious, you lost a lot of blood and your hip—"

"My hip what?" I snarl at the doctor, but from the pain I'm feeling right now, I know the words he's about to utter will be shit.

"It was shattered in the accident. Our first priority was to stop the internal bleeding. You coded in surgery. We repaired the blood vessels in your abdomen and had to remove your spleen. You've had the first surgery to repair your pelvis. You currently have a frame that's holding pins in place within your pelvis. In the next surgery, we'll insert plates to hold everything together internally. This will be performed in the next five to ten days to allow healing of your internal organs first."

"Okay, so when can I race again?" That doesn't sound too bad. A few surgeries, physical therapy, and then I'll be back in my car and racing again.

"Recovery varies from person to person, so I can't give you an exact time frame, but if you follow the rehabilitation regime, I have faith you'll be back in the car mid-season next year."

"Doc, that's too long. I need to be up and running by the start of next season."

"Marshall," Lincoln interrupts, "don't worry about racing. Worry about getting back on your feet."

"I need to race!" I yell.

"Marshall Kerr," Mom scolds, "watch your tone. I know you're hurting right now, but Dr. Kelly and Lincoln are doing their best."

"They need to do better," I snap, glaring at the doctor. Crossing my arms in anger, I huff like a petulant child. Wincing in pain from pressing on my abdomen. It's still tender from the spleen removal and surgery.

"Marshall," Dad warns, his tone meaning business.

Dr. Kelly chuckles. "What the fuck you laughing at?" I spit at the good doctor.

"Marshall," Mom admonishes me again.

"It's fine, Mrs. Kerr." He turns his attention back to me. "One of my twins is named Marshall and your attitude right now, reminds me of him when he can't play with his favorite toy. That's why I know, you'll be back in your car before you know it. Just listen to those around you and more importantly, your body."

I roll my eyes at the doctor. Racing is everything to me. It's my life. It's in my blood. I don't know how not to race, and this feeling of the unknown for my future is hard to wrap my head around. "I want to be alone," I growl.

"Marshall," Mom placates in that soothing mom tone, but right now it's anything but soothing and reassuring.

"Now!" I bellow. I know I'm being an ass, but I just want to be alone. Turning my head, I look out the window and ignore everyone, hoping they'll get the hint and piss the fuck off.

Outside the sky is gray. Rain is pouring from the dark clouds above. It's a dreary and dismal day, mirroring exactly how I feel in this moment.

Closing my eyes, I swallow down the lump in the back of my throat. My career is over in my first year, thanks to Marcus-fuck-ing-Randall. The thought of his name causes my eyes to fly open and I turn my head toward Linc. "Is Marcus okay?"

"He's fine," he replies, but I can tell there's more. I try to remember what else happened and that's when I remember a third car.

"There was another car," I whisper. "There was another car," I say louder.

He nods. "Joe Johnstone. He collided with you head-on after you landed back on the track." He pauses and rubs at the back of his neck. "He umm, ahh, he, Joe didn't make it."

"Fuck," I mumble. "Was anyone else hurt?"

"No, it was just the three of you." Nodding, I take in his words. Joe is dead and then he adds, "Since there was only one race left, they decided to end the season early. You're officially the champion."

That was my dream, to take the number one spot in my rookie year. I achieved it but now that it's actually happened, it's not so exciting. I'm number one, a man is dead, and I may never race again.

"Like that matters when a man is dead and my pelvis is shattered." The room falls silent. No one utters a word. The only sound is the relentless beeping of the machines I'm attached to. "You can all leave now. I need rest and want to be alone."

They all know I'm full of shit, but no one dares to fight me.

Mom's the first to move. She hugs me tighter and when she pulls back, her eyes are filled with unshed tears. She's thinking that I could be in Joe's position and I almost wish I was, death would be better than not being able to race again. Dad wraps his arm around her and escorts her from my room.

One by one, they all follow suit and file out. Before Linc steps into the hall, he looks back at me. "When you're ready to talk, I'm here."

Talking is the last thing I want to do right now but I nod anyway. Just before he steps out, I see pity on his face. I hate that. I don't want anyone's pity so they can all just fuck off and leave me alone.

The door closes with a click and finally, I'm alone. For the first time since I woke up, I have time to process all that's happened.

Joe is dead.

My pelvis is fucked.

I'm broken.

My career is over before it even began.

My life, much like my pelvis, is fractured but unlike my pelvis—which can be repaired with screws, plates, and pins—I'm not sure if I'll ever be whole again.

ELOISE

"Shit, shit, shit," I mumble as I calculate in my head when I last had my period. It's been far too long and going by the slight pudge of my belly, my sensitive breasts, and hating the smell of meat right now, I'm pregnant.

Rapping my fingers on my dressing table, I walk into my dream wardrobe and pull on a navy-and-white-spotted shift dress. Stepping into my ballet flats, I pull my hair up into a messy bun, grab my purse and head downstairs. I'm halfway down when I freeze at the sound of Duncan's voice coming from his office. "Shit, he's still here," I whisper.

Taking a deep breath, I continue down the stairs, and head toward his office, hesitantly knocking on the door. He looks up and frowns when he sees me. "I have an appointment that I forgot about."

"Miles will drive you," he dismissively growls, waving me away with his hand as if I'm a servant and not his fiancée.

"Okay. I'll see you later."

He doesn't reply, not that I expected him to.

Walking toward the front door, I see Miles and smile. "I have an appointment I forgot about."

"Let's go," he replies with a nod and friendly smile.

He opens the front door and we walk side by side out to the car. He opens the door for me and I climb in. My eyes drop to the floor and memories of that night come flooding back to me. I run my hand over my neck. It took weeks for the bruises on my neck to heal. I shudder at the memory and swallow down the vomit building.

Miles' voice from upfront snaps my mind away from that night, "Where to, Miss Masters?"

"Collinsville Medical, please."

"Yes, ma'am." Without another word, he starts the car, puts it into gear and heads down the long driveway. That's one of the many things I like about Miles, he doesn't ask questions or offer an opinion, even if his eyes give everything away.

The gates open and he pulls onto the main road. Resting my head back, I close my eyes. My hands automatically drift to my belly. I've always wanted to be a mom, but I really don't want to have a child with Duncan. I can handle the punches and verbal barbs from him, but a poor defenseless baby, they would have no way to protect themselves. I guess that's where I come in. I really hope my period is just late because I'm stressed but deep down I know that isn't the case, call it mother's instinct.

"We're here," Miles comments, his voice startles me and I jump in my seat. "Sorry to scare you, ma'am."

"It's fine but please, call me Eloise. Ma'am is so old-fashioned."

"I'm old-fashioned," he jokes and climbs out. He comes around to my side and opens the door for me. "I'll be here when you're finished."

"Thank you, Miles."

Looking up at the medical center, I take a deep breath and head inside.

Walking up to the counter, I see it's a girl I went to school with. I smile at her but the look she gives me in return is cold and clinical. "Welcome to Collinsville Medical, how can I help you today?"

"I was hoping I could see a doctor."

"Do you have an appointment?"

Shaking my head, I sigh. "No, it's kind of an emergency."

"And you think that because you now have money, everything will be put on hold just for you?"

"No," I refute. "I'm happy to book an appointment if you can't get me in."

"That's what you'll have to do." She looks to the computer and groans. "actually, we've just had a cancellation and there's an appointment available in fifteen minutes."

"Thank you, I'll take it."

"Take a seat and we'll call your name when it's time."

Thanking her, I turn around and as I walk away, I hear her mumble under her breath, "Bitch gets everything handed to her."

If I had brass balls, I'd spin around and tell her that it isn't all rainbows and unicorns on the other side, but I can't risk Duncan finding out that I was rude or tarnishing his shiny squeaky-clean reputation.

Instead, I take a seat and wait. Staring at the carpet, my mind drifts to a happy place where I never met *him* and I'm with a man who loves me unconditionally. I'm so lost in thoughts of my imaginary happy life that I don't hear my name being called.

Finally, I hear it and I stand up. "That's me." I smile and follow the nurse into the back.

She tells me to take a seat on the exam table. She takes my blood pressure. "It's a little elevated," she reports.

"I … I think I'm pregnant," I hesitantly utter.

This is the first time I've voiced it out loud and hearing those words pass my lips, a lump forms in the back of my throat and my eyes well with tears. How can I bring a baby into a home like this? Letting out a breath, I hope with everything I have that Aunt Flo is just late, but deep down, I know that's not the case.

"That'll do it. I'll get you to wee in this." She hands me a little cup. "The bathroom is down the hall on your left."

Nodding, I take the cup from her and make my way to the bathrooms. Stepping into the cubicle, I sit on the toilet and I'm surprised when I can pee on demand. Peeing into the cup isn't easy and I get urine all over me and the cup. I manage to wipe it and myself one-handed.

Stepping out, I wash my hands and make my way back to the room. Handing the nurse the cup. She places it on the counter and starts testing it just as the door opens and the doctor walks in.

"Eloise, I'm Dr. Jenna Miller, how can I help you today?"

"I … I think I'm pregnant," I murmur, my voice waivers on the word pregnant.

She quietly confers with the nurse and then she turns to face me. "Congrats, Ms. Masters, you are indeed pregnant."

My face pales. My eyes well with tears and I cover my mouth to hold back a sob, but I can't. I burst into tears and blubber like a baby. Covering my face, I have a mini breakdown in the doctor's office.

Composing myself, I look to the doctor and I notice she's looking at me with concern. "I take it this is unexpected?" Her tone is endearing and caring.

"Very," I confirm.

"How about we take a look?" She hands me a gown and a blanket. "I'll get you to slip this on, then climb up and lie back. Cover your lower half with the blanket while I go grab the sonogram machine."

She pulls a curtain behind her and leaves me alone to change into the paper gown. Hopping up onto the bed, I cover my legs with the blanket and lie back, waiting for the doctor to return. The silence is deafening but the doctor soon returns, "Are you ready?"

"Not really," I answer when she pulls the curtain back. She wheels the machine over. It's silent, except for the sounds of the buttons she's pressing to get the machine set up.

Lifting my gown, her eyes widen and I look down. The blanket has fallen, the bruises on my upper and inner thighs. Her eyes widen farther when she sees the remnants of a bruise on the right side of my abdomen.

"Paintball war wounds," I offer in explanation, but we both know I'm lying. The bruises on my thighs are clearly finger marks and look nothing like a paintball pellet injury.

Nodding, she picks up a blue gel, "This will be cold," she informs me. She squeezes the gel onto my belly and explains a few things. "Depending on how far along you are, I might need to do an internal exam if I cannot see anything this way." Grabbing the wand, she squeezes a little more gel onto the tip and then she places it on my stomach. She moves it around and then the silence is broken by the most magical sound.

BADUNK BADUNK BADUNK

"It sounds like galloping horses," I whisper. "Should it be that fast?"

"That's perfectly fine. Babies' heartbeats are faster than ours." She clicks a few buttons and then looks back at me. "From the measurements, you're around sixteen weeks along."

"What?" I screech. "Sixteen weeks, are you sure? That's four months." I stare at the doctor in shock.

She nods. "Give or take a few days."

Turning my head to the screen, my eyes widen when I see an image of a baby. I was expecting it to be like the movies and it just to be black-and-white speck, but before my eyes is a teeny tiny baby.

"My baby," I whisper, reaching out, I touch the screen.

Looking back at the doctor, I mumble the one statement I never thought I'd ever utter to a doctor. "I'd like to schedule a termination."

"I'm sorry, Ms. Masters, you're in your second trimester. Unless it's for medical reasons, that time has passed."

My eyes well with tears. "But I … I can't have this baby."

"Ms. Masters, are you in an abusive relationship?"

Shaking my head from side to side, I look to her. "No, I'm not. I'm just shocked to be pregnant. It'll all be fine. Nothing to worry about. Can I get dressed now?"

"Of course." She steps back from the bed and pulls the curtain closed, leaving me to get dressed. Slipping my clothes back on, I throw the gown into the trash can and pull the curtain back. The doctor points to the chair by her desk and I take a seat.

"I've gathered a few pamphlets for you. I recommend you start taking prenatal vitamins and I can recommend an obstetrician if you don't have one."

"Thank you, that would be great." I flick through the pamphlets and the last one isn't pregnancy related, it's about domestic violence. Placing the pamphlets into my bag, I ask. "Is there anything else?"

"That's everything today."

I stand up to leave when she reaches out and grips my wrist. I flinch and she immediately drops her hand. "If you need anything, please call me." She hands me her card. Taking it, I nod and slip it into my bag.

Exiting the room, I stop by reception and pay the bill. Walking outside, I look around and find Miles standing by the car, leaning against the trunk. Walking over to him, he glances up and when he sees the look on my face, he opens his arms for a hug. This is the first time anyone has willingly opened their arms for me. Openly showed me affection. The gesture overwhelms me and I break down on the sidewalk. He steps over to me and embraces me. "Shhhh, it will all be okay, Miss Masters."

Wrapping my arms around his waist, I cry into his chest. "No it won't, Miles," I blubber, "No it won't."

He pulls back and grips my upper arms. Again, I flinch. He notices and loosens his grip and gently holds on to me. I don't feel fear when he holds me, this is an affectionate embrace, something I haven't felt in a very long time, if ever come to think of it. "What can I do?"

"Just hold me," I sob.

He wraps his arms around me again and I continue to cry. This is just what I needed.

"Miss Masters, please don't think I'm being too forward, but you need to leave Mr. Montgomery, and you need to leave now."

"I can't, Miles. I have nothing."

"You have the most valuable thing growing inside of you. You need to look after them … and you."

"How did you know?"

"I may be old but I'm not a fool. If my Martha was still alive, she'd have my hide for not doing anything sooner. You need to go."

"I can't leave," I repeat, wiping at my eyes.

"Just think about it, especially now."

Nodding, we walk back to the car and he opens the door for me. Climbing in, I buckle up and like earlier, I rest my hand on my stomach. This baby is already a fighter and he, or she, hasn't even taken their first breath. I think back to the beatings from Duncan over the last four months. "You really are a miracle," I whisper.

Dropping my head back, I think about Miles' suggestion—can I leave? Am I strong enough to do that? Rubbing my belly again, I ponder what I'm going to do. I could really do with a fairy godmother right now. With a wave of her wand, bibbidi-bobbidi-boo, I'd be free and happy, but life isn't a fairy tale and I don't have a get-out-of-hell-free card. This all falls on me and now I have more than just me to worry about.

We arrive back at the house and I thank Miles and head upstairs to our bedroom. Duncan is still in his office and I hope he'll be there for the next few hours. That'll give me time to think.

Sitting on the end of our bed, I pull out the brochures the doctor gave me and start reading. I'm so engrossed in them that I don't hear him enter. It's only when he bellows, "What the fuck is this?" I realize he's here.

From the murderous look on his face, this isn't going to end well for me, or the baby.

Staring up at him in shock, I feel a fluttering in my stomach. For the very first time, I feel the baby move. I take it as a sign. It's the wake up call, or flutter, I needed. Come hell or high water, I will be leaving this house, tonight.

The time has come for me to leave.

From somewhere deep within, courage and adrenaline bubble to the surface. Climbing off the bed, I step over to him and I stare up into his evil black eyes. "I'm pregnant," I tell him. "It's yours, and yes, I'm keeping my baby. It's too late to terminate."

He steps toward me and backs me into the wall. He slaps me hard across the face. My head snaps to the side. My skin tingles from the slap. Looking back to him, I clinch my fists at my side and I snarl, "That will be the last time you *ever* touch me. You're a monster and I wish I'd never met you." Taking a deep breath, I add, "I'm leaving and you will *not* stop me."

Turning around, I walk into our wardrobe and grab a bag. Ripping clothes off their hangers, I throw them haphazardly into the bag. I have no idea what I pack, all I know is that I need to get out of here. Zipping up the duffle, I walk back into the bedroom. Picking up my handbag, I stuff the brochures I was reading inside and walk out of the room.

"Miles!" I shout as I reach the top of the stairs.

"Yes, Miss Masters?" he answers from below.

"It's time to go."

"Yes, ma'am." He nods, smiling up at me. But his face quickly morphs into fear. His eyes widen and on instinct, I turn around. Duncan's fist flies into my face, causing me to drop my things and stumble. Teetering on the edge of the top step, my arms flail about and I lose my balance. I'm about to fall backwards down the stairs but at the last second, Duncan reaches out. Grabbing me by my upper arms, he stares into my eyes. Licking his lips, he growls, "You will never leave. You are mine, Eloise. Now and forever. You need to remember that." He shakes me violently and a sinister look appears on his face.

And then I'm falling.

My arms flail about once again but this time, he doesn't reach it to save me. Flipping and flopping, I tumble down the stairs until I come to a stop on the landing with a thud.

Lying here with my eyes closed, I'm dazed and confused. I'm trying to catch my breath and calm the erratic beating of my heart. The sound of feet pounding on the stairs filters into my ears. I can't tell if it's Duncan racing down to me, or Miles racing up.

Opening my eyes, I look up and see Duncan hovering above me. He gives me a sinister smile before he rears back his leg and kicks me twice in my stomach. He bends down and roughly pulls me up by the collar of my dress. Dragging me across the landing, he stops. He tugs me so his face is millimeters away from mine. "You are mine, Eloise. Now and forever. Best you remember that dear, wife-to-be." He blows me a kiss and throws me backward down the remaining stairs. My head connects with the banister and the last thing I see before passing out is Duncan's smarmy menacing face laughing.

MARSHALL

Sitting out on my patio, I stare at the vast North Pacific Ocean. The surface is calm and flat today, the complete opposite of me. My mood is dark and stormy and once again, I'm hungover.

In the last ten weeks since my accident, my mood has soured further and further. I'm no closer to walking than I was when I first had my accident, and I've morphed into an even bigger asshole than I was before. I know it's not their fault, but the hovering and babying from everyone pisses me the fuck off.

And don't get me started on the pity looks, that's what I hate the most. I don't want your pity, I just want you to fuck off and leave me alone.

The doorbell rings but I stay where I am and continue to stare out at the ocean and sip on the beer in my hand. This used to be my happy place but now, now it's my prison.

"Yo, asshole, didn't you hear me ringing?" Grayson shouts out as he opens the side gate and walks over to me.

"I heard you."

"Well?" he snaps.

"I was ignoring you."

"Figured as much," he drawls, dropping onto the lounger beside me. "I wanted to see if you wanted to head out?"

"Do I look like I want to 'head out'?" I air quote 'head out' and roll my eyes at him.

"I don't give a flying fuck what you want. You've been moping around for the last six weeks, and quite frankly, I'm sick of your woe-is-me persona."

"Woe is me," I growl. "Woe is fucking me has a shattered pelvis and no career."

"No, you have a career on hold and a pelvis that is healing, and IF you followed the doctors' orders, you'd be up and walking again. Instead, you've turned into this entitled woe-is-me drunken asshat and I'm fuckin' sick of it."

We stare each other down, I know every word from his mouth is correct but give a guy a break—bad pun—my world was shattered—again, bad pun—literally and figuratively. I'm allowed to wallow and be an asshole for a few weeks, but the glaringly obvious part of his tirade just now is that if I had followed the plan, I would be up and getting about. I'd be that much closer to being back in my green machine and on the track. But no, because I wallowed and became a woe-is-me drunken asshat, as he put it, I'm still stuck in this chair. But you know what? I don't have it in me to care.

I'm fractured! End of story.

His gaze is focused on me and when I look over, I see concern etched on his face. And a part of me, a teeny tiny part, feels bad that I'm treating everyone like this. Then I move and a searing pain shoots through me and I remember why I've turned into this sour version of me.

Looking back at the water, I let out a frustrated sigh. He's still staring and I don't like it. Turning my head, I notice something in his expression. It's different from his usual one and it's unnerving. "You're not going to let this go, are you?"

"Nope." He crosses his arms. "So, you wanna head out?" I ignore him. "Are you going to come willingly? Or do I need to kidnap you and roll you out of here?"

"You wouldn't." He raises his eyebrows at me.

Maybe a change of scenery is what I need. What's the worst that could happen? "Fine, I'll come," I relent, affirming it with a head nod. I think the nod of agreement shocks him. "But it means you have to leave me alone afterward."

"I can do that but before we go, you need to A. Shower, because you stink worse than that dead goat we found in the quarry when we were kids, and B. Wear something other than gray sweats."

"Chicks dig guys in gray sweats."

"No! Chicks dig nonmoping guys in gray sweats."

"I'm not moping." He eyes me in that 'really' way. "Asshole," I mumble, as I spin around and wheel inside to shower and change for our mystery outing.

After showering, I pull on charcoal sweats, a black Henley, and my black Chucks. The dark clothes match my dark mood, maybe I'll mix things up and have a dark beer while we're out.

Wheeling back out, Grayson shakes his head when he sees what I'm wearing. "What? They're not gray," I nonchalantly reply with a shrug. My lips lift into a grin and I realize it's the first genuine grin in weeks.

"You really are an asshole. I think your personality crashed in the accident too."

Flipping him the bird, I grab my things and wheel toward the front door. "Let's go, asshole."

Grayson chuckles and follows me out to his Range Rover.

He's one of the few people who lets me do things on my own. Sure, it'd be quicker if I let him help but I need my independence and, thankfully, he allows that. Even if he keeps digging me over my fashion choice, but seriously, sweats are comfy and chicks fucking dig a guy in sweats. *But not a guy in sweats in a wheelchair.*

Grayson pops my chair in the back and we head off on our little adventure to who the fuck knows where.

"Where the fuck are we going?" I ask as he pulls onto the PCH, heading toward LA.

"If I told you, I'd have to kill you."

"Asshole," I mutter.

"I heard that."

"You were meant to."

Grayson is quiet on the drive and the silence unnerves me. I suddenly get the feeling that this is more than just a change of scenery. "What's up?" I ask, breaking the silence.

"Nothing's up, why?"

"You're quiet and that's never good." I pause. "Did you knock some chick up and need to talk about it?"

"You really think I'd take you out in public to discuss something like that?"

"Guess not." We both fall silent again.

A few minutes later, we pull into a parking lot and when I look around, that uneasy feeling returns with a vengeance. I don't see a bar and I've never been here before. "Are you planning on murdering me? This doesn't look like a bar."

"Never said we were heading to a bar." He climbs out and grabs my chair, leaving me to process his words. *Where the fuck are we?*

He opens my door and leans against the passenger rear door, crossing his feet, and waits for me. I appreciate his nonchalance right now. Once I'm seated, he pushes off his car, locks it, and starts walking.

"You going to tell me where we're going?"

"Nope," he sings out, as we walk down a dimly lit corridor. If I didn't know the guy in front of me, I'd seriously think I was being led to my demise.

"This feels like something that would happen in a scary movie. The unsuspecting hunk is lured down a dimly lit passageway where he will be accosted and taken advantage of."

"Thanks for referring to me as a hunk," the asshole chuckles with a wink, "but I'm not into dudes, so you won't be taken advantage of by me. Sorry to burst your bubble."

"Well damn, looks like my fantasy won't be coming true today."

We both laugh and after a few more feet, Grayson stops in front of a door. He rests his hand on the handle and hesitates. "Just remember that we care and love you." He opens the door and steps inside, I wheel in behind him and when I look up, my eyes widen. Mom, Dad, and Linc are here and I can hear Saxon's voice. I'm guessing he's Face Timing from wherever in the world he is right now. I have no fucking clue where my best friend is right now, proving that I've been a shitty friend. Some chick is in the corner, looking down at her iPad, and next to her is Jaxson, my agent from Life's Too Sport. His arms are folded across his chest and there's a murderous look on his face.

"What the fuck is this?" I snarl.

"Watch your language, Marshall," Dad scolds me.

The lady looks up. "Marshall, so glad you could join us today."

"Who the fuck are you?" I ask.

"Marshall," Dad scolds me again.

"I'm Tina Myers. We're all here today to help you."

She looks to Dad and nods at him. He takes a deep breath and mom reaches over and takes his hand. "Marshall, Son, we're all here because we care about you and it's time you pull your head out of your ass and get back on your feet."

My mouth opens and closes as my eyes dart around the room.

"Please, Marshall," Mom pleads, "please do this for me." She wipes a tear from her eyes. "I want my happy son back. I want to see you racing again. I can't handle seeing you moping around and drinking yourself into oblivion anymore."

Dad and Linc are both nodding and, on the laptop screen, Saxon is bobbing up and down in agreement too, *assholes*.

Tina walks over to me. "Marshall, your friends and family are concerned—"

"No fucking shit," I interrupt her, "my ears still work, it's my fucking legs that don't."

"Marshall!" Mom yells in that mom tone that means business. "I raised you better than that. Apologize to Tina now."

"Sorry," I spit out, but everyone in the room can tell I don't mean it. Looking around, I shake my head. "My pelvis is held together with screws. It hurts to move but most of all, I can't race. The one thing I love most in this world has been ripped away from me."

"It's still there," Linc affirms. "If you had of followed the doctors' rehabilitation plan, you'd be up on your feet by now. You'd be one step closer to getting back into the green machine."

"And how the fuck do you know that, Linc? It fucking kills me not being in my car, but it fucking hurts—"

"Boo fucking hoo." He looks to Mom and mouths sorry for the language. "There are medications to assist with the pain but you're too stubborn to see that. You have access to the best rehab facilities, but instead, you hide in your beach house and drink yourself into oblivion each and every night." He pauses and takes a deep breath. "If you want me to hold your spot at Scofield, you need to stop drinking and get yourself to rehab."

"You really think it's that easy?" I scoff. Do they not realize that this isn't going to be a walk in the park? I'm starting all over again and once I do walk again, what if I can't race? That what-if is the scariest of all. I'd rather be stuck in this chair for the rest of my life than to be able to walk and not race.

"It won't be easy but I know you, Marshall. When you put your mind to it, you can achieve anything." Linc reaffirms his belief in me. "You won the championship in your rookie year for fuck's sake."

"I only won because they cut the season short."

"Even if you lost the last two races, you still would have won. That trophy was yours and you know why it was yours?" He doesn't give me a chance to reply. "Because you," he points to me, "you put everything you had into winning and that's why you're number one. If you put that same determination into this, you'll be back in your race car, defending your title before you know it."

"What if I can't?" I quietly voice.

The lady, Tina, walks toward me and utters four words that stop me in my tracks, "What if you can?"

"Marshall," Jaxson sings in his 'I mean business' voice, he squats down so we're eye level. "We all care about you and we all want you back on the racetrack, but it all comes down to the decision you make right now. Your future is in your hands."

Staring at him, I blink and focus on the last sentence, *Your future is in your hands*. Taking a deep breath, I nod and look around the room at those who mean the most in this world to me. The concern on their faces causes something to switch inside of me and I find myself wanting what they want for me.

"Fine," I huff, "looks like I'm off to rehab."

ELOISE

Opening my eyes, it's dark except for a dull yellow light above my bed. Scrunching my face in confusion, I look around and realize I'm in hospital. Closing my eyes, they fly back open when it all comes crashing back to me.

My hand drops to my belly and I feel funny, I know something is wrong. My heart rate increases and the machine I'm connected to begins to beep erratically. Blinking rapidly, I try to focus but the room becomes blurry and my body heavy. Tears cascade down my cheeks as I remember falling and the kicks.

The door to my room opens and a nurse races in. "I need you to calm down, dear," she tells me, her tone soothing. She takes my hand in hers and gently squeezes.

"My baby. Is my baby okay?" I ask her.

"You need to calm down," she repeats.

"Is. My. Baby. Okay?" I shout through clenched teeth.

The machine beside me is really going off now and another nurse enters the room. But I just keep repeating over and over, "Is my baby okay?" My voice wavering each time I ask the question because deep down, I already know the answer.

No one will answer me and my panic increases with each passing second.

A shadow appears in my doorway. I immediately think it's Duncan but it's not, it's Miles. "Miss Masters, you need to calm down," he pleads, walking into the room and around to the other side of my bed.

"Duncan," I murmur, that one word is laced with fear and has my whole body tensing.

He shakes his head. "He's not here, Miss."

Relief floods me at knowing he isn't here. And then I think of the baby. "My baby," I breathlessly voice, "is my baby okay?" I ask, he'll answer me and without uttering a word he does.

All color in his face vanishes and he morosely utters, "I'm so sorry." He takes my hand in his and squeezes. I've only known I was pregnant for a few hours, but the loss and loneliness I feel is like nothing I've ever experienced before.

"No. No. No," I cry. "My baby. He took my baby."

"Shhhh," Miles whispers to me, pulling me into a hug, holding my head like a loving father. I wince at the pain in my side, but feeling pain is better than feeling empty and alone. "You need to press charges, Miss."

Shaking my head, I pull back. "No, I just want to leave and forget I ever met Duncan Montgomery."

"He won't let you go easily."

"Next time, it possibly will be me who dies," I cry. "I need to get away and I need to go now."

There's a commotion in the hall causing Miles and I pull apart. We stare at one another, wide-eyed, it's *him*. And no sooner do I finish that thought and he's standing in the doorway. "Eloise, honey, I'm so glad you're awake." His voice is almost sweet, too sweet. I'm on edge and he's only said seven words.

"Awake?" I question, furrowing my brows.

"You've been out since you were admitted and I approved the surgery to remove that thing."

"Surgery? Thing?" I question. I'm so confused right now.

"To remove that thing you lost when you fell down the stairs." My hand drops to my belly and I subconsciously rub it.

"Fell? Really? That's what you're going with?" I snarl, never have I ever spoken to him like this before, but I've nothing left to lose now.

"Eloise," he growls, "I suggest you think about how you're acting."

"And I suggest you fuck off." I don't know where this burst of defiance comes from, but I like this version of me. I hope she sticks around, I'll need her strength and tenacity to put up with him if I don't manage to get away.

His eyes widen at my words but before he can retaliate, my doctor, who happens to be the one from the clinic today appears. "Miss Masters, it's good to see you awake." She looks from Duncan to Miles and back to me. "Gentleman, can I ask you to leave so I can check on my patient?"

"I'm her fiancé, I'm staying," Duncan states, crossing his arms in a 'don't fuck with me' way.

"I'm her doctor and I'm asking you to leave." They stare at one another. "I'm more than happy to call security and have you escorted off the premises," she states, her tone authoritative.

"Don't you know who I am?" he growls, shocked that someone, a woman no less, would talk to him in that manner.

"I don't care who you are. My patient is my only concern and after the events of today, I need to make sure she's okay. Both mentally and physically." She emphasizes the word physically. "It will only take a moment," she stacks on to placate him.

"Fine," he huffs and storms out without a word.

"I'll get you a hot drink," Miles offers.

"Thank you, I'd love a skinny latt—"

"—latte with hazelnut syrup. I've been with you long enough, I know your drink of choice."

"Thank you." I smile and watch him shuffle out of my room, closing the door behind him.

"How are you feeling, Eloise?" Dr. Miller asks when we're alone.

Shrugging my shoulders, my eyes well with tears. "Upset. Sad. Scared. Like a failure. Take your pick."

"Why like a failure?"

"I couldn't protect my baby."

"That's not your fault."

"He, or she, was inside of me. I was their mom. I was meant to protect them and I failed."

"You did not fail. They were taken from you by a monster—"

"—he's not," I interrupt, but she gives me a look that tells me she knows I'm full of shit. "Okay, fine, he's a monster."

"So why stay?"

"Because I have nothing."

"If you stay, he will kill you."

"I can't leave," I blubber. "I have no one and nowhere to go."

"What if you did?"

Staring at her blankly, I rapidly blink, processing her words. "What?"

"What if you had a way out? What if you had somewhere to go?"

"I'd leave in a heartbeat." And I would, I only stay because I have nothing. It sounds selfish when I put it like that and my selfishness caused me to lose our, no MY, baby.

"Do you trust me?"

"Yes," I tell her, and I mean it. For some reason, I trust her, even though I've only just met her.

"Whatever you do, do not leave this hospital with him. I will get you out of here, I just need to make a few arrangements."

"Why? Why are you doing this? Why me?"

She looks at me and a wave of grief passes over her features. "I couldn't save my older sister from her monster, but I can save you from yours. I vowed when Haley died that I'd never let that happen again if I had the opportunity to help."

"I'm sorry you lost your sister."

"Helping you will ease the guilt I feel."

The door to my room slams open. "Can we go yet?" Duncan growls.

"Out," Dr. Miller spits, "I'm not finished with my patient ye—"

"When can we go home?" he interrupts, ignoring her request to leave. He's being a right royal asshole but then again, he is a right royal asshole.

"Your fiancée miscarried after taking a tumble, which resulted in her losing consciousness. Rather than allowing her to make the decision, you scheduled surgery for a D&C against my wishes. Eloise should have been the one to make the decision as to whether she tried to pass the fetus naturally, but you took that choice from her—"

"It was my baby too and I get to decide what she does."

"Regardless, she will need to stay for a few days."

"Tomorrow afternoon," he snarls. "I'll be back then and regardless of what you or anyone in this godforsaken hospital feels, she will be coming home with me." Without another word, he turns and exits my room. He doesn't say goodbye and he doesn't offer me any sweet words, not that I want anything from him.

Staring at the empty doorway, I whisper, "And I won't be here when you return." This is my chance to start repairing the fractures caused to me by Duncan Montgomery and I will do whatever Dr. Miller wants me to do to escape my monster and survive.

MARSHALL

After the intervention from those who apparently care about me—I'm looking at you Mom, Dad, Linc, Jaxson, Grayson, and Saxon—I relocate to Limitless Therapeutic Rehabilitation and Wellness Center in Brookvale, Nevada. It's a rehabilitation facility in the bumfuck of nowhere that specializes in sports injuries and most of all, privacy.

The paps can't get to me here, and I'm pretty sure that's one of the main reasons Jaxson sent me here. He assures me it's the best sports rehab center in the country, but I think he's full of shit. I've been sent here to keep out of the tabloids, to reduce my drinking, and learn to walk again, but I can't see that happening. It's just too hard.

Everyone is all upbeat and gung-ho that I can do this, but they don't know the agony I live with each and every day. It's one of the reasons I drink, when I'm numb I don't feel the pain; mentally or physically.

I've been at LTRWC for a few weeks now, I've reduced but not stopped my drinking. They can all go to hell when it comes to that. I'm still unable to walk without being in excruciating pain or walk farther than five feet unassisted. I'm broken beyond repair, both physically and mentally. I know wholeheartedly I'll never race again. I may as well end it all now.

Racing is my life, well it was, and I can't see a way back to that. They keep telling me if I get off my ass and do the work, it'll happen but they're all full of shit. They can go fuck themselves sideways with a rusty fork.

Sighing dejectedly, I look down at my arms and shake my head. I've been pricked and prodded with a needle more times than a junkie. And after all the surgeries, I will no doubt set off the sensors every time I go through airport security, thanks to the metal in my pelvis. I was lucky—I guess—that I have access to the best doctors. I was unlucky in that I needed ORIF, Open Reduction with Internal Fixation, my bones are rigidly fixed with plates and screws to prevent future displacement. It was done to allow for my rehabilitation to begin as quickly as possible, but I kinda fucked that plan up, didn't I?

Plus the reoccurring infections are a pain in the ass. We seem to get one infection under control, only for another to appear. Joys of having your spleen removed. I highly recommend it, not. And from what I've read, having no spleen is a major contributor to my slow recovery.

I shouldn't be this surly, I'm still alive. Unlike Joe Johnstone, and I did win the championship—technically—since they ended the season early but it's not a win to be celebrated.

Joe is dead and I'm stuck in the bumfuck of nowhere unable to walk.

A quiet knock at my door garners my attention and before I even look up, I know it's *her*. Lifting my head, I see I'm correct.

Standing in my doorway is E, she's kinda a gofer around here. Doing anything and everything. If a job needs doing, she jumps in. She rarely smiles and her eyes are sad, but when she does smile, fuck me sideways it's beautiful.

"Morning, Marshall," she cheerily greets, walking into my room. "Would you like to go outside? It's a gorgeous day today."

"No," I snarl.

She and I do this dance most days. She arrives, asks if I want to go outside, and I tell her to get fucked but not in so many words.

"Okay, just holler if you change your mind." She smiles and walks out, leaving me alone to wallow.

My eyes watch her ass as she exits my room. In another life, I would have hit on her but the new me, he doesn't want anyone around. It's bad enough that Linc and Grayson pop by as much as they do. Thankfully, since moving here, it's farther and not as easy. I mostly speak to Mom and Dad via FaceTime and the best thing about that, if I don't want to talk, I don't answer.

Wheeling over to the window, I stare outside. E is right, it is a gorgeous day outside today but it does little to lift my surly mood.

The day passes by quickly and before I know it, it's sunset, my favorite time of day. I stare out the window and watch the sun sink below the horizon, nothing beats a blazing sunset. I miss watching the sun set from my house in Malibu. Maybe I should just pack up and go home. I'm no closer to racing now than when I first arrived. Rehab clearly isn't for me … living isn't for me either.

Wheeling back to my bed, I maneuver myself up onto the mattress. I reach over to the side table and grab my phone. Bringing up YouTube, I torture myself and rewatch my races. I was fucking good and one accident took it all away from me. I'll never be that person again, I'm fractured beyond repair.

Throwing my phone across the room, it hits the wall and shatters upon impact. "Fuuuuuuuuck," I roar, punching the mattress in frustration.

A figure appears in my doorway and a soft voice says, "I'll pick up another one for you." She doesn't wait for my reply, she just walks away, leaving me alone to wallow and stew on the shit-show that's my currently my fucked up life.

Waking the next morning, I find a new phone in a box on the hospital bed table. Clearly I drank more than I thought last night because I didn't hear anyone drop off the phone or clean up the mess.

Them letting me drink here is one of the only reasons I'm still here. I could be doing this back home in Malibu, but at least here in the bumfuck of nowhere, there are no paps and it's a little too far for Mom and Dad to 'pop in' and check on me.

While I eat breakfast, I insert my SIM and fire up my new phone. Like the last few days, I feel her before I see her. There's a sadness inside her that reminds me of me. The new sad me, not the playboy high on life me. I watch her from the corner of my eye, she really is gorgeous in every way, but she doesn't need a broken asshole like me dragging her down.

Like we're in the movie *Groundhog Day*, she once again cheerfully greets me. "Morning, Marshall." Before walking over to the window and opening the curtains. Once again she asks the same question, "Would you like to go outside? It's a gorgeous day today."

"I'd much rather be in the gym, but I guess the garden will have to suffice," I reply like the asshole I am.

"You'll be back in there soon enough. You just need to give your body, and mind, time to heal."

"What the fuck do you know about healing?" I snarl. "You're life isn't broken like mine."

In a flash, her face blanches and she looks scared. Ready to burst into tears. "I know more than you think," she quietly whispers, her voice wavering. "I'll go get Roger to help you outside." She turns around and walks out. I feel like a dick for causing her pain but I guess my assumptions were correct, she's broken … just like me.

As if sensing I need her, my phone begins to ring and I see Mom's name on the screen. "Hey, Momma Bear," I say.

"How's my boy doing today?"

"Still fractured."

"Give yourself a break, bad pun, sorry. You were in a horrific crash, your body and mind, have been through a lot."

"I need to be up and walking again," I snap, "so I can get back on the track."

"You heard the surgeon, Marshall, with rehab it will happen but for that to happen, you actually need to get off your cute little butt and do something about it. Stop wallowing and be the Marshall I know you can be." Mom pauses and swallows back a sob. "Your dad and I love you, Marshall, and we're here for you."

The old me would have thrived at Momma Bear's pep talk just now, but the new me, well, he hates the world and everything at the moment. "Then why did you all gang up on me and send me to the bumfudge of nowhere?"

"It's not ganging up when it comes from love and it's because we care about you."

"If you cared, you would have just left me in Malibu to live my life."

"And such a life you were living." She takes a deep breath and I know I'm about to receive a KK lecture. Keri Kerr is known far and wide for her 'KK chats/lectures.' She becomes this oracle, giving advice and more times than not, she's spot-on with her suggestions. "Marshall, I've let you get away with a lot in your life, but I refuse to sit by and let you waste it away. You had an accident. You survived. It's time you pull your head out of your ass and do something about getting your life back."

Without saying anything else, she hangs up. I didn't mean to piss Mom off, or to make her swear. Lying back, I think over her words and she's right. I did survive and I need to start living again. If not for me, then for Joe.

Roger walks in, putting a halt to my thoughts. "Ready to rock, racer boy?"

"Racer boy, really?" I question him.

He shrugs. "Let's roll."

Climbing off the bed, I slide into my chair and Roger wheels me outside, we're both silent as he pushes me down the corridor. I hate that I can't do it myself outside of my room. I can't do that until my physical therapist deems me fit and until then, I have to have a staff member push and escort me around the center. It's a stupid rule, if you ask me, and having them do it doesn't do much for the so-called independence they're trying to instill in me.

Roger taps my shoulder once outside and leaves me alone. Picking up my phone, I shoot Mom a text.

MARSHALL

Sorry for being a butthead.

MOMMA BEAR

You're not a butthead, you're my beautiful son. You just need to learn to appreciate the little things again.

MARSHALL

Love you, Momma Bear

MOMMA BEAR

Love you too

Placing my phone in my lap, I look up and smile because E was once again right, it is a gorgeous day today. The sky is bright blue, there's not a cloud in sight and the temperature is perfect thanks to a gentle breeze. It reminds me of a spring day back in Malibu.

Not that I'll admit it to anyone, but being out here in the fresh air and sunlight is just what I needed to reinvigorate my soul. Mom's words about appreciating the little things play over in my mind and I think she's right—don't tell her I said that—it's time for me to start living again, hell, I've got nothing better to do so I may as well try and get my life back together.

ELOISE

acing out of his room, I find Roger coming toward me, thankful I didn't need to try and find him. "Can you take Marshall out to the garden, please?" He goes to tell me he's busy but he can tell from the look on my face that I need a moment. "Sure, why don't you take ten?" he suggests, sadly smiling at me.

Roger is one of the few people here who knows a little about my past, I would have preferred no one knew, but he walked into the office one day when Linda was giving me an update on *him*.

"Thanks," I quietly whisper before I race past him and head toward the breakroom. Entering the room, I pull the door closed behind me and take a deep breath. I hadn't realized I was holding it while I made my escape.

Walking to the bathroom, I lock myself in a toilet stall, lower the lid, and sit down. I stare at my feet, hoping they have all the answers which, unfortunately, they do not. Trying to steady my breathing, I play his comment over and over in my mind.

What do you know about healing? Your life isn't broken like mine.

"I know more than you think," I whisper, resting my hand on my stomach. My eyes well with tears. It's been six weeks since I lost my baby and left my old life behind. Not only did my baby die that day, but so did I, to an extent. The Eloise from Collinsville is gone and now I'm E, a woman trying to survive and repair the damage *he* caused. I decided to just go by my initial, making it harder for *him* to find me, but deep down I know that no matter what I call myself, one day, he'll find me. I just hope when that day comes, I'm strong enough to face him and survive.

The pain today is just as unbearable as it was on that fateful day.

Without the help of Miles, Jenna, and Linda, I'd still be stuck in hell, or worse, the morgue. I still can't believe I managed to escape. I was sure I'd be caught. If Duncan would have caught me, I have no doubt in my mind, he would have killed me. And if he ever does find me, I'm a dead lady walking. I pray to God every day *he* never finds me.

Closing my eyes, my mind drifts to the day I made my escape. Every moment is still vivid and fresh in my mind…

…After Duncan left, Jenna did exactly as she promised, she got me away from the hell I was living. She set me up with a new life and a new start, I will forever be grateful for what she did.

In the middle of the night, Miles returned and the two of them snuck me out of there. We went to Dr. Miller's house. Earlier in the day, Miles dropped off the bag I'd packed before it all turned to shit. He gave me a phone and all the cash he had. When he whispered, "I'm so sorry for your loss," that's when I fell apart. I collapsed to the ground and I sobbed for my baby.

Looking up at Miles staring down at me, I ask the one question that had been on repeat since I woke up earlier. "Why did it take me losing a baby to leave? I'm a horrible person."

"You are the least horrible person I know, Eloise. But if you remember, you were on your way out when this happened."

"I should have left sooner. If I had, my baby would still be here."

"You can't live with what-ifs," Jenna interjects. "I know I should take my own advice, considering how I feel about my sister, but you need to focus on the future. Focus on that and live the life you want. You're free now, Eloise." She pauses. "You're free."

"Free," I whisper. "I never thought I'd be free." I look over at her. "I wouldn't be free if it wasn't for you and Miles. I will never be able to thank either of you enough."

"You being free of that monster is enough for me," Miles *hugs me tightly and we say our final goodbyes.*

"No thanks is needed," Jenna adds. "Just keep looking forward. You're getting the chance Haley never got, and that's all the payment I need." Jenna hugs me tightly. "Eloise, tomorrow, you're starting your new life. Leave the past behind and focus on the future."

…Future? I've never thought about the future before but since leaving I have, many times because I have the chance to live a happy and carefree life. But I do wish I could have had it with little E. He—it was a boy … I think—and I could have been happy, just the two of us. For him, my baby boy, I vow to live a happy and fulfilling life.

Sure, I'm in the middle of nowhere, but this is the safest place to be. Duncan would never be caught dead in a little town like this.

Taking a deep breath, I compose myself and exit my hideout. Walking over to my locker, I unlock it and just as I do, my phone rings. And like I do every time it rings, I hold my breath until I see who's calling. My fear evaporates when I see the name on the screen. "Hey, Miles," I say when I answer.

"Hey, sweetheart. How are you?"

"Getting there."

Since I made my escape, Miles has called me once a week to check in. I never realized how much I appreciated having him in my life. I begged him to come with me, but he convinced me it's better if he stayed behind. That way he can keep his eyes on Duncan.

As we predicted, he took my departure how we thought he would, as in, he didn't. He trashed my hospital room when he realized I was gone. He was escorted from the premises in handcuffs and charged with willful damage of private property. I wish I could have been there to see his downfall, but at the same time I don't, because he is downright scary when he's in one of his moods.

"This should make you happy then." Hearing Miles' voice brings my attention back to him and his call. "A fed just paid dear old Dunc a visit and when they left, he was in a stellar mood."

"Wow, I always knew he was up to something but I didn't think it was on a federal level."

But his next words put the fear back into me. "He's hired another PI. He fired the last one because he couldn't find you."

"He won't find me, will he?" I hesitantly ask.

"Not if you keep your head down and stay out of the press and off social media. Why would he look in Brookvale?"

"I guess you're right, but I'm still scared that one of these days he'll find me. I don't ever want that to happen because you and I both know, it won't end well."

"And that's why I'm still here. I'll keep you updated as best I can. Since you left, he's become even angrier."

Letting out a sigh, I close my eyes. "Please stay safe, Miles. I hate that you're still there."

"Don't worry about me, dear. I'm a big boy, I can look after myself. You just stay safe."

"I will. I promise."

We end the call and I stare at my phone. Taking a deep breath, I bring up Google and punch in his name, but before anything loads, I click the search bar and type in a different name, Marshall Kerr. A picture of him standing on the podium in first place is the first image to appear. He really is gorgeous—dirty blond hair, bluest of blue eyes, muscles upon muscles and a smile that lights up a room. It's the complete opposite of him now, well, he's still blond-haired and blue-eyed but his eyes no longer sparkle and his smile is nonexistent.

He reminds me of me, broken and living in despair. Maybe we are what each other needs to glue ourselves back together so we can take on the world again. I laugh at the thought of a man like Marshall being with a girl like me. There's no way he'd ever go for a wallflower like me, besides I never want a relationship again. And I cannot have one with someone like him, the fame associated with him would cause too many issues and the biggest issue would be *him* finding me.

Damn men.

My new mantra is 'Men can fuck right off.' I don't need a man to be happy, I'm my happiness maker.

MARSHALL

I t's *Groundhog Day* number … I have no clue. Life is still the same. I'm still in this chair. My pain is still excruciating and I'm still not behind the wheel of my green machine or out on the track racing.

My moods have been improving—slightly—and I think it's to do with a dark-haired beauty I see each and every day. Sure she ignores me and skitters the other way when I try to initiate a conversation with her, but when she does open up, I find myself smiling and happy.

You could also say my mood enhancer is attributed to the non—well, reduced—drinking. I still have a beer with dinner but I max out at two … maybe three.

My phone rings and I smile when I see Mom's face grinning back at me. "Morning, Momma Bear," I say in greeting, my voice finally sounding normal. Sure, I have the odd day when grumpy asshole Marshall appears but most days now since my Momma Bear tongue-lashing, I feel like the old me again.

"How's my boy doing today?"

"Still fractured but—"

"What have I told you?" she admonishes me. I can picture her pointing her finger at me in a berating way. "You—"

"Mom," I interrupt, "if you let me finish, I was going to say, still fractured but I'm getting there."

"Ohh," she comments in shock. It's not often Keri Kerr is speechless and I find myself grinning. "What's happened to make you so chipper?"

"Nothing, I'm just feeling … good."

"Marshall, baby, that makes me so happy to hear. These past few months I've been so, so worried about you."

"I'm sorry to have caused you worry, Mom."

"Marshall, I'm your mother, I will always worry about you. When you have kids of your own, you'll know what I mean."

"I'd need a wife for that to happen." My mind drifts to E and what she'd look like with my ring on her left hand and her belly rounded and growing with our child. That thought shocks me but now I'm thinking about it, I wonder what a life with her would be like. The two of us snuggling on a porch swing, watching the sun set as our three kids—two boys, one girl—run through the sprinkler in our yard. Our dog, Boof, chasing after them and their little giggles filtering through the afternoon air.

"Marshall," Mom snaps.

"Sorry, Mom, I missed that."

"Where did you go just now?"

"Nowhere," I tell her, but I know Mom, she'll figure it out in two point five seconds. She has this sixth sense when it comes to me and my thoughts and she really should have been an FBI agent, she'd crack each and every case within a day.

"Who is she?" *See!*

"What?" I hiss, trying to play dumb.

"I may not be there with you, but I know that tone. Who is she?"

"She's no one," I tell her because really, she is. I know crap all about her. I only know her as E for fuck's sake. What does E stand for? What's her story? Why doesn't she smile all the time? Why is she frightened, especially around men?

"Mmmhmpf, well when you're ready to tell me about her, I'll be here." The line goes quiet and then she breaks the silence when she utters, "Flowers."

"What about flowers?"

"Send her flowers. Girls love receiving flowers. Did you know, flowers are how your father won me over. For weeks before we officially started dating, I'd receive a bunch every Thursday with no card. Turns out, it was your father."

"And he still does that now."

"He sure does. I hit the jackpot with him. He's the pickle to my peanut butter."

"I really hope you're referring to the food items and not what I'm currently thinking."

"I plead the Fifth," Mom laughs, causing me to shudder at the thought of Mom and Dad and a pickle.

"Mooom," I groan, "I don't want to be thinking about that."

"And on that pickle note," she teases.

"Ugh," I grumble and make gagging noises. Mom's laughter fills my ears and I can't help but smile.

"I'm going to go, she tells me. "and you're going to order some flowers. Sunflowers are pretty."

"They're your favorite, Mom."

"I know they are, but sunflowers will brighten any girl's day."

"I'll see what I can do. Bye, Mom."

"Bye, Marshall, love you."

She hangs up before I can tell her I love her too. I think about her words, should I send E flowers? It might brighten her day but do I want to start something here? Maybe a rehab fling is what I need to get the cylinders firing. It's been a while since I got laid and E does have a killer body. I'm sure she'd be a firecracker between the sheets, the quiet and shy ones are always the kinkiest. My dirty thoughts are interrupted when the girl in question appears. "Morning, Marshall."

Something in her greeting today does something to me and before she can open the curtains and ask if I'd like to go outside, I beat her to the punch. "I'd like to go outside, please."

She smiles, and fuck me sideways, it does something to me that I haven't felt in a long time. "I'll go get Roger."

Shocking myself, I ask, "Can you do it?"

"I ... umm ... ahh, sure."

She walks into my room and opens my curtains. She turns back to me and smiles again but this time, it lights up her face. I've noticed when she really smiles, the dimples on her cheeks become more prominent, and I find myself wanting to lick and kiss the cute little indents. "Let's get you outside."

"Let's."

She grips the handles on my chair and pushes me out into the hall. We're almost outside when someone yells, "Yo."

E freezes and her eyes widen. I peer around E and grin when I see Grayson walking toward us. "Hey," I greet him, "what are you doing here?"

"Came to visit you, hoping to smack some sense into your stubborn ass."

"Hardy har har," I retort. "I'm about to head outside."

"Sweet," he agrees and starts walking past us, leaving me with E.

Grayson is almost to the door and I realize that E is still frozen. She hasn't moved a muscle and her smile has been wiped from her face. In its place is an expression I've noticed mars her face often, fear.

"E," I say but she doesn't move. "E!" I yell, this time a little louder and she jumps five feet in the air in fright. "You okay?"

"Yeah, umm, sorry." Without saying anything further, she begins to wheel me outside. By the time we arrive, Grayson has two coffees waiting. When he notices us, he walks over. "I've got him," he informs E.

Looking over my shoulder, I see her nod and without uttering a word, she spins on her heel and quickly turns away from us, racing back inside as if her ass is on fire.

"She's fucking hot," he states.

"Back off," I growl through clenched teeth. "And what would Soraya say about you flirting with E?"

"I have no clue what you are referring to with Saxon's big sister, besides, what are you going to do about it from that chair?" he cheekily teases.

"My arms still work and I'm at the perfect height to punch you in the dick. Plus, I'll call Saxon and let him know you two are bumping uglies."

"Where's Marshall and what have you done with him?" I flip him the bird. "No, seriously, what's got you so chipper? The last time we spoke you were still asshole Marshall, today you're like Marshall Marshall." I shrug.

"Ahhhh," he singsongs, nodding. "You're tapping that?" His head flicks toward the door E just stepped through.

"No—"

"But you want to," he taunts.

Again I shrug. Not liking the direction of this conversation, I turn it back to his surprise visit. "What are you doing here? Midweek, no less."

"I was coming here to try and get you to pull your head out of your ass, but it seems like your head has been removed already."

Again, I flip him the bird. "Can't a guy just be happy?"

"Yes, but for the last few months you've been the complete opposite of happy. You've been a grumpy asshole laced with a dose of douchecanoeitis."

"Douchecanoeitis isn't a word," I retort.

He shrugs at me. "I hope I'm not stepping over the line here, but I … umm … ahh, I've been looking into recovery methods for those who suffer from douchecanoenesitis after an accident like yours and I have a plan, if you're interested?"

Staring at him, I smile. "If you'd been here last week, yesterday even, I would have told you to shove it up your ass sideways, but not today. The time for wallowing is over, Grayson. It's time for me to pull on my big boy panties and focus on my recovery."

"You don't know how happy that makes me." He takes a sip of his coffee. "I'd hate to see all that you, me, and the team have worked so hard for thrown away because you were a—"

"—douchecanoe," we both say, and then we laugh. It feels good to be laughing and not wallowing.

"I didn't get to where I was by being a pussy, I got to where I was, at the top of the leaderboard, through hard work and determination. Not to mention, I have a fan-fucking-tabulous team behind me, #TeamKerr. The days, weeks, and months ahead will be tough but I'm tougher. My pelvis may be fractured and held together by pins, screws, and plates but my mind, soul, and the rest of my body isn't. It's time to get out of this chair, up on my feet and back into my green machine. My sole focus is to get back behind the wheel and out on the track again."

"Wow, that was some speech, but if anyone can do it, it's you."

Grayson heads out to his car and returns with his laptop and together we go over his plan. He's been conferring with a Dr. Michels, the team doctor for the NY Crushers. After informing him of everything, the good doctor informed Grayson he'd be more than happy to help put together a recovery plan. He's been developing techniques to help athletes get back on their feet quicker and I think some of his ideas have merit. It also helps that he's a fan of mine, so he has both a professional and personal interest in my recovery, or lack thereof right at this moment.

After finalizing the plan, Grayson and I call Linc.

Linc is stoked that I'm finally pulling my head out of my ass, and said he'd do all that he can to make this happen for me. With his approval, we seek out Nancy, my assigned physical therapist here. Together, with the assistance of Doc Michels, we tweak my recovery plan. He thinks that if I stick to this new regime and with hard work and determination, I can be back on the track before the start of the next season.

The coming weeks are going to be tough, but I'm tougher. Like my career, this is a marathon, not a sprint but this is a race I need to win and my preparation starts now.

MARSHALL

"**C**ome on, Marshall," Nancy, my physical therapist from hell shouts, "my nana can do this and she's ninety-four."

"Your nana doesn't have a shattered pelvis," I growl through clenched teeth. Sweat beading along my hairline. I'm red in the face and huffing and puffing like Nancy's nana.

"No, but she's had two knee reconstructions and doesn't whine like a little bitch."

"I'm doing my best," I snap. Raising my hand, I signal I'm done and she helps me back into my chair.

"Really? That's your best? You, sir, are full of shit. You're three weeks into the new program, you should be able to walk along this without whining like—"

"I'm done!" I scream at her and before she can stop me, I pull off my chair's brake and wheel out of the therapy room—thankful that my 'wheel myself' privileges have been granted. If I'd had to wait for someone to wheel me away right now, I'd be even more pissed off.

My emotions are up and down like a freakin' yo-yo at the moment. One minute I'm all 'Yes, I can do this' and then next I'm back to wallowing and hating the world. I wish there was a magic pill, and poof, I'm all healed and back in my car, but no, there is no pill and I'm stuck in hell confined to this fucking chair.

Angry at myself, I don't look before I enter the corridor and I knock into someone as soon as I wheel out of the room. "Watch where you're going," I seethe.

"I … I … I'm sorry," E utters, her voice wavering. "I-i-i-I … it won't happen again." She presses herself into the wall and closes her eyes, wiping at her cheeks.

"Just watch it," I snap at a visibly shaking E, who is pushing herself tightly against the wall, trying to make herself invisible. Her body is tight with fear. Her beautiful face scrunched up and scared. Tears welling in her eyes.

"Fucking hell," I mumble as I angrily wheel down the corridor. I'm pissed at Nancy and her words. I'm pissed at me for not being able to recover quicker. I'm really pissed that I haven't been on a racetrack in months and there's a part of my that's pissed that I was so mean to E just now.

Looking up, I realize I'm at the opposite end of the center from my room. Spinning around, I hurriedly wheel back the way I came. Rather than wheeling to my room, I decide to head outside. Hoping the fresh air will clear my head and remove this shitty mood I seem to have found myself in.

Wheeling to the edge of the cement, I stare out at the sky. The sun is about to set and it's a fiery orange mixed with reds and yellows. It's really stunning, reminding me of the scene in my reoccurring fantasy about E and me on our porch swing, but after the way she reacted just now, I know hell will freeze over before that ever happens.

"Marshall," Nancy voices from behind. Turning to face her, I wait for the lecture that I'm no doubt about to be given. "I know I push you but I do it because I know you can. What are you afraid of?"

Her question stumps me, I expected to be berated, not to have to think. "I … what … I …"

"I … what? Talk to me, Marshall, I may be your physical therapist, but I'm a pretty good listener too."

"What if I can't race again?"

"But what if you can?" she throws back at me.

Her response once again stops me in my tracks. She's right, what if I can? Only I can determine if I can or cannot. Sure, the doctors think it's unlikely but they don't know how much I want this. They don't know me, when I'm determined to achieve something, I do it. Hell, I set out to win my rookie year and I did. Well technically, I won it, but I did what I set out to do and this is no different.

Looking over to Nancy, she's pulled one of the outdoor chairs over to me. She leans forward, her elbows resting on her knees, her chin on her palm and she looks at me, waiting for my reply.

"Nancy, you're right. I can do this. I'm just frustrated 'cause it's slow going. I live my life in the fast lane, suddenly being in the slow lane is hard to take but I promise, I'll do whatever it takes so I can race again." I grin at her. "I will race again," I reiterate to confirm that I mean business.

"You're all talk, Marshall Kerr—"

"I mean it," I interrupt her, "I *will* race again and I *will* win another championship."

She eyes me, scrutinizing me as she processes my words. "Then pull your head out of your ass and do it. In there," she points back inside, "I want to see that killer attitude you have on the racetrack in full throttle. I honestly believe you'll beat the odds and do this, but you need to stop with the woe-is-me bullshit and start pushing yourself. You need to push yourself harder than you've ever pushed before."

"You don't hold back, do you?"

"It's not my job to blow smoke up your ass. It's my job to repair you. To push you and get you back in your race car."

I laugh. "It's refreshing to have someone other than my family and friends do that."

"So now that your head is out of your ass, should we get back in there," She flicks her finger over her shoulder, "And finish today's session?"

"Sounds good, but first, I need to apologize to E for growling at her."

"You can do that after I work you out. Now get back into the therapy room and let's get you out of that chair."

"You really are a bossy bitch, you know that?"

"Yep, now hop to it, Kerr."

Twenty minutes later, I'm on my fourth lap between the parallel bars. I can't believe it's taken me this long to walk four laps. The pressure in my hip is excruciating and pain is radiating down my dominant leg, but I'm going to push through because Nancy is right, I can do this. I just need to keep on pushing myself and work through the pain. *No pain, no gain.*

Sweat lines my forehead as I place one foot in front of the other and shuffle along. I'm huffing and puffing as if I'm running a marathon and not trying to walk eight-freakin-feet.

"Take a seat," Nancy tells me when I finally finish my fourth lap. "I have an idea for your mobility training."

"A magic wand and bibbidi-bobbidi-boo I'm fixed," I suggest as I take a drink of water. I worked up quite the sweat with my four whole laps.

"Not quite bibbidi-bobbidi-boo but how about, splish-splash aqua therapy?"

"Like in a pool?"

"Yep. The water will ease the pressure on your body and allow you to get the motions going. We can even do the repetitions in the water too. I think the water's resistance will help ease things and get your movements more fluid without the pressure of standing."

"Why didn't you suggest this weeks ago?"

"Well for one, we needed to wait for your incisions to heal, but most of all, I like seeing you suffer."

"Sadist."

"That's why they pay me the big bucks. So tomorrow, let's give aqua therapy a go."

"Sounds good to me. I need to upgrade these wheels," I say, doing a spin in my chair.

"Upgrade to your feet?"

"Nope, my race car."

"That's quite a jump from that," she points at my wheels, "to that." She mimics steering and I laugh. "But it's a goal we can work toward. In six to twelve mon—"

"Nope, mid-to-end of this season," I inform her.

"That's a bit of a stretch bu—"

"I *will* be there," I interrupt her, my words forceful and determined. "I've already missed most of this season, I won't be missing the whole thing. Mark my words, Nancy, by the end of the season, I'll be back on the podium. And next season, I will dedicate my season win and honor Joe Johnstone."

She doesn't say anything to that but what can she say, I'm determined to be there, and with my newfound confidence I know I'll get there. Only missing half to three quarters of a season is all I will allow, I will not settle for anything else. My mind is made up and when I set my mind to something, nothing will stand in my way.

Waving goodbye to Nancy, I exit the therapy room and head back to mine to shower and change before dinner. I round a corner and once again, I wheel into someone.

Lifting my gaze I look up at E. We stare at each other for a few seconds. Both of us frozen and then she snarls, "How about you look where you wheel." Throwing my words from earlier back at me. "Men think they can do what they want when they want." I swear I hear her murmur, "Men can fuck right off."

Before I can ask her to elaborate, she storms away and down the corridor, pulling the door to the kitchen open, slamming it into the wall with a thud.

"What the hell?" I mumble to myself as I continue down the corridor.

Once in my room, I head into the shower and decide that tonight I'm going to try to shower unassisted. Wheeling my chair in, I strip off my clothes and use the rails to pull myself up. Turning the faucet on, I flinch at the cold water hitting my skin. It quickly heats so I shuffle farther under the spray, the hot water beating down on my aching muscles feels phenomenal.

Closing my eyes, I drop my head back, the water cascades down my face and a vision of E appears before me. My cock twitches, it's the first time I've felt anything in my nether regions since the accident. I was starting to wonder if he was broken too. My hand lifts on its own accord and I grip my shaft. I begin to stroke myself, up and down. I fist my cock with a vision of E in my head. Sooner than a grown man should, I spray cum all over the tiled wall.

"Well that was embarrassing," I whisper.

Grabbing my body wash, I pump some gel in my hand and begin to clean up. Rinsing off, I grab a towel and dry myself. Flopping into my chair, I redress. This is the hardest part and one of the reasons I wear sweats, they're easy to slip into while sitting down.

Wheeling back into my room, I'm looking out the window when our resident chef enters my room. "Tony, my man," I call out, as he places my dinner on my bed trolley. "Personal delivery tonight, it must be my lucky day."

"It's your lucky day every day that I cook for you." He winks at me and then his face turns serious. "You need to apologize to her."

My face scrunches in confusion. "Huh?"

"Tomorrow you need to apologize to E for being an asshole. She doesn't deserve that."

"I know, I do. I decided while in the shower," *pleasuring myself to images of her*, "that I would."

"Good because I'd hate to have to beat a cripple's ass for upsetting a pretty lady." A laugh escapes me. "Don't be laughing, racer boy, no one makes my girl upset."

Him calling E 'his girl' pisses me off, but before I can say anything to him, he's exiting my room, whistling to "Tuesday's Gone" by Lynyrd Skynyrd.

Wheeling to the bed table, I dive into my dinner.

When my plate is licked clean—sorry mom—I decide that tomorrow I'll find E and apologize for being such a dick, but most of all I want to find out why she thinks men are scum.

ELOISE

Why are men such dicks?

They think they can do what they want when they want. When Marshall bumped into me and growled, I was taken back to when I was living with *him*. I froze with fear, something that's been occurring a lot lately. Ever since the dreams started after my call with Miles. Most nights now, I dream that *he* finds me and it doesn't end well.

Today, I waited for the hit to come from Marshall. For the verbal lashing for being stupid and in the way. Then I remembered I'm not there anymore. I'm safe and it was Marshall, *him*.

As I watched Marshall wheel away, anger built within because I'm not the frail, weak, and scared woman I once way. Now, I'm strong, independent, and I don't cower to anyone … or so I thought.

Shaking it off, I start on my second to last task for the day and then I can head home. *Home*, I finally have a place of my own. Sure, Jenna arranged it for me but it's mine. It's been really refreshing working here, I may be a gofer doing this and that, but I'm doing something for me.

It's kind of funny, I'm broken like many of the residents. The only difference is, I'm mentally broken. I don't know which is harder to heal but somedays, it feels like we help each other mend. That's one thing I'm sure about, I will heal and one day, I'll be Eloise Masters again … who ever she may be.

I've learnt a lot about mindset from my time here. From listening in during group sessions when I'm setting up the refreshments. I know I shouldn't be eavesdropping, but it's not like I'm listening to pertinent information that could bring about the end of the world. I'm taking the bits I need to heal myself.

I've finished setting out the refreshments when I'm called into the director's office. My heart races as I walk toward her door. I feel like I'm being summoned to see the principal. I knock and when she looks up, I can tell from the look on her face it's not good news.

"Please, take a seat, Eloise." My eyes widen at the use of my actual name. It's odd hearing it in full, I've just been E since I left.

"I'm not going to like what you tell me, am I?"

She shakes her head as I close the door behind me. "I don't think so. I just got off the phone with Jenna—"

"Is she okay?" I ask, dropping into the seat across from her.

"She's fine, but it looks like your medical file from her office has been taken."

"Duncan," I murmur, biting my lip. I wring my hands in my lap and then I hesitantly look up. "Do you want me to leave?"

"No!" Linda protests, shaking her head from side to side vigorously. "Not at all. You're one hell of a worker and I don't want to lose you. The staff and residents love you. As long as the past doesn't affect the now, you can stay as long as you like. I just wanted to let you know."

"Is he going to find me?" I ask her, my voice meek and fragile. I hate that he still has this power over me.

"I don't think so," she reassures me. "Jenna said there's nothing in the file to indicate where you are now so you're safe, but you need to be vigilant."

"Vigilant is my first name since escaping but knowing this I'll be even more so now."

"Good. Now, I want you to take the afternoon off."

"No, I'll be fine." Shaking my head, I continue, "I need to work, otherwise I'll think about *him*." Silently I add, *or Marshall.*

"It wasn't a suggestion, Eloise."

"There's no point in arguing, is there?"

She shakes her head again. "Nope. I'll see you bright and early tomorrow morning."

Nodding, I rise and walk toward the door. With my hand on the knob, I look over my shoulder. "Thank you for everything, Linda."

Turning the handle, I step into the hallway and leave her office in a daze. Taking a left, I head toward the staff lounge. I need a few moments to compose myself before I leave. Turning the corner, a staff member bumps into me and they drop the files they were carrying.

"Watch where you're going," they snarl, the tone of their voice cuts through me and fear envelops me.

"I … I'm sorry," I mutter, my voice wavering. Wiping at a stray tear, I mumble, "It won't happen again."

"Just watch it," they grumble as they bend down to collect the papers. From the tone of their voice, my body begins to shake. They mutter under their breath as they continue down the hallway, leaving me a quivering mess.

With my head down, I race toward the locker rooms. Pushing the door open, I walk over to my locker, and rest my head on the metal. Another tear drops and I let out a frustrated sigh. Will I feel like this every time Duncan is mentioned? Will I cower anytime someone raises their voice at me? I thought I was doing better, but clearly I'm just as weak as I was when I was back in Collinsville.

"Miles," I whisper to myself. Opening my locker, I grab my phone but when I look at the screen, I freeze and it slips through my fingers, hitting my foot before coming to rest on the tiles below.

There are dozens of text messages and voicemail notification ... from *him*. I'm glad I had the foresight to input his number when I left.

Sliding down the lockers, I drop to the floor and pick up my phone. Taking a deep breath I click on the voicemail icon. "Eloise, you fucking bit..." As soon as I hear his voice, a lump forms in the back of my throat and the urge to throw up hits me. Jumping up, I race into the closest toilet stall and empty my stomach.

Tears cascade down my cheeks and the fear that enveloped me earlier tightens its grip on my body. My skin becomes clammy. My vision blurs and I visibly shake as I slide to the floor. Bile gurgles in my stomach and I vomit again.

If he has my number, it's only a matter of time before he finds me. I should never have run away. I should have stayed. I should have sucked it up, married him, and played the dutiful wife. Maybe it's not too late to go back to him. Maybe I can fix this and the consequences won't be so bad. *Ha*, I think, if I went back now he'd kill me for sure.

Standing up, I walk over to the sink, rinse my mouth, and wash my face. Looking at myself in the mirror, the girl staring back at me is not the one from Collinsville. The one staring back at me is strong, ish.

I got out of there.

I'm my own person now.

I'm much tougher than he *ever* gave me credit for.

I will not let him win.

I refuse to let *him* ruin my future. I did not lose my baby or run away just for him to waltz back in and take control of my life again.

This is MY life and I will live it how I want. Walking back over to my locker, I pick up my phone and delete all of his voicemails and text messages. Feeling brave I send him a text message.

> You don't control me anymore, Duncan. I control my life, not you. Leave me alone. Forget you ever knew me. You have more to lose than I do, don't push me. Goodbye.

As soon as I hit send, my confidence soars, that is until my phone vibrates in my hand and I see the reply from Duncan aka Prickface.

> You cannot hide from me forever, bitch. I will find you and when I do, you will regret the day you left me.

> Mark my words, your days are numbered.

> Remember, Eloise, you are mine, now and forever.

With three text messages my brief moment of bravery vanishes. Once again, meek and shy Eloise is back. Without thinking, I call Miles. He answers on the third ring.

"Hello, this is Miles."

"It's me," I meekly say. "He has my number."

"How?" Miles asks, his voice laced with concern.

"Jenna's office was broken into and my file was accessed. I'm guessing my number was updated."

"You need to hang up, turn off the phone, remove the SIM, and get rid of it."

"Okay, I'll do that, and I'll be sure to message you my new number when I get it."

"No, we can't risk him knowing I'm in contact with you."

"But I need you," I cry.

"You don't need me, sweetheart. You're stronger than you think."

"I don't want to say goodbye."

"Let's go with see you later then. I know where to reach you if I need to."

"Miles," I blubber, "please don't leave me."

"For your safety we need to do this, but you're strong. Remember that." He pauses and then says two final words that gut me. "Goodbye, Eloise."

Before I can say anything, he hangs up. I call him back immediately but it goes straight to voicemail. He's turned off his phone, or he's blocked me. Doing as he told me to, I remove the SIM card and flush it.

Wiping under my eyes, I take a deep breath, ever so thankful I have the afternoon off because I'm an emotional mess right now. Grabbing my bag, I wipe under my eyes again and exit the locker room. Pulling the door open, with my head down and my mind a jumbled mess, I step out into the hallway. Someone wheels into me.

Looking up, I see it's Marshall. *Freakin' men crashing into my life all the time.* "How about you look where you wheel," I growl. "Men think they can do what they want when they want." Stepping around him, I walk toward the kitchen and mumble, "Men can fuck right off."

Pushing the door to the kitchen open with more force than I intended, it slams into the wall with a thud. "Easy there, Tiger," Tony, the chef, says to me.

"S-s-s-sorry," I stutter, "b-b-bad day." Tony is much like Miles, I'm not frightened around him and I know he unequivocally has my back.

"Will this cheer you up?" He hands me a plate with his famous caramel slice on it. I'm addicted to the sweet treat Tony has perfected. I mean, caramel, chocolate, and a crunchy cookie base, what's not to love?

"It definitely will help." Lifting the slice to my mouth, I take a bite, close my eyes and moan as the chocolate and caramel flavors dance and melt on my tongue. "This is soooooo good." I groan.

"How about I wrap you up a few slices for later tonight?"

"I love you, Tony."

"Just like all the boys do." He winks and goes about wrapping up my dessert. He hands it to me and grips my wrist. My eyes widen and I flinch at the contact. He immediately drops his hand. "I'm sorry," he quickly interjects, offering me a comforting smile. "One of these days you need to tell me who I need to kill. No one should ever make a woman cower like that."

"I'm fine," I reassure him.

"Don't bullshit me, E. Just know, I'm here anytime you need me."

Smiling, I take his hand and squeeze. "I promise I'm fine. Just a few men have pissed me off today." I pause. "If you feel like helping me, feel free to give Marshall Kerr a case of severe food poisoning."

"Now why would I poison a fine-looking man like that?"

"Because he's an asshole."

"Why are the assholes always good-looking?"

"He's not that good-looking," I protest, but it's a complete and utter lie. Marshall Kerr is H O doubt T hot. I've always thought he was attractive when I saw him on the news, but in the flesh, holy freakin' hotness, Batman. It's a pity he has a giant chip on his sexy as sin shoulders.

"The tinge of pink on your neck and face tells me otherwise."

"Fine, he's good-looking, but I don't need a man in my life."

"Girl, you always need the P, nothing beats a good pounding." I shudder at his words because the last P I got was against my will. Actually, most of the poundings I've received were against my will. I've never had sex for pleasure, guess that happens when you live with a monster.

Not wanting to dwell on that, I lift my hand and wave my fingers. "I don't need a P when I have these ... or my rabbit." Then I add with an eyebrow wiggle. "Or both."

"Girl, I knew you were a kinky one. One of these days, you and I are going to drink cosmos and you're gonna tell me everything."

"Yes to the cosmos. No to the history of E. The past is the past and I'm all about the future."

If only I was as confident about what I just declared, I thought I was strong, but maybe I'll never be whole again. Maybe, I'm just too fractured.

MARSHALL

"Who knew all I had to do was get you in a pool to aid in your recovery?" Nancy teases me as I walk—yes, walk—another lap of the pool. I'm currently on lap nine, it may not be many but three weeks ago I struggled to do one. My speed is getting faster and faster each day. By the end of the month, I want to be doing this out of the water. Nancy thinks it's a bit optimistic, but that fire inside of me has been lit and I'm determined to get better and back out on the track.

"I know, right?"

"Think you can do this on dry land, starting next week?" Nancy throws at me, totally shocking me because she doubted me when I broached it yesterday. "Let's kick that chair to the curb and get you closer to your new wheels."

"New wheels?" I question as I walk back toward her.

"Your race car."

"Those wheels are a far way off yet, but I can see them in the distance now. It doesn't seem so grim anymore."

"Hence why I think you can do this on dry land." I eye her. "I know I doubted you when you touched on the subject yesterday, but you've changed. Your mind is focused on your goal, but I've also seen a change in YOU as a person. Anything you care to tell me? Or maybe *someone* you care to tell me about?"

"You sound just like my mother," I retort and roll my eyes. Mom is like a dog with a bone when it comes to E.

"Your mother and I had coffee when they were here last week."

"Of course you did. What wild stories did you two share with one another?"

"What happens during coffee, stays at coffee."

"Is that some coffee fight club rule?" I tease.

"Yep, now give me three more laps and we can call it a day or you can tell me all about—"

"Sorry, can't talk, I have laps to do. My physical therapist is a real hard-ass who will kick mine if I don't finish this set."

Nancy laughs. "Come on then, hop to it, racer boy."

As I finish my laps, I think about what she said. E and I have been getting closer these last few weeks. After I apologized for running into her and being a grumpy asshole all the time, an unofficial truce was called between us. We've become friendly and since the run-in where I'm sure I heard her whisper something about not needing a man, I've been secretly watching her but not in a creepy way. But it seems it wasn't so much of a secret since Mom, and now Nancy, have noticed me admiring her.

There's also the fact that each afternoon for the last week, before she leaves for the day, the two of us have watched the sunset together.

We chat, well, I chat and she listens. Whenever I ask her personal questions, she clams up and deflects, but one of these days, I'll get her to tell me her story.

I've tried looking for her online but with only her first initial to go on, it's hard. I'm not very sleuthy. If only I knew what the E stood for, and her last name, it would make my stalking that much easier.

"Good job," Nancy praises me as I hobble up the ramp and over to her. Taking the outstretched towel from her, I wipe myself down. Once dried, I go to grab my chair when Nancy pulls it away from me. "Uhhh ah, you're walking back to your room today."

"But I just did twelve laps."

"And now you can add a lap of the facility to today's workout as well, unless you want to wuss out?"

"Did anyone ever tell you you're a sadist?"

"Yep, you did last week when I made you do the same thing."

"Sadist," I mumble, shuffling away from her. Looking over my shoulder I throw back at her, "If I remember correctly, I didn't make it to my room and I 'wussed out' as you so eloquently put it."

"But you tried," she states matter-of-factly. Flipping her the bird, I continue toward the exit. "Same time tomorrow, Kerr," she shouts at me.

Waving over my shoulder, I push the door open and step into the corridor leading back to the residents' wing. Who would have thought I'd be shuffling around like this so soon?

I certainly didn't.

To be honest, I was starting to think I'd never get back on my feet. Sure, after I get back to my room, I'll be done for the night, *but* I'm up and moving about. That's more than I was doing three weeks ago.

Nancy was right, the aqua therapy has been a game-changer for me.

A smile graces my face when I turn the corner and see E bent over, picking up something she dropped. My eyes roam over her khaki clad ass. She somehow manages to make khaki slacks look amazing.

She stands up and turns around, catching me checking her out. Her cheeks darken in embarrassment, or maybe arousal.

"Hey," I offer in greeting, walking over to her.

"Hey, how was aqua therapy?"

"Wet," I reply to her. "How you doing?"

"Did you just Joey me?"

"Unintentionally, yes … unless you want me to Joey you?" I raise my eyebrows at her but she just stares blankly at me. The air around us thickens the longer we stare at one another. She bites her bottom lip, my eyes drop and I watch her teeth sink into her skin. The action causes my dick to twitch, I'm only wearing board shorts so I can't hide what she's doing to me.

Her eyes drop to my crotch, then quickly she averts her gaze. Her cheeks darken again and her breath hitches in her throat. "I … umm … ahh, better go … I have to, umm, go." She spins on her heel and quickly walks away from me and I can't help but admire her tight taut butt. With my eyes glued to her backside, I stand here and appreciate the view as she races into the staff locker room.

"You hurt her, and I'll hurt you." I turn toward the voice and find Tony staring intently at me. The look on his face means business.

"I'd like to see you try, chef boy." I tease to try and lighten the mood.

"Chef boy," he repeats, "I like that," his voice much smoother than moments ago. Then his face turns stern. "But seriously, be careful with E. She's precious to me and I'd hate to have to maim a pretty boy like you." His gaze roams over me and my cock deflates, quickly. I have no problem with gays but they just don't do it for me. He steps to me so we're nose-to-nose. "Just remember, I know how to use a carving knife and I know people who know people."

He taps the tip of my nose, steps around me, and heads into the kitchen. Leaving me standing here confused about his threat and wondering what he knows about E that I don't. I need to get E to open up to me. I want to know everything there is to know about her.

Finally I make my way to my room and I head straight to my shower to wash off the chlorine from the pool. Turning on the water, I remove my board shorts and T-shirt and stare at myself in the mirror. My gaze focuses on the left side of my abdomen. Specifically, underneath my rib cage. The scar from my splenectomy is still red but thanks to the Bio-Oil E recommended, it's not as vicious anymore. My mind drifts to the day she gave me the oil…

…Sitting on the edge of my bed, I stare at myself in the mirror by the door. The scar from my splenectomy is red, raw, and ugly. It's staring at me, waving its jazz hands at me and reminding me of all that I lost with the accident. My spleen. My hip movements. My calm and cool persona. My career. My life. That accident screwed up everything.

The ugly scar matches my ugly mood and mars my perfect abdomen. I run my finger gently over it.

"Bio-Oil will help with that," a sweet voice says from the doorway.

"Huh?" I respond like a goofball.

"Bio-Oil, it helps scars to fade quicker," she advises, placing new towels on the shelf in my room.

"What do you know about scars?" I throw back at her.

"More than I should," she quietly admits before turning around and exiting my room, leaving me to wallow in self-pity.

Grabbing my shirt, I pull it over my head and climb into my chair. My stomach grumbles as I wheel myself toward the dining room for lunch.

Returning to my room with one of Tony's caramel slice pieces balancing on my lap, I pause mid-wheel when I see, sitting on my bed, a brown paper bag. Wheeling over, I place my slice on the rolling bed table and grab the bag. Opening it, I pull out a white box with orange writing. "Bio-Oil," I whisper as I read the box. For the first time in a long time, my lip lifts and a smile graces my face and it's all thanks to E and her thoughtful gift.

…I've used the Bio-Oil every day since she gave it to me and she was right, the scar has faded. If only an oil could help my hip heal as quickly.

Stepping under the shower spray, I soap up and when I wash my cock, it hardens under my touch. In the last seven days, my cock has acted like a horny teenager again. He's always hard and I'm jerking off like no tomorrow. Lack of sex drive is apparently a side effect from the surgeries I had, but it seems my cock didn't get the memo. He's popping up to wave hello each and every day … and it's generally after I see E.

I don't have time to whack one out right now, so I turn the water to cold and step back under the freezing spray. I finish soaping myself up, avoiding my cock. I rinse off the suds and turn the water off. Grabbing my towel, I dry myself and realize I didn't grab any clean clothes.

Wrapping the towel around my waist, I hobble back into my room. The towel brushing against my cock has it hardening once again and I can't take it. Taking a seat on my bed, I lie back and grip my cock in my fist. Closing my eyes, I imagine it's E's delicate hand wrapped around my shaft and I begin to stroke myself.

Up and down I pump my cock and before long, I come with a grunt. Thick ropes spray my abdomen and chest and then I hear a gasp.

Lifting my head, I look to the doorway and I see a startled E. Her gaze is on my dick and the mess I made on my chest. "Can I help you?" I ask, not bothering to cover up.

"I … ummm … ahh, I'll come back." She quickly turns around and races out of my room, slamming the door closed behind her.

Laughing to myself, I wipe off my chest, stand up, and walk over to the wardrobe. Opening the closet, I lean in and grab my briefs when there's a knock on my door and it begins to open.

Spinning to see who it is, my towel slips from my fingertips. I try and grab it but my nimble fingers miss, both the towel and my briefs fall to the floor. Not even thinking, I reach down to pick my briefs up. My eyes widen and I cry out when a searing pain radiates from my hip down my thigh.

"Dude, put some fucking clothes on," Linc teases, but when he sees the look on my face, his morphs from joking to concern.

"I'm fucking trying but I can't move right now, my hip's…" I snarl through clenched teeth not finishing my sentence. "I think I just tore my insides open," I cry and let out the breath I didn't realize I was holding.

"Shit, what can I do?" he asks, walking over to me.

"Help me to the bed before I die standing here with my dick out."

He drapes my arm over his shoulder and when he turns me, I scream out in agony. "Fuuuuuck," I shout, my eyes welling with tears.

"I'm sorry."

"Just get me to the bed."

After what feels like an eternity, Linc finally has me back in bed. He races out of my room to get the doctor. They return a few moments later and I'm still in pain. The doctor checks me over and thinks I just bent the wrong way and my healing groin did not like it. He's not concerned but fuck me does it hurt.

He prescribes me a pain reliever and a sleeping pill. He also arranges for me to have scan tomorrow to make sure there's no internal damage—thankfully, my scan comes back.

After apologizing to Linc because we were meant to spend the afternoon together, but he waves me off and tells me he'll be back tomorrow, I take the pills the doctor prescribed. They kick in immediately and I drift off to sleep, dreaming about E and her delicate hands roaming over my body and cock.

ELOISE

Holy shit!

He's naked. And there's cum all over his abdomen.

And I'm staring at his dick.

His dick is perfect … and I wouldn't mind getting a closer look.

Holy shit, I'm thinking about a dick.

Oh My God, I'm drooling over a dick, a beautiful, gorgeous dick.

Why am I still focused on his dick? His long, thick, veiny dick.

My brain finally kicks into gear and I stop staring.

Shaking my head, I spin on my heel and race out of his room quicker than Speedy Gonzales.

My head is down in embarrassment and I bump into someone in the corridor. Reaching out they grab my upper arms to steady me. My eyes widen at the contact. I'm frozen with fear. Panic courses through me. My body tenses. I want to curl into myself and make myself invisible.

Lowering my head, I close my eyes and wait for the hit.

Wait for something horrible to happen.

Waiting.

Waiting.

Waiting.

"Where's the fire, sweet cheeks?" His voice startles me.

Lifting my gaze I stare at the man before me. My vision is hazy. My heart rapidly beating within my chest. I can feel and hear the blood pumping through my veins, the sound whooshes through my head making me feel giddy and nauseous.

Pulling my arm free, I step backward and mumble, "I … ummm, ahh, I … I need to go." The need to flee overtakes my body and I run for it, accidentally bumping into his shoulder as I race away. With each step I take, I wait for it. I wait for him to grab me … but it never comes.

On autopilot, my feet keep moving of their own accord. They take me away from the danger that seems to only be in my head. The door to the staff locker room comes into view and I head toward it.

Stepping inside, I make my way to my locker. Leaning against the cool metal, I close my eyes and breathe deeply. The coldness is a relief on my heated body. Leaning my head back, I look to the ceiling before spinning around and sliding down, dropping to the floor in a heap.

Pulling my knees to my chest, I begin to rock back and forth. My breathing is hurried. I'm on the verge of a panic attack. My vision starts to dot when someone drops in front of me. They grip my shoulders, squeezing in a reassuring way.

"E, what's wrong?" Blinking rapidly, Nancy comes into focus before me. "Babe, what's wrong?" she asks again, her voice laced with concern.

"I … I … I can't breathe," I tell her, dropping my head back to the lockers. I close my eyes and continue to hyperventilate.

She takes my hands in hers and gently squeezes. "Look at me, E." I lift my head, open my eyes and stare at her. "Good girl," she soothes. "Now breathe in through your nose and out through your mouth." She breathes along with me and after a few breaths, my breathing begins to slow down.

My heart rate returns to normal.

My vision clears and now I can clearly see a worried Nancy before me.

"Thank you," I tell her once the panic attack dies down.

"You're welcome." She drops to her butt, crosses her legs and stares at me.

"I'm fine," I assure her, "I just ..." *I saw a beautiful dick and it's the first dick since* him, *and it didn't freak me out and that in itself freaks me out, because I didn't freak out at seeing a dick, a glorious, beautiful dick.*

"Just what?"

"I saw his dick and it was beautiful. And then someone grabbed me and I freaked out."

"Whose beautiful dick did you see?"

"It doesn't matter whose. What matters is that I saw it and now I can never look him in the eye again. I'm going to have to leave."

"I'm sure it'll all be fine." I nod but I don't think it will be. "Okay, beautiful dick aside, who grabbed you? And do I need to get Tony's carving knife?"

"No, no carving is necessary. Some guy grabbed me as I was freaking out over the beautiful dick, and then I freaked out some more."

"Why did you freak out?"

"I ... I ..." But I drift off, I've kept this part of me a secret because if no one but me knows, it never happened—an out of sight, out of mind kinda thing. As I stare at Nancy, I see nothing but worry etched on her face. She's staring at me like a concerned friend, not someone who wants the gossip.

For the first time since I ran, I want to tell someone my story.

Closing my eyes, I take a deep breath and then I begin. "I was in an abusive relationship before I came here. Whenever people grab me, men in particular, I tend to freak out. Especially when they grab my upper arms. He used to grip mine and shake me," I swallow deeply as the memories flood my mind, "he'd ... he'd shake me before throwing me to the ground and he'd either beat me or fuck me senseless."

"Ohh, E," she coos, "do you wanna talk about it?" Shaking my head no, I smile and sigh again. "Just know, I'm here anytime you want to talk."

"I know and thank you, but really, I'm fine. The dick just surprised me."

"So we're back to the dick then … wanna talk about that?" She waggles her eyebrows at me.

Again I shake my head from side to side. "Thanks, but I'm good."

"Can you at least share whose dick you saw so I can try and get a peek? I love a good dick, just like the next girl."

"As do I," Tony interrupts, walking in at just the right moment. As soon as he sees me on the floor, he shakes his head. "I'm going to carve him, I told him if he hurt you I would hurt him."

"Who?" Nancy and I ask in unison.

"Racer boy."

"Marshall?" we both say at the same time.

"Yep, I warned that pretty boy not to mess with you."

"What? Why?"

"I've seen the way he looks at you." He laughs. "It's the same way you look at him."

"He doesn't look at me like that." *Does he? And do I really look at him like Tony is suggesting?* He annoys me more than anything. He has the world at his feet and rather than facing his issues head-on, he's sulking like a petulant child … well, he was until recently. I know it's a pot-kettle situation since I ran away from mine, but mine is literally a life-or-death scenario, his is just 'I'm a douchehole woe-is-me' scenario.

"Ahh, yeah he does, and so do you for the record," Nancy states matter-of-factly.

Now it's Tony's turn. "Well, if it wasn't him who turned you into this," he circles his finger in front of me, "who am I carving?"

"You don't need to carve anyone. I just freaked out."

"Over seeing a dick?" he questions, his face scrunching in confusion that I would be freaked out by the male appendage. "Why on Earth would a dick freak you out?"

"It's complicated," I tell him. "Seeing a dick was the catalyst that started my freak-out."

"And whose dick freaked you out?"

"She won't share that information," Nancy sulks, crossing her arms and huffing.

"Come on, girl, you gotta share the good dick." He drops to his ass and sits on the other side of me. "It's slim dickings around here, so you need to share the dick deets."

"See, I'm not the only one who wants the dick deets," Nancy confirms, shuffling around to sit beside me.

This causes me to laugh. "My lips are sealed on the owner of said dick, but I will tell you, it was a beautiful one."

"You're such a dick tease, E," Tony whines. He reaches over and takes my hand in his and squeezes, just like Miles did the last day I saw him. "Dicks aside, are you sure you're okay?"

I nod. "I'm sure. I just overreacted. My life before here was less than stellar, and occasionally, I get taken back to that time and I freak out."

"Seems like I need to carve someone from your past," Tony grumbles, and I laugh. I'd love to see Tony carve Duncan, but Tony is too pretty for prison and orange really isn't his color, so we'll keep the Tony carving Duncan as a fantasy.

Shaking my head, I smile at Tony and his carving threats. "As much as I'd appreciate you carving him, orange really isn't your color and if you went away, who would feed my caramel slice addiction?"

"So you only want me around for my slice?" he teases.

"And to save you from a fashion disaster."

For the next few minutes, the three of us sit on the floor and chat about anything and everything. It's the perfect distraction.

Later that night I wake from another horrible nightmare, but this time when Duncan found me, it didn't end well for me … or Marshall. And that's why I cannot pursue anything with him, he has too much to lose if I invite him into my life. I lie here and stare at the ceiling, afraid to go back to sleep because even though it's just a dream, I hate it.

Why can't I dream of rainbows and unicorns … or Marshall's dick?

The next day flies by in a blur, I don't have a chance to scratch myself. After my restless night's sleep, I'm surprised I can function. I like busy days like this because it keeps me occupied and my mind doesn't wander to a certain race car driver … and his dick.

Since walking in on him, twice now, I see him in a different light. He seems nicer and now, he's actually making an effort with his recovery. The thought of him leaving hurts, and that shocks me. I hardly know the guy, but I'm already mourning his departure.

It's finally Friday and it's been a pretty good day. It's going to end on a high because when I finish, I'm going to watch the sunset from the patio before I head home for a relaxing bath. The sunsets from the center are pretty phenomenal and I have a feeling tonight's is going to be spectacular.

Grabbing my things, I head out to the patio and pull out a chair. Sitting down, I look to the sky and watch as the sun starts its descent toward the horizon. I used to love sunrise but now, sunset is my favorite time of day. The sky tonight is putting on a pretty epic show, it's like the universe knows I need this. Rich hues of red blend with oranges, purples, and crimsons. From just watching this for a few short moments, my spirits soar and I feel rejuvenated.

"Mind if I join you?" Marshall asks, as he walks, yes walks, over to me but I smile when I don't see his chair.

"No wheels this evening?"

"I'm in the process of upgrading so in the meantime, I'm hoofing it."

"That's good, I guess you'll be leaving us soon." At the thought of him not being here, my heart stutters. I'm sad at the prospect of him, and his dick, leaving. I'm not ready for him to go.

"Trying to get rid of me?" he teases. "You see my dick and then boom, I'm tossed out on my naked ass." My eyes widen at his words. My mouth drops open in shock. I'm at a loss as to what to say to that. Then he adds, "You know, you've seen me naked, it's only fair that I get to see you naked too now."

"Where in the friendship rule book does it say that?"

"We're friends, are we?" he throws back at me.

Nodding, I smile up at him. "Yeah, we are." I motion to the seat next to me and he lowers himself down. Wincing as he gets himself comfortable.

"Well, friends show each other their, umm, ahh bits." His eyes drop to my breasts and between my legs before he lifts his gaze back up, staring into my eyes. "It's like an unwritten rule," he nonchalantly replies before he turns his attention to the sky. He stares out at the sunset, leaving me to process his words and pondering if I *want* to show him my 'bits' as he so eloquently put it.

Returning my attention back to the sunset, I notice a silhouette of birds flying across the now magenta sky. They flap their wings without—I presume—a care in the world. The sun is half into the horizon now and I really wish I had a camera to capture the moment.

He breaks the silence that has fallen between us, "So, how about it?"

Playing dumb, I shrug. "How about what?"

"About showing me your bits?"

"Ohh, that," I nonchalantly reply. "Your friendship book and my friendship book seem to be different versions." I glance over to him. "Let's stick with mine … for now."

"We can do that … for now, but I will say, anytime you want to show me your bits, I won't mind at all."

My cheeks heat at the thought of showing him my bits, and between my legs pulsates in a way that it hasn't for a very long time. Swallowing down the desire building, I nod. "I'll keep that in mind."

Focusing on the sunset, I bite my bottom lip as Marshall and I quietly watch the sun finally disappear, leaving behind the darkness of the night ahead. The biggest star appears, paving way for thousands of others to appear in the inky black sky.

The stars twinkle above us and I keep thinking about Marshall, his dick and showing him my bits. I grin and realize that I wouldn't mind showing him my bits, but after Duncan, can I open myself up to a man in that way again?

MARSHALL

Watching the sunset with E tonight has been the most fun I've had since the accident. We didn't say much, not after I asked to see her bits but before we parted ways, we did agree to watch the sunset again together.

After we say our goodbyes, I walk the long way back to my room because what's one more lap? Climbing into bed, I lie back and flick the television on. *Fast and the Furious* is on, I love this movie, and in my opinion, it's the best of the franchise.

When the movie finishes, I turn the television off and drift off to sleep, dreaming of being back in my green machine and having E by my side as I do it.

When I wake the next morning, I feel refreshed and ready to tackle the day ahead. My mind drifts to E and last night and my heart feels full. I'm looking forward to watching it with her again. *Is tonight too soon to ask her to watch it with me?*

After breakfast, I'm in my room and since the cramping incident, Nancy is giving me every second day off from therapy to rest up. I'm at a loss as to what to do. I've been so focused on my therapy these last few weeks, I've forgotten what it's like to have free time.

My eyes land on the Bio-Oil bottle and I smile.

"What's got you grinning like a lovesick fool?" Linc's voice from my doorway startles me, snapping my thoughts away from Bio-Oil and E.

"I'm not a lovesick fool," I scoff in reply.

"But you are grinning."

"I just realized that I'm not in all that much pain this morning. Maybe I can go a whole day without using my wheels?"

"You think that's a good idea after how I found you the other night?"

"If I want to get back on the track and into my green machine, I need to keep on going. And I'm fine, really. I'm listening to my doctor and Nancy and I'm not pushing myself too hard." *Kinda, sorta.*

"Look at you go. If you keep this up, you'll be back out on the track before you know it."

"That's the plan," my grin widens. "Fuck, I can't wait for that day. I always knew I loved racing but not being in the car these last few months has been painful."

"You need to fix you before I'll even allow you back in your car and on the track."

"You sound like Mom."

"That mother of yours is a wise woman, you should listen to her." He pauses. "Speaking of women, what's the story with that hottie that works here?"

Feigning ignorance, I answer nonchalantly, "Which hottie?"

"The hottie you eye-fuck all the time. The hottie you're always with. The hottie you mention and quote often when we chat. Shall I go on about the hottie?"

"I'm not always with E."

"So you admit she's hot?"

"Blind Freddie can see she's hot," I retort and I mean it, E is stunning but what makes her the most beautiful woman in the world, she doesn't realize just how stunning she actually is. And that adds to her hotness.

"So, you gonna tap that?"

"Tap that? Really?" He shrugs. "In a heartbeat I would, but she doesn't see me that way. We're just friends."

"She eye-fucks you just as much as you eye-fuck her."

Why do people keep saying that? And why don't I see it? Does she? Does she see me the way I see her? Come to think of it, her eyes were glued to my dick the other day but I do have a nice dick—not lying there, I've had several people tell me so. But do I want to start something with her? I mean, as soon as I'm healed, I'll be heading back to Cali and she'll still be here in Brookvale, in the bumfuck of nowhere. Unless I can get her to fall for me and come to Cali with me, it's not like we can have a future together.

"Yo, earth to Marshall," he clicks his fingers on front of my face. "I said, do you wanna get out of here for the day?"

Nodding my head, I smile. "Yeah, let's blow this joint."

Grabbing my things and cane, we head out. *Not* taking my chair for an outing is a first for me and I cannot wait to see if I can do it.

We exit my room and Linc bumps into E, she drops the towels in her hands and stumbles from the force of Linc smashing into her. Reaching out, he grabs her upper arms to steady her. Her eyes widen at the contact and I notice her breath hitch.

"E," I voice, her head turns toward me and when she sees me standing here, she begins to breathe again. "You okay?" I ask, my voice laced with concern for her.

She nods. "Yeah, you, just, ummm, ahh, you guys scared me. I was in my own little world." She says all of this in one breath.

Dropping to her knees, she begins to collect the towels. If I could easily bend, I'd help but I stand here and watch. Her breathing is labored and her face is etched with fear whenever Linc hands her a towel. He looks at me confused, I just shrug because I have no idea why she's acting like this. She stands up and I notice, her eyes are full to the brim with unshed tears. Before I can ask her anything, she mumbles, "Excuse me," and races off.

Standing here, Linc and I watch her hustle down the corridor and into the laundry room.

"That's the second time I've run into her and both times she's reacted the same way," Linc informs me.

"I wheeled into her one day and she went off on me. Like crazy went off."

"What do you think that's about?"

"I'll tell you what I think over a burger and a beer."

"Deal."

Linc and I walk to his car, much slower than we normally would but I did it without the use of my chair. "Look at you go," he teases when we finally reach his baby.

"Fuck off, asshole," I grumble.

Opening my door—myself—I lower myself into his car, flinching in pain as I fold my body into the passenger seat of his McLaren GT. Clicking in my seat belt, I realize, this is the first time I've been in his car since my accident. My wheelchair didn't exactly fit into this sexy sleek machine easily, or at all. Being low to the ground like this with the leather seat enveloping me, feels like coming home.

Linc starts the engine and even though I'm not in the driver's seat, my body comes alive, just like it does when I'm behind the wheel of my race car. My heart begins to thump with excitement and I smile as the happy memories come back to me.

"I haven't seen you smile like that in a long time," he pops the car into reverse and backs out of his spot.

"I've missed the rumble of an engine beneath me."

"Are you going to jizz your pants in my car?"

"No, but I think the first time I'm behind the wheel of my green machine again, I just might."

Linc laughs as we head toward the exit. I catch a glimpse of E leaving. She looks up and our gaze connects. Something passes between us, and with that brief look my heart skips a beat yet speeds up at the same time. She looks sad and unnerved and I decide I'm going to make it my mission to make her smile brightly again. When E smiles, the world is brighter and beautiful. Plus those dimples of hers are sexy AF … don't get me started on the dirty delicious things I want to do to them.

"You're grinning again," Linc razzes, as we pull onto the street and he heads into the main part of town.

"There's lots to be thankful for."

"I think you mean someone to be thankful for."

"Well, there's that too, but I don't think anything will happen." As I say those words, my heart—that only moments ago was soaring—aches at the thought of not getting a chance with her.

"She's definitely spooked around men."

"I can't find anything about her," I tell him, "it's hard when all I have to search is E."

"Stalker much?" Linc teases.

"It's not stalking when you genuinely care for someone."

"So you DO like her?"

"Yes. No. I don't know," I admit to him. "There's something about her that I'm drawn to, but she's guarded by an impenetrable wall."

"Well, you need to figure out how to smash through that wall and get her to let her guard down."

"That's easier said than done, Linc."

"I didn't take you for a quitter."

"I'm not quitting, just at a loss on how to proceed."

"I know what you need."

"And what's that?" I ask, as we pull up outside the local burger joint.

"You need a KK chat."

I laugh because he's right, if anyone has the right advice for me, it's my mom. "Fine, after you feed me, I'll call Mom."

"You better, or I'll swoop in and rescue the damsel in distress myself."

A growl forms in the back of my throat and the urge to kill my friend and team owner is strong. Linc laughs and then climbs out, I follow, but at a much slower rate.

The two of us spend the afternoon and evening eating freakin' amazeballs burgers, drinking beer and talking shit, just like old times. Since I started this new exercise regime, alcohol has been banned from my diet, but one afternoon off the wagon won't hurt. A few months back, I wouldn't have survived a day without a drink, but now that my head is in the game and not up my ass wallowing, it's easy.

Linc drops me back to the center and before I close the door, he reminds me to call Mom. I salute him and watch him drive off, it's been great having him here.

Even though he's my boss, he's also a good friend. I offered for him to replace me permanently at Scofield Racing, but he reassured me my place will be waiting for me as soon as I'm medically cleared to race again. All going well, I should be ready toward the end of the current season, and I cannot wait to get behind the wheel again and defend my title.

Shuffling to my room, I collapse onto my bed. I may have overdone it today, especially at the burger place. Rather than taking the ramp inside—the easy way—I took the front stairs—the hard way. Sure, there were only eight steps but after what I've been through, it felt like I had walked the Spanish Steps, twice.

Lying back in bed, I find a comfy position and call Mom. "Marshall, how are you?"

"I'm good, Mom. I went out with Linc earlier and I didn't use the chair."

"That's wonderful to hear. How you feeling now?"

"I feel like I ran a marathon and all I did was walk to the car, into the burger joint, and back again."

"For someone who had major surgery not that long ago, that's a big outing."

"Pffft, I should be able to do it without feeling like this."

"You never were one to take things easy. You always pushed yourself to the limit."

"Geez, Mom, I wonder where I get that from?" My mom is just as much of a go-getter as I am.

"Must be your father," she teases.

I laugh. "Yes, must be from Dad." He and Mom are polar opposites but they somehow work. I guess she pushes him and he keeps her in line. I love seeing the two of them together because even though Mom is a foot shorter than Dad, she has him wrapped tightly around her little finger. They have the kind of relationship I aspire to have.

"So, how are things with that girl who has you all knotted up?"

"I'm not knotted up," I protest but Mom's right, E does have me in her grasp and all we've done is watch the sun set together.

"Deny it all you want, but Mom knows best. Now, did you send her flowers like I suggested?"

"No," I tell her, waiting for the lecture.

"And why not, Marshall Kerr?"

"Because I'm an idiot, but I …"

"I what?" Mom pushes.

"I think she's hiding something and on a few occasions now, she's frozen around me and Linc."

"So you've finally met a woman who doesn't drop her panties at the sight of you. I like her already and as I've already said, flowers. Flowers are the way to any girl's heart."

"Fine," I relent, "I'll send her some flowers."

"Good, now get off the phone with me and go woo my future daughter-in-law."

"That's racing a bit far ahead, Mom."

"Nope, I feel it in my bones. This girl is 'the one.' For starters, she's got you all twisted up and I've never seen you like this with a woman before. Not even with that Stefanie Jenkins, if I remember correctly, you were going to marry her when you grew up."

"Mom, I was ten years old."

"Just trust your mother on this."

"Yes, Mom," I say to placate her. "I'll call you later in the week."

"I love you, Marshall."

"Love you too, Mom."

Hanging up from Mom, I bring up Google and call a local florist but they're closed. I leave a message asking them to call me back.

Ten minutes later, my phone rings and it's the florist. I tell her I want something teal, I'm sure, well pretty sure, it's her favorite color. E has a bracelet with teal on it and at least once a week she wears a teal item of clothing. The lady tells me she can do a teal chrysanthemum bouquet. I have no clue what a chrysanthemum is, but I go with her recommendation.

With the flowers ordered, I lie back and watch Netflix but my mind can't focus. I keep thinking about E and what the future may or may not hold for us. *Damn you, Mom, planting seeds of the future in my head.*

ELOISE

Nancy walks toward me with a gorgeous flower bouquet in her arms. "Someone's a lucky lady," I singsong, admiring the stunning arrangement.

"Yes, you are," she replies, handing the flowers to me.

"Huh?" I question, scrunching my eyes in confusion.

"It's for you."

"Who's it from?"

"Read the card and see."

Plucking out the card it just has my name on it. "There's nothing except my name." *Well, my initial since no one here knows me as Eloise.*

"Ohhhhhhh, looks like someone has an admirer," she teases and my eyes widen, I immediately think that Duncan has found me. I go to ask her who delivered it but by the time I look up, the door to the staff locker room is closing and I'm alone with my flowers.

Reading the card again, I deduce they're not from Duncan. Not only are they addressed to E but this isn't his style. He'd storm in, chest puffing and he'd drag me out of here kicking and screaming by my hair. If he did send me something, it would be something sinister like a shredded black rose … or a dead cat.

Staring at the flowers, I smile and wonder who they could possibly be from.

"I love seeing you smile like that," Marshall's voice startles me and I flinch in fright. "Sorry, I didn't mean to scare you."

"No, you're fine. I'm just trying to deduce who would send me flowers."

"Do you not receive them often?" he questions me.

Shaking my head, I stare at my flowers. "Uhhh, no, Dunc—" but I stop before I finish that sentence. "I've actually never received flowers before."

"Never?" he probes.

"Nope," I honestly tell him and shocking myself, I add on, "I've never had someone care enough to send me anything special like this."

"Well, it looks like someone cares now."

"Yeah, seems so." I smile and realize that for the first time in a long time, my heart is racing, not with fear but with excitement. Biting my lip, I think about who they could be from but I come up blank.

"Marshall, did you send these?"

He shrugs, turns and walks toward the dining room. Before he enters, he looks over his shoulder and winks. Once again, my heart races and I become giddy.

Standing here staring at the dining room entrance, I realize that I have myself a crush ... and an admirer ... and I really hope Marshall is my admirer.

The next day, almost to the exact minute, I receive another flower delivery but this time, it's a single teal chrysanthemum and there's a quote on the card.

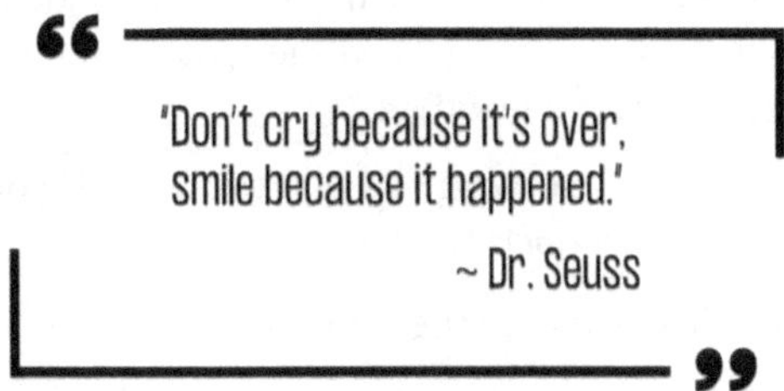

The quote tugs at my heart and my eyes well with tears.

Whoever is sending these seems to know that I'm struggling with my past, but no one here knows anything about me and my history.

Who is sending these to me?

Two days later I receive another gorgeous arrangement.

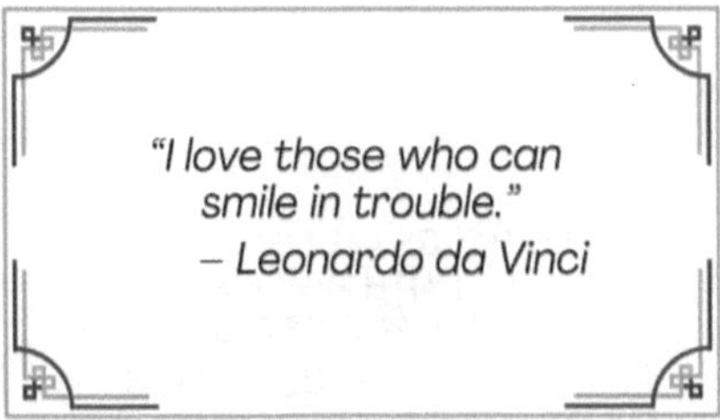

It's like the person sending these knows that I'm sad and in need of cheering up. *But who is it?*

"You really are beautiful when you smile," Marshall offers as he wheels past me. My smile and steps falter when I see him back in his chair, he's been doing so well lately. "Why are you back in your chair?" I call out.

"I pushed myself in my session this morning and didn't stop when Nancy told me to. I've pulled the muscle in my groin and now I need to rest it for a few days."

"Marshall," I scold, "you need to listen to Nancy if you're going to get back on the race track."

"Not you too. I just had a lecture from my mom."

"You should listen to your mom too."

"What is it with women riding my ass today?"

"Don't do stupid shit and we wouldn't have to."

He laughs and continues down the hallway. Before he turns the corner he shouts, "We need to watch the sunset together again … and soon." He winks and wheels around the corner.

"I'd like that," I quietly whisper with a grin on my face.

Three days later, I receive another flower arrangement. This time the quote is from Joel Osteen.

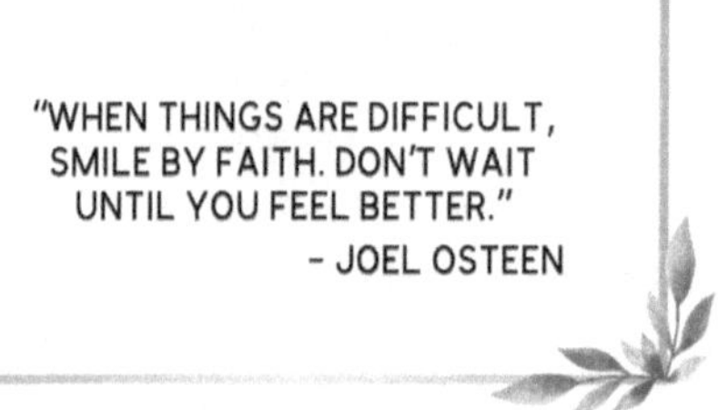

Once again, I find myself smiling. I don't think I've ever smiled as much as I have this past week. People used to say that my smile could light up the darkest of rooms and I feel like the person who used to smile like that is slowly returning.

It's largely due to my secret admirer. I wish I knew who he, or she, is. I want to thank them for making me happy again. For making me feel like me again.

I haven't felt happiness like this since the early days with Duncan. This could have been something he would have done in the beginning, but I now know his charm and suaveness were all a ruse to get me under his thumb and control.

Everyone is teasing me about my secret admirer and if I'm honest, I love that I have one. I almost feel guilty for smiling so much when not everyone here is smiling. A new patient arrived, Dylan, a teenage boy who was injured in a horrific car accident. He was predicted to be the next Michael Jordan but after his accident, well, it's not looking good for him. His physical injuries are very similar to those of Marshall's but Dylan's demeanor and attitude is off the charts surly. He's seriously surlier than Marshall's when he first arrived.

I'm going to make it my mission to make Dylan smile again. *He needs to get himself an admirer.* Then I remember words one of the counselors here said a few weeks back, "Life goes on. We can morn our losses but there's no guilt in surviving or being happy. Those we have lost, our inner self included, want us to continue to live life and be happy."

Those words ring true in regard to so many things and today as I stare at my latest gift, I come to the conclusion that it's okay for me to smile and live my life. It's okay for me to be happy and look to the future. I can't let little E's passing be for nothing so I make a decision, I'm going to live each and every day for him, and me. It's the least I can do.

It's been a week since my last delivery.

My flower surprises have stopped and if I'm honest, I'm a little upset, but when I walk into admin the front door opens and the delivery boy is back.

He smiles at me. "I have another one for you, E."

Taking them from him, I smile. "Can you please let me know who they're from?"

Before he even opens his mouth, I know exactly what he's going to say. "I would if I could but I'm just the delivery boy." Then he tacks on, "I'm sure if you called the store they might be able to help you."

"No, no, it's fine." I shake my head. "As much as it's killing me not knowing who's sending these to me, I'm also scared to know."

My answer confuses the boy but he doesn't hang around to probe me. He leaves and I reach into the bouquet and pull out today's card.

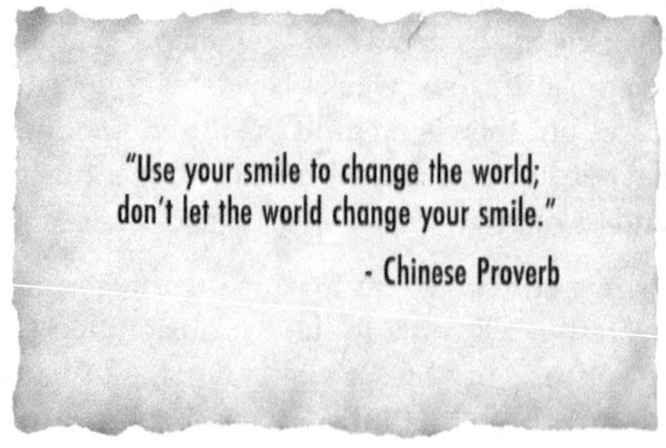

Today's message confirms my earlier thoughts, it's okay to smile ... and live. I think that maybe this is the start of my happy future.

A week later, I receive another delivery. This is now the sixth time I've received flowers and today's bouquet holds six chrysanthemums and the card's quote is once again about smiling but this time, it's accompanied by my favorite MAC lip gloss.

A laugh escapes me when I read today's quote.

"I love your laugh," Marshall voices as he walks toward me. Looking up, I smile when I see him. "And when you smile, like really smile, it lights up your entire face."

Before I can reply, he walks into his therapy session.

It feels good that people, specifically Marshall, are seeing the real me. And it's damn good to be happy once again. I think it's time for people to get to know E, the real E. No more hiding. Eloise Masters is going to start living again … and I'm going to start by taking a chance with my heart.

Looking into the therapy room, I focus on Marshall. He's talking to Dylan and for the first time since the kid arrived, he's smiling too. And it reaches his eyes.

As I watch the two of them together, I realize that I want Marshall to be my admirer.

Then I quash that thought because a guy like him would never go for someone like me. Besides, we can never happen. I need to remain in the shadows. The fame that comes with being with him would cause Duncan to find me and I can never let that happen. It's too dangerous for me, and I refuse to let *him* hurt those I care about. Shaking my head, I dejectedly sigh.

Once again, Duncan is messing with my life, but this time I have the power to control what happens. I'm stronger now and I will never let him hurt anyone else because of me.

MARSHALL

Seeing the smile on E's face each time a delivery arrives makes the secrecy totally worth it. She hasn't been this vibrant since I arrived. It's nice to see a glow on her face and a pep in her step.

I'm working my way up to revealing it's me, but when I overhear her telling Tony that 'she's not ready to date and she doesn't think she ever will' it crushes me. It hurts more than I care to admit and it puts doubt in my mind on me revealing that I'm her admirer.

I've never felt like this about a woman before. I'm usually a 'wham-bam-thank-you-ma'am-don't-let-the-door-hit-you-in-the-ass-on-the-way-out' kind of guy but with E, I want more. And if my daydreams are anything to go by, I'm talking about the whole shebang—white picket fence, two point five kids, and a dog named Boof. I don't do that mushy crap, but clearly, when it comes to E, I do because I want her by my side as Mrs. Kerr.

At that thought, I begin to wonder what the E stands for. Elenore? Ellie? Elizabeth?

"Yo, Romeo," Nancy commands. "You owe me twenty minutes of actual riding on the bike, not twenty minutes of contemplating the world, now get moving or I'll double it."

Looking down at the screen, I frown. I've been sitting here for fifteen minutes and I've only ridden two-hundred feet, I should be up around the two-mile mark. Prior to my accident, I could ride ten miles in forty-five minutes but these days, it's a little slow going.

Gripping the handles, I focus on a spot on the ground in front of me and get to it. I've been pushing myself lately and my body is hurting, but it's hurting from overexertion and not from the accident. I forgot how good it feels to hurt so good, and yes, I totally said it in a George Thorogood way. If I keep this momentum up, all going well, I'll be out of here in the next month or two.

I can't wait to get back to California and into my normal routine. Linc is still banning me from getting behind the wheel. But if I keep this up, I reckon within the next three months, I'll be back where I belong, behind the wheel of my green machine and out on the track doing what I love most in this world.

"Where's your head at today?" Nancy roasts me. Leaning against the wall next to me, she continues, "I've had to push you to get everything completed today. It's like you've checked out."

"I'm thinking about when I get out of here. I reckon within the month, I'll be back in Cali and on my way to racing again."

"A month, really?" she questions, her tone giving away her true feelings.

"You don't think I'm ready?" I quiz.

"I didn't say that, but if you keep sitting here like a grandad, you'll still be here in a year. You need to focus, Marshall."

"I'm focused," I snap and it reminds me of Chance's words about focus. "I'd also like to point out, I'm currently in a position that none of you so-called experts," I air quote experts, "thought I would be. I WILL race again, Nance, I will."

"There's the fire I want to see."

"You baited me?" I question. Hopping off the bike, finally reaching my target but I wince with my first step.

"Yep, and the wince just there," she circles her finger in my face, "tells me you aren't as healed as you think you are." She hands me my cane. "I believe you can do it, Marshall, but I don't think it will be in the time frame you're hoping for." I try to interrupt her but she raises her hand to stop me. "You *will* get there, I'm not saying you won't, but don't put a deadline on it. Let your body guide you. I'd hate to see you push yourself so far that you end up back in the chair."

"I'm going to do it. Watch me," I growl at her and hobble out of the workout room.

Turning the corner, I bump into someone and from the breath hitch, I know who it is before I lift my head. "I really should watch where I'm going, I seem to bump into you all the time."

"Yes, you should," she scolds me, but it's not as venomous as her usual berating. Then she shocks me when she adds, "I'm starting to think you do it on purpose."

"On purpose, huh?" She nods. "And why would I bump into you on purpose?"

"So you can touch me."

"You've got that all wrong, E. I think you," I point to her, "are bumping into ME," I point back at me, "so YOU can touch me."

"Guess we'll never know."

"Guess not," I reply. "Can I ask you a question?"

"You can ask but whether I answer or not, that's another thing."

"Okay, well, can I ask what E stands for?"

She stares at me blankly, I think she's going to ignore my question then she shocks me. "Guess?"

"Really?" I question and she nods. "Okay, Elizabeth?"

She shakes her head.

"Edith?"

Again she shakes her head.

"Elaine?'

"Nope."

Tapping my chin, I throw out, "Elodie." Her eyes widen in surprise but she shakes her head. "Am I close?" She shrugs and smiles. Fuck me sideways, that slight movement of her lips upward lit her face up in a way that has my heart racing, just like it does when I'm on the starting line, waiting for a race to start.

"Keep guessing," she teases, tapping me on the chest, she steps around me and continues walking down the corridor.

Turning around, I watch her saunter away. Her hips swaying side to side, taunting me. She stops and just before she walks through the doorway, she looks over her shoulder. We have one of those moments like in the movies. You know that romcom moment when everything around the couple stills. It's just them, well technically it is just us in the hallway, but semantics. She winks at me and all the blood in my body rushes to my cock. Then she's gone. She steps into the dining room, leaving me with a semi and a goofy grin on my face.

Shaking my head, I return to my room. I need a shower before dinner because I stink after my training session. On the way to my room, I decide to throw caution to the wind, I'm going to confess it's me sending her the flowers. And I have the perfect way to do it … I just hope Tony won't carve me into a million pieces when I ask him for his help.

ELOISE

I t's been three days since my last delivery and I still have no clue who my admirer is, but whoever they are, I thank them profusely. My happiness is increasing by the day and I can attribute some of that happiness to Marshall. He's still trying to guess my name and his guesses are getting worse. Today's guesses include Earlene, Elsa—yes, that Elsa—and my favorite, Egberta. He must have access to a baby name book because the guesses are ridiculous.

The other day when he said Elodie, my heart stopped. One letter different and he would have guessed correctly. I'm not sure what I'll do when he does, I'll cross that bridge if, when, it happens. I mean, there has to be at least five hundred different E names out there. I think we're twenty in, so there's a lot of names to go through before he gets to Eloise.

Closing my locker, I pick my bag up off the bench and head home. I cannot wait to soak in the tub tonight. Today was grueling but I have to admit, my run-in with Marshall earlier made me giddy. When I flirted with him, it was fun and exhilarating but he didn't flirt back. He either feels nothing for me or my flirting techniques suck. But seriously, why would a guy like him want someone like me? A wallflower with baggage in the form of a psycho ex, whom she ran away from and is hiding from. Sounds like I'm a winner, not.

A wave of sadness hits when I think about Miles. After Duncan reaching out, he's kept true to his word and has ceased all contact with me. I miss him. I'm lost in my head and it isn't until someone taps my shoulder and yells my name that I'm snapped to the present.

Spinning around, I see Nancy staring at me, holding the biggest bunch of teal chrysanthemums I've ever seen. "Your admirer strikes again."

"Oh My God, this bouquet is stunning."

"He's really upped his game with this one, what does the card say?" she excitedly asks. Nancy is a romantic at heart, you wouldn't pick up on that from her tough as nails exterior, but underneath she's a soft teddy bear. My recent admirer and subsequent flower deliveries are making her swoon harder than when she read *Unseen* by Cassie Laelyn. The hero, EJ, had her gushing the whole time she was reading it … and I admit, EJ is swoony but he's nothing compared to my mystery admirer.

Plucking the card out, my eyes widen and my breath hitches when I read it.

"He wants to meet me," I whisper.

"What did the card say?" she excitedly prods.

"He asked me out on a date."

"Girl, you have to go. When? And where?"

"Here at sunset." As soon as I utter that sentence, I know who my admirer is. "Marshall," I murmur. My lips lift into a grin at the thought of him doing all of this for me. "I think Marshall is my admirer," I tell Nancy.

"No way," she screeches. "Who knew Mr. 'I-want-to-get-back-on-the-track' was so sweet. Are you going to go?"

"I … I … I don't know," I stammer, "Should I?"

"Do you want to?"

Do I want to? That's the million-dollar question. A part of me wants to but there's also a part of me, a biiiig part that's afraid. Duncan was nice in the beginning too but look how that turned out.

Looking at her, I ask, "Are you free tonight? I think I need to … talk."

"For you, I'm free and happy to 'talk.'" She air quotes talk and I laugh. Nancy has been trying to get me to 'talk' for months, so I dare say my request just made her week. Without a doubt, I know she cares and that's why I'm willing to open up.

"Thank you," I tell her. "Meet you at my place at seven. I'll cook."

"I'll bring the wine."

A laugh escapes me. "I might need lots."

"Okay, I'll bring lots of wine … and tequila."

"Ugh, no tequila. How about vodka?"

"Ugh, no vodka."

Then together we shout, "Jägermeister!"

"Wine and Jägermeister it is then." She hands me my flowers and we go our separate ways.

Stopping at home, I drop off my flowers before heading to the store to get the ingredients to make pesto chicken pasta for dinner. I also grab a bottle of wine, I need to start preparing myself for my 'talk' with Nancy.

Once home, I whip up the pasta and pop it into the oven to stay warm. I quickly shower and change into leggings and a Colorado Dragons sweater with their cute dragon holding a hockey stick emblem.

Turning on the TV, I put the game on in the background and take my first sip of wine. My stomach churns at what I'm going to reveal tonight, but I know that I need to talk to someone if I'm going to take a risk with Marshall, or whomever my admirer is.

A knock at the door startles me and I spill my wine—sacrilege I know. "Shit," I grunt as I stand up, shaking off the spilled wine on my hand.

Opening the door, I smile when I see Nancy is dressed similar to me but the traitor is wearing a LA Legends sweater. "Remove that thing," I point to her jersey, "immediately after putting the wine and Jäger down."

"No jersey, no wine or Jäger."

"You drive a hard bargain but I'll allow you to enter because I see you got the good wine."

She laughs and enters my apartment. Once inside, she heads straight to my kitchen. She places the wine on the counter, grabs a glass, and helps herself to the bottle I opened earlier. She pours herself a glass and then freezes when she sees me.

"Why do you look like your puppy died?" At the mention of death, my eyes well with tears and I cup my stomach. "Ohh, E," she utters.

Walking over, she envelops me in a hug. When her arms wrap around me, I completely break down. Tears steak down my cheeks, soaking her jersey. When I settle down, she pulls back and holds my hands in hers. "Okay, babe, you're freaking me out. What's going on? And do I need to borrow Tony's carving knife?"

"Maybe," I tell her. "Let's sit down."

Nodding, she leads me to the sofa and we sit down but immediately she jumps up again. She goes back to the kitchen to get the wine and our glasses. Placing the bottle on my coffee table, she then heads back to the kitchen and grabs the second bottle of wine and the Jäger. "I think this is a two bottle of red and possibly Jäger conversation."

Nodding at her, I take my wine glass which she topped off and take a sip, and by sip, I mean gulp. I empty half the glass in the one mouthful. Without saying a word, she tops my glass back up and takes my hand in hers. She squeezes it reassuringly and smiles. "When you're ready."

Taking a deep breath, I close my eyes. "I'm originally from a town called Collinsville and my life has been a roller coaster, a really shitty roller coaster ride..." I'm transported back two years...

...I'm sitting at the bus stop and I people watch while I wait for the bus to take me back to the less than stellar side of town. Sometimes I wonder what it'd be like to never have to want for anything. To have the world at my fingertips. Luckily for me, dreams are free. I've had to work hard for everything I've ever gotten and even with all the hard work, I still have very little.

Looking at my watch, I realize the bus is late and knowing my luck, it's probably not going to come at all. "Looks like I'm walking," I mumble.

Standing up, I start the long arduous walk home. I feel so out of place here, I don't know why I torture myself and come to this part of town, but people-watching is one of my favorite things to do. It transports me to a world where I'm not me. I'm not poor Eloise Masters. I'm just Eloise.

Waiting to cross the street, I look at the people around me. A woman in her late fifties looks down her nose at me. "Riffraff," she not so quietly mutters to her husband. He looks to me and sadly smiles, clearly he doesn't feel the same way.

The light changes and we cross the road. Once we reach the other side, where most turn right, myself and a few others head left, toward shanty town, also known as Trenton. Sure, it's nothing flashy but it's home, it's the only place I've ever known. It's safe ... ish but it's comforting because people here stick to themselves and never pass judgement, to your face anyway.

Lost in my thoughts, I'm not watching where I'm going and a group of teenagers approach me. Recently, these assholes started to think that they rule the streets here. Spinning around, I pick up my pace and walk back the way I came. Why are they on this side of the tracks? They never venture this far, but I guess today is my lucky—unlucky—day.

Turning the corner, I smack into a hard body. They reach out and grip my upper arms, steadying me. Fear courses through my body but when I look up, that fear disappears. The man before me is gorgeous. Dark eyes. Dark hair. He has this aurora about him. And when he smiles, I swear the angels in heaven sing.

"You okay, little lady?" he asks, the timbre of his voice deep, yet calming.

"I ... I ..." I look behind me and notice the boys following me are now walking the other way, "I'm ... I'm okay, thank you," I murmur. "I'm sorry to have disturbed you."

Pulling myself free from his grasp, I turn to walk back the way I came, but he stops me in my tracks with his next question, "Will you join me for dinner?"

My eyes widen at his request. I look down at my torn and ratty clothes, then I look over my shoulder back at him. He's in a pristine suit that I'm sure is worth more than everything I have in my little apartment combined.

Shaking my head, I decline, "Thank you, but I'm fine, really."

"I didn't ask if you were fine, I asked if you'd join me for dinner."

"I'd love to but I'm not really dressed for the places you dine at."

"We can fix that," he offers. He smiles and instantly, it puts me at ease.

· · ·

…"Accepting his dinner invitation was the first mistake I made when it comes to Duncan Montgomery. In hindsight, I wish he'd let the hooligans have me."

Nancy's eyes widen when I say that. "You would have rather faced a bunch of thugs than have dinner with Prince Charming?"

"He's no Prince Charming," I growl, "He's a wolf in sheep's clothing."

Nancy nods. "Okay, do you want to keep going or do you need a break?"

Shaking my head, I breathe deeply. "No, I can do this." Taking another gulp of wine, I continue…

…That evening Duncan wined and dined me. I've never had a meal as decadent as I did that night. After dinner, he offered to drive me home. Reluctantly, I accepted and when we pulled up to my building, he was aghast when he saw where I lived. In that moment, he decided that I'd live with him. He was the first person to openly care for me. To show me any affection and I was under his spell. I thought all my Christmases had come at once so I agreed but on the provision that I worked for him. He accepted my terms and hired me as his personal assistant.

Duncan and I grew close and six months later, I became more than just his assistant. My days started and ended with him. Finally, I was living a fairy tale life. I had everything at my disposal. I got everything I wanted, everything I dreamed of. My man adored me and I was finally happy.

Three months after we officially started dating, he proposed and of course I said yes, but as soon as his ring was on my finger, things started to change. With him. With me. With us. I put it down to stress from work but I now know, he's just a prickface."

…"Prickface, ha, love it but E, why didn't you just leave?"

"I had nothing to go back to. I thought I was safer where I was. I know that sounds shallow and conceited, and I guess, it was but I was safe … ish."

"No one can judge you for what you did and if they do, fuck them."

Laughing at her statement, I take another sip of wine and continue…

…As time wore on, Duncan became more and more aggressive and less like the man I met. Slowly, I became a former shell of myself and morphed into someone I didn't recognize anymore. I smiled when I needed to play the dutiful fiancée. I took the punches, both physical and verbal. I was existing and my fairy tale became a living nightmare. Then I discovered I was pregnant. I was well into my second trimester before I found out so I couldn't terminate. It was the wake-up call I needed, but it came too late.

When Duncan discovered I was pregnant, it spectacularly fell apart. A small part of me was hoping that he'd be over the moon and elated with the news, but that wasn't the case. I decided there and then that I was leaving. I packed my bag and my driver, Miles, was willing to help me get away but before I could leave, Duncan pushed–well threw—me down our stairs and I lost my baby."

…"Holy shit, E. You're lucky to be alive. How did you get away?"

"While I was in hospital my wonderful doctor, Jenna, and Miles got me out of there. Jenna secured me the job at the center and Miles is my eyes and ears back in Collinsville."

"Aren't you worried he'll find you?"

Nodding, I tell her honestly, "Every day, but if I don't keep living, he wins and I refuse to let him take anything more from me. It's my life to live."

"Well, I think that's your answer concerning your admirer."

"But what if …"

"No, don't do that," she interrupts shaking her head. "Do not live with what-ifs. If Marshall is your admirer, like you think, there will be no what-ifs with that man. He is sex on a stick and he has a heart of gold. And if it's someone else, trust your gut."

"That was Duncan at the beginning too. I trusted my gut and look where it got me."

"Do you really think Marshall is hiding an evil alter ego?" I shake my head, "no, I don't think that at all. He's genuine, through and through." And I know this with all my heart. I've seen him with Dylan. He pushes him daily but not in an abusive way, he pushes him so he can get back on his feet, just like he did.

The timer on the oven beeps and I'm thankful for the reprieve. It was hard recounting my time with *him*. Standing up I walk into the kitchen and dish up our dinner. Handing Nancy her plate, I top up our wines and sit back next to her.

Tucking my feet under my ass, I stare down at my plate. "I think I'm going to give it my all with my admirer, even if it isn't Marshall. Surely fate wouldn't be a bitch and hand me two assholes?"

"Just know, that if your admirer **cough**Marshall**cough** tries anything, and I mean anything, Tony and I will be there with his carving knife and a shovel to protect you."

"I have no doubt that you two will have my back." And I believe her, one million percent. I've finally found my people but now, it's time for me to open my life and my heart to the possibility of more.

MARSHALL

For the first time ever, I'm not the confident cocky guy when it comes to pursuing a woman. For the first time ever, I'm a bumbling bundle of nervous energy. My mind is all over the place and I'm a fumbling fool.

Clearly I'm off my game because earlier in my therapy session, Nancy was on my ass every second. She seemed to be riding my ass harder than usual today. She definitely kept me on my toes and now, my body aches. I'd be okay with feeling achy and sore like this but with my date tonight looming, I don't have time to be aching.

Slowly I hobble back to my room, hoping that a rest and a super-hot shower will ease my muscles. Walking into my room, I close the door and begin to strip off. Pulling my shirt over my head, I drop it to the bed. Then I slide my shorts and briefs down my aching thighs, over my knees and with a wiggle, they slip to the floor.

Standing back up, I'm met with an open-mouthed and gaping E. She's standing in the doorway of my bathroom.

"Shit," I gasp, "I didn't realize anyone was in here." But I make no move to cover my junk.

Our eyes are locked on one another as I stand before her buck naked, again. She swallows deeply and her eyes drop. Ever so slowly they roam over me, I feel the heat in her gaze as she takes me in. Her tongue darts out to lick her bottom lip and when her eyes land back on mine, her cheeks are tinged pink.

"I … ummm, sorry," she mumbles. Without another word, she races out of my room.

If this was a cartoon, there'd be an E-shaped hole in my door and smoke tracks on the floor from her hasty exit.

The door clicks closed behind her and I grin, that was just what I needed to calm my nerves. I just hope I still feel like this tonight so I don't fuck up my date with E.

For the rest of the afternoon, I laze about in my room until it's time to prepare for our date. When I approached Tony yesterday afternoon, he was more than willing to help me and as usual, he warned me, "*You hurt that girl in any way with your playboy rookie ways and I will end you. I don't care how famous you are. Orange may not look good on me but when it comes to that girl, I'm not afraid of the consequences.*"

I assured him that I didn't plan on hurting her. That I planned to woo her and make her smile each and every day. That seemed to appease him because he went on to say that he hadn't seen her happier since I started sending her the flowers. I begin to wonder if he knows her secrets since his warning is pretty strong but regardless, I'm glad she has him on her side. Hopefully after tonight, She'll have me too.

If the guys could see me right now, they'd be razzing the piss out of me at me becoming such a pansy-ass when it comes to a woman. I don't think I've ever worked this hard in regard to a chick. Normally they throw themselves at me, but not E. If anything, she seems afraid of the opposite sex but after tonight, I hope to change her opinion of men, specifically, me.

While I'm dressing for the evening, those nerves from this morning return with a vengeance. I'm so nervous that it takes me forever to button up my dress shirt. When I look to the clock, I curse because I'm late. I wanted to get to the patio early to make sure Tony did as I asked.

Quickly I make my way to the patio. I consider wheeling since it's faster but the stubborn ass in me tells me no and I walk. Well, shuffle.

Walking into the dining room, I notice it's empty. For this time of night it should be full, everyone chowing down on dinner. From the window into the kitchen, I see Tony. He's grinning like a proud father and gives me two thumbs-up.

Nodding at him, I head over to the patio doors. With my hand on the slider, I take a deep breath and slide the door open. Stepping outside, I pause midstep and it's not from what Tony created for me this evening, but it's E. She's here and she's fucking stunning. She's gorgeous at the best of times but tonight, I have no words.

With the sun starting to set behind her, she looks like she's glowing. Her dark locks hang loose down her back. She's wearing a little black dress that accentuates every curve on her body and shows off her sexy as fuck shoulder blades. I've never really noticed a woman's shoulder blades before but as I stand here taking her in, I want to lick and caress them.

She spins around and startles when she notices me but when she registers it's me, her face breaks out into a killer smile that punches me right in the chest. It turns my thumping heart all mushy. If this were a cartoon, arrows shot by Cupid would be flying above my head and hearts would be pulsating out of my chest.

"I'd hoped it was you." She beams, breaking the silent stare off happening between us. She walks toward me. "You've really outdone yourself, Marshall, but how did you know I'd come?"

"I didn't," I honestly tell her, shaking my head, "but I hoped like hell you would."

She smiles and looks around at the fairy lights adorning the roof line. Her gaze lowers to the picnic blanket and beanbags, with candles in mason jars along the patio edge. Tony has put together a cheese platter with olives and cured meats. A bottle of bubbly sits in a wine bucket with two flutes waiting to be filled. "No one has ever done anything like this for me before."

"This is a first for me too." I don't elaborate because I don't want her to think that I'm a slimeball 'wham-bam-thank-you-ma'am' kind of guy. "Shall we?" I ask, nodding to the picnic.

She nods and grins.

Stepping over to her, I offer my elbow and we walk the few steps before each of us takes a seat. It takes me longer than I hoped to get comfortable and E notices the strain on my face. "What can I do to help you?"

"You being here is enough." I shuffle around and finally, I find a position that doesn't hurt but then I realize that if I have to move again, it's going to suck donkey balls. She notices the confusion on my face when I keep staring at the food and drinks. Without saying a word, she grabs the bottle of champagne and pops the cork, it flies up into the air. She squeals and laughs, it's pure music to my ears to hear the joy emitting from her. "I love that sound," she states.

"Me too, especially when I'm on the podium after a win."

She pours two glasses and hands one to me.

"Cheers," I toast, tilting my glass toward her.

She taps her glass against mine and repeats the toast. With our eyes locked on one another we sip. She closes her eyes and savors the crispness of the cool liquid. She opens her eyes and finds me staring at her. Her cheeks darken at my ogling.

She snuggles back into her beanbag and I'm envious that she can maneuver herself so easily into a comfortable position. I'd love to recline in the beanbag laid out for me too but I'd never get up, so I awkwardly sit on the ground on the rug next to her.

"This is perfect in every way, Marshall. Thank you for tonight and for the flowers. It's been thrilling to receive them. I've been trying to guess who my admirer was but I had no clue, not until yesterday anyway." She laughs and once again, it's music to my ears.

"Thrilling, huh? I'll have to up my thrill game then."

"Well, you're off to a great start."

"Duly noted and since we're being honest, it's been pretty thrilling for me too."

"Everything to do with what you do for a living is thrilling, I can't see how flowers and a sunset picnic can compare."

"Yes, I have a pretty thrilling job, but it's nice to jump into the slow lane every once in a while." She nods in agreement. "Maybe when I'm back on the track you can come see me race one day and feel the thrill trackside."

Her eyes widen at my suggestion and the hand holding her drink visibly shakes. She lowers the glass from her lips and places it next to her. "I … ummm, I'm not really a people person so I'll be fine watching you on the television."

Not liking the unease my suggestion invokes, I turn her attention to the sunset. "Look," I point over her left shoulder, she cranes her neck to look where I'm pointing.

"It's beautiful," she murmurs.

"It sure is," I confirm but I'm not referring to the blazing sky. All I see is the beautiful woman sitting in front of a sunset.

She looks back toward me and all the unease from moments ago is nowhere to be seen. "Me? Or the sunset?" she brazenly asks, biting her lip and lowering her head in embarrassment.

Leaning over, I place my finger under her chin so she's looking at me. "Both."

ELOISE

Both.

That one word causes my heart to beat faster and my blood to sizzle within my veins. Never have I ever had a reaction to a man like this before. Who knew one word could evoke such a reaction?

Marshall has certainly brought his 'A' game tonight. As much as I thought I was ready to let someone in, now I'm in the moment, I'm not sure I'm ready. If I freaked out at the prospect of attending a race with him, how can we be anything more? Maybe I need to quit while I'm ahead, enjoy what has been and continue on with my life as it is. Hiding and alone.

The sound of his voice brings me back to the present. "I'm sorry, I missed that."

"I asked if you'd like to move this to the table?" My face deflates at the prospect of moving, this setup is straight out of a romance novel and perfect in every way. But then he adds, "I hate to ask, but from sitting on the ground my hip is killing me, and if I have any hope of getting back on the track, I need to look after it."

He's in pain, of course he is.

This isn't about me, it's not always about me.

Nodding, I begin to stand up. "Of course we can, I don't want you in pain. Besides, we can still see what's left of the sunset from there."

He groans and grunts as he tries to lift himself up. "Would you like a hand?" I offer.

"Please," he grits through clenched teeth.

Stepping over to him, he places his hand in mine and a spark jolts through me at the connection but it quickly morphs to pain when he grips my hand tightly to pull himself up.

Once he's upright, he loosens the grip on my hand but he doesn't let go. He threads his fingers through mine and with his other hand, he cups my cheek. We stare at one another. The air around us zinging and pinging with desire. Now *this* is a scene from one of my romance novels.

With his thumb, he traces the pad over my bottom lip, lifting his gaze back to mine, I notice his eyes are a gorgeous Caribbean Sea blue up close. I've never seen blue eyes like this before, they are simply gorgeous.

"You're eyes are gorgeous."

"As are yours," he replies. "Up close like this I can see flecks of gold around your irises."

Swallowing deeply, my tongue darts out and I lick my bottom lip. We both lean forward, the moment perfect for a kiss. Our lips are a hairs width apart when the patio door slides open. "Shit," a voice growls, "I missed it."

Marshall and I quickly pull apart. Looking over, I see Dylan in the doorway. He glances around. "What are you two doing out here?" he asks when he notices us. His gaze then moves to the picnic and then back to us. His eyes widen when realization of what he interrupted hits him. "Ohh shit, did I interrupt a date or something?"

"No," I say shaking my head, as Marshall hisses, "Yes," his tone a little on the angry side. His tone unnerves me but it doesn't create fear like when *he* growled.

Without saying anything more, Dylan begins to close the slider. He pops his head back out. "I knew you were smitten with her," he teases Marshall before disappearing back inside, leaving us alone once again.

"Smitten, eh?" I tease, turning to face a slightly blushing Marshall at being outed by a teenager.

"Smitten might be a bit strong," he denies, "more …"

"More what?" I press.

"Just more," he states, and those two words affect me in a way that I've never felt before. Those two words confirm to me that I really want more with this man.

Marshall takes a seat and I grab the food items. Placing them before us, I notice he's in pain. "Are you okay? We can call it a night if you're in pain."

He shakes his head. "No, no, I'll be fine." He grabs an olive from the platter and he pops it into his mouth. "I need to get back to doing things I used to do."

"So you set up sunset picnics quite often, do you?" The thought of him doing this with anyone else doesn't sit well with me. It's irrational to feel this way since we aren't even a couple but that animosity is there regardless.

"I'll have you know, this is the first sunset picnic I've arranged … and I hope it's not the last … with you."

This guy really is smooth. "I bet that line works with all the girls."

"I don't know, did it?"

Raising my eyebrows at him, I pick up a sliver of cheese and eat it. Smirking at him, I grab my drink and bring it to my lips. We watch each other as I sip my drink until it becomes too much. That's when I notice the sun has set and now the only light is from the fairy lights above. He really went all out tonight.

Lifting my gaze, I notice him staring at me intently. "What?" I ask, "Do I have something on my face?"

He shakes his head. "No, nothing on your face. I'm just admiring you. I like seeing you smile. You seem happy."

"I like smiling and I am happy. I haven't felt like this in a very long time." As soon as I say those words, my mind drifts to

Duncan. I hate myself for thinking about *him* right now but that prickface—thanks Nancy for the new nickname—always pops into my mind at the most annoying times.

Marshall places his hand on mine and snaps me back to the present. "Where did you go just now?"

"Nowhere that needs mentioning." Pulling my hand from under his, I rest my palm on top of his. "Thank you for tonight. It was everything I hoped for and more. I hope we can do it again sometime."

"I'd like that too." We stare at one another and then he guesses, "Emory?"

"I was waiting for a guess but again, you'd be incorrect." I ponder what to do. I like this guessing game with him, but it would also be nice for him to know me, the real me. Do I tell him? Or do we keep playing the name game?

"Do I get a hint?"

Tapping my chin, I decide this is too much fun so we will keep it up for a little longer. "Well, it starts with E—"

"No shit," he interrupts me.

I stick my tongue out at him. "As I was saying before I was rudely interrupted, it starts with E and it has six letters."

"That narrows it down. Kinda. Sorta. Not really." He concentrates. "Edwina."

I shake my head.

"Emma."

I laugh. "Emma only has four letters.

"Not if you prolong the m's Emmmma."

"Nice guess, but once again no."

He guesses a few more, all of them incorrect. He also includes a few not even staring with E.

We fall silent and stare at one another. Like earlier, the air around us thickens. We begin to lean closer to one another. He lifts his hand and cups my cheek. A magnetic force pulls me to him. I'm helpless to stop it. I want this kiss with every fiber of my being. I close my eyes and then it happens, his lips touch mine and my body comes alive. My tongue slips out and presses against the seam of his lips. His lips part and I slide my tongue into his mouth. Sliding his hand around to the back of my head, he cups the nape of my neck and gently nudges me closer, deepening the connection.

As first kisses go, this one is pretty spectacular.

Our tongues slide against one another. In and out of each other's mouths. Around and around in an erotic, sensual dance.

Marshall pulls back and rests his forehead against mine, we're both breathing heavily. "Wow," he whispers.

"Wow indeed," I murmur back.

MARSHALL

My forehead is resting against hers.

My heart is racing.

My cock is rock hard.

The old me would have swooped E into my arms, taken her back to my room and fucked her into a coma. The new me, well, aside from the fact that I couldn't physically do that, wants to take it slow. The new me wants to wine her and dine her. I actually want to know her name before we take that step. That in itself shocks me. In the past, I couldn't care less about their name, as long as I got my dick wet, that's all that mattered but with this woman, I want it all.

"Wow," I whisper.

"Wow, indeed," she murmurs back. "That was some kiss."

Nodding my head up and down I stare at her. "You continue to surprise me, Evangeline."

She bursts out laughing. "Not even remotely close."

"Are you ever going to tell me?"

"Depends," she nonchalantly teases.

"Depends on what?"

"If I trust you." She leans back in her seat, grabs her glass and takes a sip, staring out at the pitch-black night sky.

"Who hurt you?" I ask. Her head snaps to me, her eyes wide open like a deer caught in headlights.

"What makes you think someone hurt me?"

"I see things. I pay attention."

"Yeah, and what do you see, Mr. Stalker?"

"I see a broken woman who is slowly gluing the fractures in her facade back together. I see a woman who lights up a room when she walks in. I see a woman who makes the world a better place because she's in it. I see a woman who, when she smiles, it's infectious and makes others smile. I see an amazing woman with a heart of gold who will help anyone in need, but most of all, I see a woman who I could quite easily fall in love with."

Her mouth opens and closes. I've stunned her silent with my words. "You don't see all of that."

"Yeah, I do."

She bites her bottom lip, her teeth digging into the plump flesh. Reaching out, I pull her lip free and run the pad of my thumb over her skin. "I really want to kiss you again."

"I really want you to kiss me again too," she whispers.

That's all the encouragement I need. Leaning forward, I grip her cheeks in my palms and press my lips to hers. She places her hands over mine and moans into my mouth. It's the sexiest sound ever and my cock agrees, he twitches in my pants as I continue to assault her mouth with my tongue.

Where our first kiss was languid and slow. This kiss is fierce and demanding. Each of us wanting more.

She pulls away first but she keeps her hands on top of mine. "I really like kissing you."

"I like kissing you too, maybe we should kiss some more?"

She nods and starts kissing me again.

The door to the patio opens and Tony pops his head out, interrupting the best night—and kiss—of my life. "Sorry to intrude, lovebirds but I'm heading out now. I trust the two of you will tidy up."

"Of course," E says.

"Fabulous," he singsongs. "Leave the rug and beanbags, I'll deal with them in the morning. Night, guys … and don't forget to use protection," he cajoles with a wink and closes the door.

E's eyes widen and I laugh. "He's really something," I tell her. "Thankfully there's only one Tony. I don't think the world could handle two."

"No truer words have ever been spoken," she agrees. "As much as I'm loving tonight, I need to get home. I have an early shift tomorrow."

"Of course," I reply, but secretly I'm gutted, I don't want tonight to end.

"Marshall, tonight has been incredible. Maybe we can do it again sometime?"

"I'd like that."

"And maybe next time, we can actually eat."

"Maybe," I agree with her.

We stare at one another for a few beats then she leans forward and kisses my cheek, her lips lingering before she stands up and starts to pack up our picnic. I sit here frozen and watch her as she cleans up. She's smiling and her eyes are bright and glowing.

"What?" she queries, noticing me watching her. "You're staring."

"Just admiring your beauty." Her cheeks darken at my compliment and she becomes bashful and shy. "You're not too fond of compliments, are you?"

She shakes her head. "Over the years, I haven't received too many. My last partner was all about himself."

This is the first time she's mentioned her past. I want to push her so I can know her better, but I can tell from the change in her face and demeanor, her past is a touchy subject.

"Well, he sounds like a douche but his loss is my gain." She smiles at my choice of words and once again, she's glowing. "Do you have any plans this weekend?" She shakes her head. "Would you like to go out on a date with me?"

Nodding, she bites her lip. "I'd like that very much."

"Do you like burgers?"

"Who doesn't like burgers?"

"I knew I liked you for a reason. Linc takes me to this amazeballs burger joint and I'd like to take you."

"Sounds delicious and I'd love to." She steps over to me and since I'm still sitting, she cups my cheek. "Thank you for a wonderful evening, Marshall Kerr. I can't remember the last time I had this much fun."

"It was my pleasure, Elvira." She laughs. "Emme?" She shakes her head. "Elle?" Again, she shakes her head. "Ezra?"

"That's a boy's name."

"Well I'm running out of girls' names."

"Clearly not as you're yet to guess mine."

"As much as it's frustrating not knowing your real name, this guessing game is fun … Eliza."

"I kinda like it too. I guess when you guess correctly, we'll have to come up with another guessing game."

"Game on," I tell her and once again, she laughs.

With the picnic all packed up, we grab the basket and head inside. I switch off the outside lights and E returns the basket to the kitchen. We meet back up and start walking to the exit.

Opening the door for E, we step out into the cool night air. She turns to face me. "Thank you again for a lovely evening, Marshall."

"Thank *you* for an amazing evening. The first of many, I hope?"

She nods and then we fall silent. Under the moonlit we, we stare at one another. The air around us thickens, she swallows deeply. "Well, I better get going."

"Where's your car?"

"I don't have one."

"How do you get home?"

"I walk."

"At night? Alone?" She nods. "Is it safe?"

"It's Brookvale."

"So, bad guys can be anywhere."

"Marshall, I grew up in a place where it wasn't even safe to check the mailbox after dark. I've been walking home and everywhere, daily since I arrived here. It's fine and safe, trust me."

"I trust you, it's others that I don't." I pause. "Will you at least text me that you got home safe?"

"Is that your roundabout way of getting my digits?"

"If it means I know you've gotten home safely, then yes."

"Give me your phone."

Pulling my phone from my pocket, I unlock it and hand it to her. Our fingers brush and a spark zaps between us. She enters her phone number and then from her bag a chime rings out.

"Texted myself so I have yours too." She hands me my phone back but she doesn't let go when I go to pull it away. "Thank you again for a wonderful evening, Marshall."

"You are most welcome, Eliza."

She shakes her head. "You already guessed that one." She backs away from me. "Good night, Marshall. Sweet Dreams"

"Good night, E."

Standing here, I focus on her walking backward and away from me and subconsciously, I start humming "Sweet Dreams" to myself, the Marilyn Manson version cause it's better than the original … sorry Eurythmics.

When she's halfway into the parking lot, she spins around and I continue to watch her. This woman is everything I thought she'd be and more. I whisper into the night sky, "I'm going to win you over, E, if it's the last thing I do."

ELOISE

Tonight with Marshall was everything a first date should be and more, I feel like I'm floating. And the kisses, holy kiss, Batman. That man can kiss. I don't think I've ever had a kiss, well kisses, like that before.

Entering my apartment, I kick off my shoes and place my bag on the hall table. Grabbing my phone, I text Marshall.

Walking into my bedroom, I place my phone on the bedside table and I change into my pajamas. Then I brush my teeth.

Staring at myself in the mirror, I see a smiling Eloise and I like the person I see looking back at me. It's been a long time since I felt that looking at my reflection. I can see happiness in my eyes. I never thought I'd get to this point. I thought I'd be a frail fearful woman for the rest of my life.

Running my fingertip over my lips, I think about Marshall and his kisses. My phone pings with a text and my grin widens because I know it's Marshall. Turning off the light, I walk into my room and climb into bed. Grabbing my phone, I unlock it and bring up the message.

E

Elmo. Really?

MARSHALL

Ernie???

Ernest???

It must be something truly embarrassing if you won't tell.

Elissa?

Engrid?

E

Ingrid is with an I

MARSHALL

Please tell me????

E

Good night, Marshall

MARSHALL

Good night, Dimples

E

Dimples?????

MARSHALL

It's my new name for you

E

But Dimples???

MARSHALL

When you smile, really smile, you get these cute little dimples on your cheeks … therefore you will forever be known as Dimples.

E

You're a dork

MARSHALL

You say the nicest things to me, Dimples

E

Good night, Marshall

MARSHALL

Good night, Dimples

Placing my phone down, I turn the light off and snuggle under the covers. I toss and turn, unable to sleep as I play the events of the evening over and over in my head. Rolling to my back, I stare at the ceiling and think about Marshall's lips on mine. It really was the best date of my life, once I got over my little freak-out. I was sure the night was ruined when I freaked out but it wasn't the case. He sensed my unease and quickly turned our attention to something that made me happy.

That's one of the things I love about him, he can read situations and people and then he fixes it. It's probably why he's a brilliant racer and if I wasn't such a chickenshit, seeing him race in the flesh would be amazing, but am I brave enough to open myself to something like that?

MARSHALL

"**M**orning, Dimples," I greet E as she walks into the center. She looks radiant this morning. Don't get me wrong, she's gorgeous all of the time but today, she's glowing.

"Morning, Wheels."

"Wheels?" I question.

"Well, since you call me Dimples, I now call you Wheels."

"I don't hate that, but you know, if you just tell me your name, we could avoid all these nicknames and just be Marshall and Effie."

"But if I tell you, then I'd have to kill you, and if I kill you, I wouldn't be able to do this." She grips my cheeks and kisses me. Her tongue pushes into my mouth and I open willingly. Our tongues duel together in a sexy dance.

Breaking the kiss, against her lips, I whisper, "Morning."

"You already said that."

"I know but when you do things like that, my brain forgets how to brain."

"Your brain forgets how to brain, really? Maybe once you leave here, you need to head back to kindergarten so you can learn to speak properly too."

"I don't need more schooling because I'm one-hundred-percent certain, my braining issues are because of you. When you're around, Edna, I lose all control of my sense and braining."

"Does that line work on all the girls?" she asks me.

"I don't know, does it?"

She shrugs at me. "PS. Edna is not even in the ballpark."

"Elena?"

"Nope."

"Evan."

"That's a boy's name."

"Also a girl's name."

"Well either way, not mine."

"How about…"

"E," Linda interrupts our banter and my name guessing. "Can I see you when you get a moment, please?"

"Sure, I'll be right there," she responds.

"No rush, take your time." Linda replies, before continuing on to her office.

"Ohhh O, someone's in trouble," I tease, "the headmaster wants to speak to you."

"You're such a child at times."

"You love it," I point out with a shrug.

"I can take you or leave you," she cheekily replies, a grin forming on her gorgeous face. I seriously love it when she smiles, it brightens up any room and has the power to bring me to my knees.

"Kerr," Nancy sternly bellows as she walks toward us, "less flirting and more training. You were supposed to be in the weight room two minutes ago."

"Ohh, no, not two minutes," I sass at her.

"Now who's in trouble with the headmaster?" Dimples teases.

"She's not the headmaster."

"No, but I'm the master of your rehab, now get to it or I'll make you do extra today."

"Bring it," I goad her. Looking back to E. "Wanna do lunch later?"

She nods. "I'd like that."

E heads toward the big boss's office and I follow Nancy into the weight room. This week she has me on the seated leg press with no weights. She's currently working on building the muscles in my legs back up without weight and in the process, stretching me to my limit. It kills my hips on this machine but at the same time, it makes me stronger and gives me a good workout.

Climbing onto the contraption from hell, Nancy stands to the side and stares at me, it's unnerving. "What?" I finally snap and ask her.

"Nothing," she teases.

"Nothing my ass, you're staring and it's creepy and unnerving."

"You're glowing."

"Am not," I scoff, "and guys don't glow."

"Well you definitely are and can I say, it's great to see you both happy but you—"

"—you hurt her, Tony will carve me. I've got the memo and the commemorative shirt. I will not be hurting her. How anyone could hurt someone like E, I will never know." Nancy's face changes when I say this. "What?"

"What has she told you about her past?"

"Not a lot. She's a closed book. Hell, I don't even know what E stands for. I'm trying to guess but she's keeping that info locked up tighter than a nun's cu … vagina."

"Nice save there, Kerr," she chides. "Just … just be careful with her okay."

"Her past is bad, isn't it?" She nods. "I wish she'd open up to me."

"She will, when she's ready." She pauses. "I only found out a few weeks ago. I'm still coming to terms with what she told me but I do know, I won't let anything like that happen to her again. Since you've been wooing her, she's smiling more and is opening up. I think you're good for her … just like she's good for you. You two are healing each other's fractured hearts."

"My heart isn't fractured."

"It's a figure of speech but you're good for each other. Is all I'm saying."

Nodding my head, I agree. I do feel whole again and I think a part of that is to do with her.

Later that day, E and I are out on the patio enjoying a late, really late, lunch. Looking over at her, I decide to just go for it. "E," she looks up at me, "will you have dinner with me tomorrow night?"

"A dinner date?" she repeats.

My heart is racing while I wait for her answer. A million scenarios run through my mind. She says yes. She says no. She laughs in my face. She jumps me and fucks me here on the patio. "What about burgers?"

"We can do burgers another time, I … I have something else in mind. So, what do you say? Dinner? With me?" I pause. "Please, Evelyn, wi—"

"Nope," she states and my heart deflates. Then I realize she's saying no to the name, not my date request … I think.

She looks to the ground, suddenly shy. Lifting her gaze to mine, I flash her my million dollar smile, "Dimples, will you do me the absolute honor and go on a date with me tomorrow night? Please."

"Sorry, I missed what you said."

"Dimples," I repeat again, "will you go out with me tomorrow night?"

When her head moves up and down indicating a yes, my nerves disappear. "Yes, Wheels, I'd love to go on a date with you tomorrow night." She bites her bottom lip and I'd love nothing more than to bite it too. I'm about to lean in for a bite, I mean kiss, when Dylan wheels over to us. My brows furrow at seeing him back in his chair.

"Sorry to interrupt, but ummm, ahh, Marshall, will you help me in the weight room please?"

"Why you back in the chair, buddy?" I ask him.

"I fell in the shower and reinjured my hip."

"And you want back in the weight room because?"

"I need to get back on my feet and out of here," he snaps. Wow, I wish I had his attitude when I first had my accident. If I was as gung-ho as he is, I'd possibly be out of here by now. Then he adds, "I have a life to live." and the tone implies he just wants out of here. "Please?" he begs when I don't answer. I look to E and she gives me the 'go, it's fine' look with her eyes.

"Okay, let's do this." Turning to E, I smile. "See you tomorrow night. I'll text you the details later."

"Okay, I'm looking forward to it." She smiles at me and fuck me sideways, who knew a little smile could hold so much power, I'm screwed when it comes to this woman. "Bye, Marshall. Bye, Dylan." She waves to him, but he's already off, determined to get out of here.

"Later, E."

Bending down, I place a quick kiss on her cheek and follow after Dylan. As we walk down the corridor, I start to get nervous because I'm going on another date with E. This is uncharted territory for me. I don't date and I definitely don't try and guess names or send flowers or organize sunset picnics. But there is something about E, she makes me want more, and as exhilarating as that is, it also scares the absolute shit out of me.

ELOISE

S itting here, I watch Marshall follow Dylan. That young man looks up to Wheels and it's great to see him encouraging the kid. When I first met Marshall, I thought he was an arrogant egotistical jerk only out for himself but as I've gotten to know him, I realize I completely misjudged him. Quite harshly to be honest. After my previous encounter with the opposite sex, it's little wonder I was so jaded and judgmental. *He* would never do anything like what Marshall is doing with Dylan. Unless *he* benefited from something, *he* never lifted a finger and *he* never went over and above what was expected. *He* is the egotistical jerk, how I ever fell for *him* I'll never know.

Leaning back in my chair, I start thinking about tomorrow night. I'm nervously excited for our date. This guessing game is fun, but I think it's time I tell Wheels the truth. I'm going to tell him all of it. My name. My past. *Him.* Everything. But what if it scares him away? I have enough baggage to fill a 747 airplane … twice. Will he want to stick around after I confess everything?

Shaking my head, I grab our lunch plates and head back inside to finish my shift. I'm so busy that I don't see Marshall again before I leave. Stopping at the liquor store on the way home, I grab a bottle of wine and decide to have a bath to clear my mind.

Slipping into the tub, I lie back and let the aromatic bubbles work their magic. The little heart-shaped bubble bar turns my bath into a floral meadow with an explosion of soft yellows and the fresh, soothing scents of gardenia, jasmine, and honey permeate the air. The scents envelop me and instantly I relax.

Closing my eyes, a vision of Marshall appears before me but it quickly morphs into an image of Duncan and he's lunging for me. Sitting bolt upright, I splash water everywhere as I push myself away from the vision.

Blinking rapidly, the room comes back into view and I realize it wasn't real.

Sighing, I fall back and stare at the wall before me. Just when I think I'm free of *him* and the memories, *he* comes crashing back into my mind like the wrecking ball that *he* is. *Will I ever be free of him? Or will his memory taunt me for the rest of my life?*

No longer enjoying my bath, I reach forward and pull the plug. Climbing out, I wrap my towel around my body and step over to the vanity. I stare at my reflection in the mirror and for a brief moment, I see the girl I used to be reflecting back at me. I see that weak woman who cowered and let *him* control her.

Closing my eyes, I take a deep breath and when I open them again, I see me, the new and improved version of me. I'm not that woman anymore. I'm strong and brave. Sure, I'm still a little fractured, but with time those fractures are healing. Marshall is the glue slowly piecing me back together. He brings out the real me and I know, it's time. It's time to confess all to him. If he doesn't like what I have to say, then so be it. I refuse to live my life in fear and with what-ifs. Me and me alone is the controller of my destiny.

ELOISE

Today is my day off and I'm ever so thankful, I've been a nervous Nelly from the moment I woke up. I'm excitedly nervous about my date with Wheels. I know we've had a date before, but this time it feels more, so much more. Add to the moreness—it's totally a word—I've decided to tell him about my past.

I'm scared that when I tell him who I really am and what I'm running from, he'll turn around and wheel out of my life. Once again, leaving me alone in this world. I should be used to being alone, but clearly, I'm a glutton for punishment because I keep opening my heart.

Standing in front of the floor-length mirror, I look at myself and see the real me reflecting back. I'm wearing the same black dress from our sunset picnic, it's the only nice item of clothing I own. If tonight goes well, I guess I better buy myself a few more nice outfits.

A knock at my door startles me. "He's here," I whisper. Taking one last look in the mirror, I nod and as I walk toward the door, I give myself a little pep talk. "You can do this, Eloise."

It feels like I'm walking to my execution. I'm nervous but at the same time excited for the night ahead. It feels like a tsunami is building in my stomach. Taking a deep lungful of air, I turn the handle and pull the door open. All the breath in my lungs disappears when my eyes land on the godlike man before me.

"Hi," I breathlessly let out.

"Hi," he nervously replies. "You ready?"

"Yeah," I reply with a nod, "I just need to grab my purse." Turning, I pick it up off the table by the door and sling it over my shoulder. Looking up, I take a moment to gaze at Marshall. He's wearing dark denim jeans and a dark Henley. He's dressed casually, then I look down at my dress and furrow my brows. "I think I might be a little overdressed."

His gaze roams over me. I can feel his stare deep inside and those butterflies in my stomach, take flight. "You look perfect." He bends his arm, offering me his elbow. "Shall we?"

"We shall."

Walking to him, I slide my arm through the crook of his elbow and we exit my apartment. Closing the door behind me, we head out of the building and into a waiting car.

"You didn't drive?" I ask, as the driver pulls away from the curb.

He shakes his head. "Nope, I haven't been cleared to get behind the wheel yet, but hopefully it won't be too far away."

"You're doing so well with your recovery."

"I am now. I wish I hadn't been such a dick when it first happened, I could possibly be back on the track by now."

"You can't live life with what-ifs," I inform him. "I … I used to think what if I never met *him* but then I wouldn't be where I am now. Instead, I look to the future."

Looking over, I see him staring intently at me. He lifts his hand and cups my cheek. "What did he do to you?"

"Everything," I whisper. Closing my eyes, my body trembles as I vividly remember everything *he* did to me during our time together. My hand subconsciously moves and rests on my stomach.

Opening my eyes, I see concern in Marshall's staring back at me. My mouth opens to start telling him my story when the driver's voice announces, "We're here."

The sound startles me but neither of us move. We continue to stare at one another. Lifting my hand from my stomach, I cover his that's still cupping my cheek. "Once we're inside, I have something to tell you."

He nods. "Okay."

We climb out and enter the restaurant. We're seated in a corner booth, Marshall sits across from me and stares. The intensity in his gaze calms me and I utter my name, "Eloise," breaking our silent stare off.

"Huh?"

"My name is Eloise Masters."

"Eloise," he repeats, and hearing him say my name is the sexiest thing I've ever heard. "I like it but I still think I'm going to call you Dimples." A smile graces my face. "And there they are," he tells me, "those dimples of yours really pop when you smile." My smile widens. "See?"

"Stop it, Wheels," I chastise him just as the waitress arrives.

"What can I get you both this evening?" Her gaze locks on Marshall and I find myself getting angry that she's ogling him.

"Can we have a few more moments please?" Marshall requests. His gaze is still on mine, he doesn't give the waitress any of this attention

"Sure thing," she singsongs. I watch her walk away and notice that she swings her ass from side to side. She looks over her shoulder but her face drops because Marshall is still staring at me. Internally I high-five myself.

"So, what's good here?" I ask Marshall, picking up my menu looking it over.

"The company I have," he croons and once again those butterflies in my stomach swarm.

The waitress returns and we place our orders. As soon as she walks away, the atmosphere around us changes. "Okay, Dimples aka Eloise Masters, what were you going to tell me earlier?"

Swallowing deeply, I take a breath. I'm just about to tell him everything when the waitress returns with our drinks. She places a glass of wine in front of me and a water in front of Marshall. He's in training mode so that means no alcohol. I was going to have a water too but I need liquid courage to tell him everything.

Picking up my glass, I take a sip—well, a gulp. Dropping my gaze to the table, I focus on the grain of the wood and I begin. "As I said earlier, my name is Eloise Masters. I'm originally from Collinsville…" For the next ten minutes I tell him everything about my childhood, my family, Duncan, the abuse, losing the baby and making my escape.

After I finish my story, I lift my gaze and I'm shocked at the expression I see on his face. It's not anger. It's not pity and it's definitely not sadness. It's awe. His mouth opens and closes a few times. Reaching across the table, he covers my hand with his. "Shit, Dimples, I had no idea. You're amazing. You've been through so much, yet you're still here and you're stronger than ever. Smiling. Bright. Bubbly and simply perfect." He pauses. "It goes to show, I was right about you."

"How so?" I ask.

"You worry about everyone else before yourself. Take for example your concern for Miles. You're more worried about him than yourself. At any moment, that doucheknuckle could appear and you're worried that he'll find out Miles helped you."

"But—"

"No buts. You have a super big heart, Eloise." He squeezes my hand in a reassuring, I've got you way. "I hope there's room in your heart for me too."

Staring at him, I nod. "I think there's definitely room for you, Wheels."

"Good, because you already have a spot in mine."

Holy fucking swoon, Batman, this man is smooth. I can tell he's being honest and for the first time since *him*, I'm open to trusting a man with my heart. However, if this turns to shit, my heart will irrevocably be fractured and it will never be fixed.

With our meal finished, Marshall settles the bill and offers to take me home. He laces his fingers with mine and we leave the restaurant hand in hand.

I'm on cloud one million right now. Tonight was everything and more. I confessed and not once did Marshall make me feel ashamed and he didn't show pity. He showed me empathy and understanding.

Since it's a nice night out and I'm just around the corner, we walk back to my place. The pace is slower than I normally walk but with Marshall by my side, it's perfect.

We arrive at my building and I turn to face him. "Thank you," I honestly tell him. "I had an awesome time with you tonight."

"I did too but then again, I always have a great time when I'm with you."

We stare at one another. The air around us thickening the longer we stare at each other. He takes a step closer, closing the distance between us. He reaches up and cups my cheek in his palm. He lowers his head and ever so gently, he presses his lips to mine.

Closing my eyes, I cover his hand with mine and kiss him back. We've kissed a few times now, but this kiss, it's the best of my life. My leg lifts like in romantic comedies and I giggle into his mouth.

"Something funny?" he wonders, resting his forehead against mine.

"My leg lifted," I whisper.

"Huh?"

"In romantic movies, when the hero and heroine kiss epically, her leg lifts."

"So we just kissed epically, huh?"

"You know it was epic."

"My leg didn't lift."

"It's a girl thing," I explain with a shrug.

"Well, let's see if we can epically kiss again."

Reaching up, I capture his cheeks in my hands and bring his lips down to mine. I lick along the seam of his mouth before pressing and seeking access into his mouth. He opens and I slide my tongue inside. He quickly takes control of the kiss and once again, my leg lifts.

"Yes," he murmurs against my lips, "I felt you lift your leg."

"Shut up and kiss me ag—" Before I can finish my request, he's kissing me senseless once again.

He severs the connection and stares at me. His gaze is so full of hunger, I'm about to invite him up when he breaks the silence, "I'm going to go before I take you upstairs and do all the wicked things I want to do to you."

"I'd be okay with that," I admit, totally surprising myself with that comment.

A growl emits from him. "As much as I want to, I'm trying to be a gentleman here."

"Fine," I relent, but if I'm being honest, I think it's for the best. I need to remember … baby steps. I don't want to rush things with Wheels, I want every moment to be perfect, like tonight was. But there's a part of me that's waiting for the bomb to drop because after all, this is me … and it seems, I don't have to wait too long.

MARSHALL

Waking the next morning, I find myself smiling before I've even had coffee and I'm pretty sure it's all to do with E aka Eloise Masters. My Dimples. Last night wasn't what I expected, but I'm glad it played out the way it did. After our date, I know her all the more better and it cemented my feelings, I'm falling for her.

Climbing out of bed, I wince in pain but it's not as bad as the previous day. After dressing, I head to the dining room for breakfast before I'm scheduled to meet Nancy in the weight room.

With my breakfast sandwich in hand, I take a seat. Pulling out my phone, I go to send Dimples a good morning text when I notice a Google alert notification. I haven't had one since Linc and I went out for burgers the other week so I wonder what it could possibly be. Clicking on the notification, it takes me to WtB —What's the Buzz—and I see a picture of Eloise and me from behind, walking back to her place after dinner last night. I read the article, well the first few lines, and roll my eyes.

Marshall Kerr, the notorious playboy who had a career-ending accident earlier this year has been spotted with a mystery woman. Our source tells us the brunette and race car driver have been seen together on several occasions now.
Who is she? And how long will she stick around?
pic of us walking together down the street

"Several occasions now?" I voice out loud. "What the hell? Damn public sending shit in to that gossip site."

"Move it, Kerr, we have training in thirty," Nancy bellows from beside me.

"Plenty of time," I retort.

"Just don't be late." She squeezes my shoulder and walks away. My eyes drop back to the article. Shaking it off, I finish my breakfast and then go and join Nancy for my session. She's in a particularly hellish mood today and she's really putting me through my paces but I'm invigorated this morning.

I'm smashing each and every task she throws at me.

"Dude, you're on fire this morning," she praises when we take a drink break.

"Just in a good mood."

"Would that mood happen to be because of a brown-haired lady who works here?"

Nonchalantly I shrug my shoulders. "Maybe."

"Maybe yes," she teases, and I find myself grinning behind my water bottle. "You keep this up and you'll be back in Cali and behind the wheel of your green machine in no time."

Taking a sip of water, I stare at the floor and process her words. This is what I've been working toward but now that it's in sight, I'm not as excited as I thought I would be. When I head home, it means I'll be leaving Dimples behind. The thought of that guts me. I'm snapped back to the present when I hear Nancy's voice. "I've seen a change in her recently too and it all started when you two began canoodling."

"Canoodling? Really?"

"Well, what do you call it then?"

"Dating."

"According to WtB, you don't date. You hook up," she throws back at me. And she's right, the old me did that but then I met Eloise Masters and it all changed.

"Well, clearly I do, because Dimples and I are dating."

"Does she know that?"

"I … I think she knows."

"You might want to clarify that."

Nodding, I think about her words and she's right. Not only do I need to clarify what we are but I also need to gauge if she'd be open to returning to Cali with me when I leave here. Sure, we've only been together—I think—for a short period of time, but everything feels perfect with her. The thought of her not wanting to return with me would suck donkey dick. I'd be gutted but at the same time I'd understand, especially now that I know about her past.

We hardly know each other and the last time she trusted a guy, he royally fucked her over. Maybe I'll wait a bit, see what happens between us before I possibly scare her away with my invitation to return to LA with me.

As if she senses I need her, she pops her head into the weight room. "Lunch?"

"Sounds good," I answer with a nod. "Twelve thirty work for you?"

"Perfect," she looks to Nancy, "give him hell, Nance."

"Always, E, always."

"Hey," I protest, "I thought you were on my team?"

She shrugs and I find myself laughing. "See you at lunch … if you survive," Dimples teases.

Before I can reply, she's gone.

For the next hour, Nancy puts me through hell but I manage to keep up with everything she throws at me. Just before twelve, she releases me from her clutches and I head back to my room to shower before lunch with Dimples.

While Dimples and I are having lunch, we're joined by Dylan and a few other residents. As much as I wish it was just the two of us, it is nice to mingle and laugh again. Dimples sits by my side and touches me as much as she can, well as much as is appropriate when you're in a dining hall with relative strangers … and at her place of employment.

She has to get back to work and we agree to watch the sunset together later. As I'm heading back to my room for a rest, my phone rings and I grin when I see Jaxson's name on the screen. "Well, if it isn't my favorite agent, how you doing, Jacky boy?"

"Don't call me Jacky boy," he snaps down the line and I chuckle.

"Hello, Jaxson, how are you today?" I reply back with a hint of sarcasm in my tone.

"I'm doing great but wondering why I'm fielding calls about you dating someone?"

"Well, I am … I think."

"You think you're dating someone. Care to elaborate?"

"I met a girl and she's everything. We've been out a few times and that's all there is to tell."

"Who are you? Marshall Kerr is a womanizing playboy who doesn't date. Did they do something else to you while they were repairing your hip?"

"Hardy har har, Jaxson."

"I'm just busting your balls, dating I can work with. Give me the deets and we can issue a statement."

"Nope," I vehemently deny, shaking my head. "No comment, I want to keep this just us."

"That's a bit hard when WtB already has an image of the two of you together and you know how relentless Margaret can be when she doesn't have all the information. She's going to speculate, then she'll piss you off, and you'll do something stupid. Then I'll be fielding a million calls as to why you snapped."

"Look, just gimme time to speak with Dimples. There's—"

"I knew there'd be something, there's always something with you."

"It's not bad, per se, but just lemme get back to you before we say anything."

"Fine," he huffs, "but please get back to me before this all blows up in our faces, okay?"

"There's nothing to blow up." *I hope.* "And I promise, you will be my first call once I know more."

"Good. Now, how's the recovery coming along?"

"Good," I tell him, "hoping to be back in Cali soon and back behind the wheel of my car."

"That's great to hear. Just don't fuck up, Kerr. These last few months not having to deal with your little fires have been great and I'd like to keep it that way."

"Roger that," I confirm, but my mind drifts to what Eloise told me last night. Our relationship could lead to an inferno but for the first time in my life, I'm happy to run directly into the flames. As long as Dimples is by my side, I can face anything thrown at me.

ELOISE

The last few weeks with Marshall have been everything a relationship should be, fun, loving and without violence and abuse. There have been a few times when I've felt he's been holding something back but as quickly as that feeling appears, it vanishes. Maybe I'm overthinking things due to my last relationship. Who knows? What I do know is that I'm happy, blissfully happy.

Wheels makes me feel alive in a way that I've never felt before, not even in the beginning with *him* when I thought all my Christmases had come at once. I've even officially met his mom and dad. I'd seen them in passing when they visited in Marshall's early days here but as he got stronger their visits have become fewer. One thing has remained the same though, the love they have for their son.

Bouncing into Marshall's room, I stop midstep when I see an ashen look on his face and then I hear his name mentioned on the television. When I look up, I see WtB is on and there's an image of him and a woman's silhouette with a question mark on the head. The reporter, Margaret, is talking about Marshall and his mystery woman.

"What's going on?" I ask, just as from the television, I hear, "Who is this mystery brunette that Marshall has recently been seen with?"

Turning my head to the screen, I see a picture of Marshall and me from the back, holding hands. I think it's from when we first went to dinner together. Spinning back to him, I raise my eyebrows. "Maaarshall, what's going on?"

"Dimples," he draws out my name, "it's not that bad."

"What's not bad?" I ask, my heart rate accelerating as I wait for him to explain.

"For the last week, WtB have been reporting about me and my mystery brunette."

"What the hell, Marshall?" I shout. "You should have told me when the first picture surfaced. What if *he* finds me?"

"He won't."

"You don't know that. *He* already has a PI looking for me. This is like handing *him* an invitation to my whereabouts."

"No," he growls and limps over to me.

"You're limping."

He shakes his head. "I'm fine." He stops before me and grabs my hands. My skin heats at his touch and the anxiety begins to fade as he stares into my eyes. "Eloise," he whispers, *I love it when he says my real name.* "I will not let anything happen to you. You mean everything to me."

As I stare into his baby blues, I believe him. "I believe you," I tell him and I wholeheartedly believe he will never let anything happen to me but I know Duncan, he'll never stop looking for me.

Leaning into him, he wraps his arms around me and I feel safe.

Lifting my head, I gaze up at him. "Please don't keep things from me, Marshall, I'm not weak anymore but how can I handle things that don't I know about?"

"I promise, no more secrets." He places a kiss on the tip of my nose.

"I ... I want to see what else is out there about us."

He looks hesitant but eventually, he nods. Taking my hand, he leads us to his bed. He takes a seat and I sit next to him. Picking up his iPad, he taps the screen and hands it to me.

Marshall Kerr, the notorious playboy who had a career-ending accident earlier this year has been spotted with a mystery woman. The brunette and racing playboy have been spotted together on several occasions now.
Who is she? And how long will she stick around?
pic of us from behind walking together down the street

Marshall Kerr and his mystery lady were spotted watching the sunset earlier this week. Sources tell us this isn't the first sunset these two have watched together.
pic of us gazing at the sunset

Marshall and his mystery lady spotted kissing over burgers
pic of us from behind, Marshall cupping my face and kissing me

Marshall and his mystery lady take a stroll through local park
pic of us holding hands walking in park from behind

Marshall Kerr and parents have lunch with his mystery lady.
Could wedding bells be around the corner for the former playboy?
pic of the four of us having lunch

Who is Marshall Kerr's mystery lady?
They've been spotted together on numerous occasions now. His social media is still inactive but it seems he's busy with this woman. Who is she? And is she the one?
Our source also confirms he is about to make a comeback. The stars seem to be aligning for him both personally and professionally.
Watch this space for more details
pic of Marshall in his rookie season
montage of previous images

"Shit-shit-shit," I hiss as I continue to scroll. There are pages and pages of images and articles about us. The wording is always the same, with tiny differences, and they all wonder who I am. At least my identity is still hidden. *But it won't stay that way forever.* How long until a shot of me from the front is posted online? "How? Why? Shit! Why didn't you tell me this was happening?" Covering my mouth, I cry, *"He's* going to find me."

"No, Dimples, I won't let that happen." He pulls me into his side and places a kiss on my head. "Jaxson is on standby to help."

"Who's Jaxson?"

"My Agent. He called me after the first picture appeared and I told him to say no comment. I don't want this to come between us."

"This didn't but you keeping it from me makes me wonder what else you're keeping from me."

"Nothing, I'm not hiding anything. I didn't tell you because I wanted to protect you. Dimples, you mean everything to me and I want to shield you from this shit."

"Shielding and hiding are two different things. You should have told me, Marshall. You should have told me when the first image surfaced." Rising from the bed, I shake my head and walk to the door. I feel him stand but I turn to face him and raise my hand in a stop motion. "No," I vehemently hiss. "I need to be alone right now." Before he has a chance to reply, I exit his room and race to the staff locker room.

Stepping inside, I walk to my locker and rest my forehead against the cool metal. The first tear drops and I let out a guttural sob. I knew this was all too good to be true. I finally find happiness, true happiness and once again *he* is going to tear it away from me. Duncan Montgomery is a thorn in my side. "Am I ever going to be free and safe?" I tearfully mumble.

Arms wrap around me from behind and his head rests on my shoulder. "You are free and I promise to keep you safe." He kisses my neck. "I'm sorry I kept this from you. I was trying to protect you."

Spinning in his arms, I look up and see anguish written all over his face. "I don't need you to protect me, Wheels. I just need you to be honest." Reaching up, I cup his cheek. "I'm not made of glass, I won't shatter and I know that with you by my side, if he finds me, I'll be fine." I laugh. "I'm stronger than he realizes."

"Hell yeah you are. You're Eloise 'Dimples' Masters, badass babe, and … and I love you."

My eyes widen. "Did you just say you love me?"

He nods. "Yep. I'm hopelessly in love with you, Dimples."

Biting my bottom lip to suppress the grin trying to break free, I decide to throw caution to the wind and once again, follow my heart. "I love you too, Wheels." Gripping his cheeks, I kiss him. He covers my hands with his and deepens our kiss. Pulling back, he rests his forehead against mine. "I promise not to hide anything from you ever again."

Nodding, I close my eyes and wrap my arms around his waist. He hugs me back and I hope my heart is right this time because I will not survive being hurt a second time.

MARSHALL

The last six weeks with Dimples have been great. Her discovery of me hiding the media surrounding us somehow brought us closer together. Hell, it was when I told her I loved her and much to my surprise, and delight, she loves me too.

In a way, I'm thankful to have been featured on WtB because I don't know if I would have had the balls to truly voice how I felt about her.

When she ran out of my room, I thought I'd ruined it all but Lady Luck was on my side and Dimples and I turned a corner in our relationship. We've officially been 'in love' for six weeks now. We've yet to have sex and this is the longest I've ever gone without sex. My balls are bluer than my eyes and my hand just isn't cutting it anymore. I can't wait until we get to that. I can't wait to taste her on my tongue. To slide between her thighs and have her pussy hug my cock, but most of all, I want to lick and worship every inch of her body from head to toe. I don't want to push her into it but I'm not sure how much longer I can keep this up. I haven't jacked off this much since I was fifteen and discovered Playboy magazines.

"Fuuuuuck," I groan, my dick is rock-hard and I'm in my workout shorts, which hide nothing. Thankfully, I'm in my room, about to have a shower.

Stripping off, I throw my clothes at the hamper. My dick is harder than steel. Dropping to the edge of my bed, I reach down, grip my dick. Closing my eyes, I begin to stroke. I'm mid-tug when the door to my room swings open.

"Knock kn—" My eyes pop wide open and I see an open-mouthed and shocked Dimples in the doorway. This is the third time she's caught me naked in my room, and it's not the first time she's caught me pleasuring myself.

She slips into my room and closes the door behind her. She leans against the wood and I grab my pillow and cover my lap with it.

"Well, that wasn't what I was expecting to find when I came in here."

"What were you expecting to find?"

"Not that." She points toward my crotch and spins her finger around.

"Do you barge into all rooms like this? Or just mine?"

"Just yours."

"So you haven't seen anyone else's bits here?"

"Just yours."

"Lucky me. And now that I think about it, you need to show me yours. Friends show each other their bits, it's…"

Together we both say, "…an unwritten rule."

"Exactly," I reply.

We stare intently at one another. The air in my room heating rapidly and my already hard cock is getting harder by the second. The look Dimples is giving me right now is carnal. I'd love nothing more than to bend her over my bed and sink myself balls deep inside of her.

"How about you come to my place for dinner tonight and … then …"

Fuck yes, I immediately say in my head but I need to play this cool, I am Marshall Kerr after all. "Are you sure?"

She nods. "Yeah, I'm sure. And as you said, friends show each other their bits and since we're a little more than 'just friends.'" She air quotes just friends and swallows deeply. "I think it's time for me to show you mine. After all, I've seen your bits a few times now."

"Three times. You've seen my bits three times now."

"Who's counting?" she sasses. "Be at my place around seven." Pushing off the door, she turns the handle but before she exits, she looks over her shoulder. "I'm looking forward to tonight."

Without another word, she departs and the door clicks closed behind her.

With my cock still hard, I collapse to the mattress and stare up at the ceiling, grinning like a carnival clown. *Holy shit, I'm going to see Eloise's bits tonight.*

ELOISE

I f I thought I was a Nervous Nelly the day of our first date, I was wrong. Today, I'm, I have no clue how to describe how I feel. When I walked into his room and saw what he was doing, my libido immediately kicked into gear. The urge to step toward him, drop to my knees and take over the stroking of his cock was strong.

Thankfully, my brain kicked in and I refrained, after all, I was at work. But holy hotness, Batman, watching Wheels do that to himself is the hottest thing I've ever seen.

Clearly my brain was still in La-la Land because I invited him over for dinner with an offer to finally show him my bits, since I've seen his bits a few times now. *What the hell, Eloise?* Now I need to cook an out of this world dinner and prep my body for what I hope will be a fantabulous night.

Leaving work early, I stop and grab the ingredients to make pesto pasta with grilled chicken, a garden salad and garlic bread because what's a pasta dish without garlic bread? This meal is simple. Easy to cook but ohh so delicious.

Flicking on the television, I roll my eyes when I see Margaret from WtB once again speculating about Wheels and me. This woman is like a rabid dog. Marshall assures me that he and Jaxson are all over it and my identity will be kept hidden for as long as possible. I believe him. But there's also a part of me that's scared and freaking out. When *he* finds out about my new relationship, shit is gonna hit the fan. And this time, it could ruin someone's career. A career that he's worked so hard for. He's literally been to hell and back and his comeback is so close to happening. I just hope my baggage doesn't ruin it for him.

Before I know it, there's a knock at my door. My nerves ramp up with each step I take to let Wheels in. No longer am I worried about Margaret or *him*, now I'm nervous and anxious about what's going to happen when I open the door.

Running my hands down my sundress, I take a deep breath, place my hand on the door handle and swing it open. When my eyes land on his, any and all nerves I had, float away. My body is now filled with desire, want and need for the man standing in my doorway.

"Fuck me, Dimples. You look stunning." Before I have a chance to reply, he slides his arm around my waist, pulls me into him and covers my mouth with his for an amazing hello kiss.

"Hello to you too," I breathlessly reply when we pull apart. We gaze into each other's eyes. Something passes between us but the oven timer begins to beep. "That'll be the garlic bread."

Pulling away from him, I walk into the kitchen and open the oven to save the garlic bread from burning, no one wants burnt garlic bread.

"That smells delicious." Marshall closes his eyes and breathes in deeply. Opening his eyes again, he places a bottle of white wine on the countertop. "Hope Pinot Grigio goes with what you're cooking."

"It's perfect," I tell him. "Glasses are on the table, you pour the wine and I'll bring everything over."

Placing the pasta on the table, I sit next to Marshall and notice him grinning. "What?" I ask, self-conscious at the intensity of his stare.

"You are ..."

"Are what?" I ask him, as I begin to dish up the pasta and chicken.

"Everything," he states, so much emphasis and meaning is held in that one word. "You are everything, Eloise Masters."

Pausing mid-scoop, I look up and my mouth opens and closes in shock. I'm at a loss for words. No one has ever said anything like that to me before. "Thanks!" I quietly reply and as soon as the word passes through my lips, I shake my head. *Thanks? Really, Eloise*, I internally scold myself.

"You are so very welcome." Reaching out he picks up his glass of wine and raises it up. "A toast."

Picking up mine, I smile over at him. "What shall we toast to?"

"Everything and us."

"I like it."

"To everything and us," we both repeat, tapping our glasses together.

The butterflies in my stomach take flight once again and I cannot wait for dessert … him.

"That was the best pasta I've ever eaten and I've been to Italy," Marshall shares with me. Leaning back in his chair he runs his hand over his stomach. His flat and ohh so toned stomach.

"Thank you," I reply. I seem to be thanking him lots this evening. "I'd love to go one day."

"And one day you shall."

We finish our wine and then I stand to clear up the dishes. Marshall stands too. "Uhhh uh," I warn. "You're a guest and guests don't clean up. Take your wine into the living room and I'll join you in five."

"Are you sure?"

"Yep."

Marshall heads into the living room and I quickly clean up. As I place the last dish into the dishwasher, an idea forms in my head.

"Be right back," I tell him and I quickly head down the hallway to my room.

Lifting my dress up, I remove my panties, leaving myself bare underneath. I'm not wearing a bra due to the neckline of my dress, not that my itty bitty titties need one.

Looking in the mirror, I give myself an internal pep talk. "You can do this, Eloise. Go out there and ravage that man. Do what friends do and show him your bits." Nodding at my reflection, I wink and head out to do what friends do—I'm going to show him my bits.

MARSHALL

That was the most scrumptious meal I've had in a long time. Don't get me wrong, the food at LTRWC is great but nothing beats a home-cooked meal—just don't tell Tony I said that. I'm sure he'd use his knives on me if he heard this.

Dimples is taking a while in the bathroom and I'm starting to wonder if I've overstayed my welcome. No sooner do I finish that thought and she walks back into the room. I watch intently as she walks toward me. She really is the most beautiful woman in the world. Stopping next to the sofa, she reaches down and takes my wine from my hand. Bringing the glass to her lips, she drinks the rest and places the empty glass on the coffee table.

She stares down at me, the air in the room thickens and my heart rate begins to accelerate. My tongue darts out and licks along my bottom lip. Her eyes track the movement and then she makes her move. She steps around the corner of the sofa and with her eyes locked on mine, she swings a leg over and straddles me. Placing her hands on my shoulders for balance. "As you've previously said, friends show each other their bits and you are a few—"

"Three."

"Okay, three up on me." She takes a deep breath. Removing her hands from my shoulders, she grips the hem of her dress and lifts it over her head, dropping it to the sofa next to us.

My eyes roam over her body and widen when I realize she's naked.

"You're … you're naked." She nods. "Like naked-naked." Again she nods. "Why?"

"Because friends …"

"…show each other their bits," I finish for her, grinning from ear to ear. "I can unequivocally say, I love being friends with you."

"I love being friends with you too, Wheels. But do you know what boyfriends and girlfriends get to do?" I shrug and shake my head. She leans in, her breasts brushing against my chest and the contact is everything and more. She whispers into my ear, "Boyfriends get to play with their girlfriend's bits."

Leaning back, she takes my hand and covers her breast. My skin sparks alive at the contact and without any thought at all, I begin to massage.

A small moan erupts from Dimples and the sound encourages me. Leaning forward, I cup her tit and suck her nipple into my mouth. My tongue circles the taut tip, garnering a guttural moan from her. Sucking harder, she runs her hands through my hair.

"More," she pants, swiveling her hips in my lap.

Lifting my hand, I massage her other breast as I continue to suck and nibble on the first one. "Maaaaaarshall," she coos, adding five extra a's to my name and never has my name sounded so amazing.

The scent of her arousal is hedonistic. My already hard cock twitches, it's painfully straining against the zipper of my pants. Popping her nipple out of my mouth, I stare up at her. "As much as I'm loving this, I need you to hop off me." Her face falls. "No," I quickly defend, shaking my head, "my cock is about to combust and I need to make room for him."

She nods in understanding and shimmies back. She drops to her knees between my legs and makes quick work of flipping opening the button on my jeans and lowering the fly. Her dainty hand slips inside and frees my dick. She licks her lips and leans forward. Her tongue slides across the head and I hiss at the connection. Then she shocks me by opening her mouth and sucks my cock into her mouth.

"Fuuuuuuuuck," I growl, as she begins to slide her lips up and down my shaft. Ever so gently she scrapes her teeth along the underside. It's the most amazing feeling ever. My balls tighten and I'm close to coming.

"Dimples, if you keep that up, I'm going to come." I add a few extra o's to come.

My cock pops free and she utters three words that I will never ever tire of hearing when they come from her lips. "I want you to." The minx that she is, lowers her mouth back to my dick and begins to suck harder. Pressing her finger to that magic spot between the base of my shaft and anus. Her head bobs up and down, faster and faster and sucks and strokes me.

Over and over, my cock slips in and out of her warm, wet mouth. It's like sliding into heaven. My balls tighten and before I can warn her, I explode. I come down her throat, groaning as she sucks every last drop from me.

My cock pops out of her mouth. "Fuck me," I breathlessly pant, completely spent.

"I want to," she huskily purrs from between my legs.

Looking down, I stare at her and I see nothing but adoration and lust in her gaze.

"I want to too," I agree.

Standing, I offer her my hand. She places her palm in mine and I pull her into my embrace. I wrap my arm around her waist and press my lips to hers. My tongue pushes into her mouth and she slips hers into mine, I give myself over to her and the kiss.

Kissing Eloise has always been impressive but standing here with her naked and my cock out, it's so much better than all our previous kisses combined.

With our lips fused together, we make our way into her bedroom. Stopping at the end of her bed, I step back and stare at her. Her cheeks are flushed. Her chest rises rapidly and she breathes deeply.

Gently, I push her back onto the mattress. Her eyes widen as she falls and I quickly cover her body with mine.

She's frozen. Staring into space, her chest no longer rising. Reaching up, I cup her cheek and she flinches. "Dimples," I quietly whisper. The sound of my voice snaps her back to the present and she begins to breathe again.

"I … I … I'm sorry," she cries, covering her face as she begins to sob.

"Hey, hey, what's wrong?" I ask, hovering over her.

"I … he … he used to throw me on the bed and the sensation from falling took me back there."

"Shit, Dimples," I say. Lifting myself up and off of her, I shuffle to the side and sit on the mattress next to her. With my knees bent and ankles crossed, I rest my arms on my knees. "I'm so sorry," I honestly tell her. "I feel like an utter asshole right now." Shoe doesn't move, she just lays there, covering her face.

"I got lost in the moment and I—"

"Do not apologize, Dimples," reaching out, I uncover her face and the utter look of hurt and defeat crushes me. "It's me who needs to apologize—"

"It's not your fault," she interrupts, "this is all me and my head. I hate that *he* still has this control over me." She rolls to her side, away from me. She curls into a ball and begins to cry.

Lying down next to her, I gaze at her back. She looks so small. So broken. "I hate that he's done this to you."

Moving her head, she stares at me over her shoulder. "I hate that I'm letting *him* control me like this. I know you're not *him* but in that moment—"

"Shhhh," I comfort her, pressing my finger to her lips. "You don't ever, E V E R, need to apologize for how you feel, Dimples. A relationship is between two people and when you hurt, I hurt. When you're happy, I'm happy. I can say, right now, I'm the happiest I've ever been and that's because of you. You helped me heal mentally and now it's my turn to return the favor. I will do everything in my power to help you forget all about him and for you to feel love like no one ever has before and I do. I love you to the moon and back, Eloise Masters."

I mean every word I just said. Seeing her falling apart, it broke me. If I ever run into him, it's not going to end well for the asshole. No one hurts my Dimples, no one.

ELOISE

Staring over at him, I process his words and one phrase keeps repeating over and over in my head, *when you hurt, I hurt.* No one has ever had my back in that way before, not even my parents. I've never had someone love me unconditionally like Marshall loves me. I know deep down he'll never hurt me and I hate that I've let *him* ruin our evening. However, I'm hoping there's still time for me to turn this around.

"I love you too, Marshall." I stare over at him. I've finally found my Prince Charming, my real Prince Charming. "Can we snuggle for a bit?" I ask him.

"We can do anything that you want, Dimples. I have nowhere else to be and for the record, I don't want to be anywhere else."

Rolling to face him, he falls to his back and I shuffle over to him. I slide in beside him. He slips his arm underneath me and I rest my arm on his abs and throw my leg across him. Cuddling into his side, our bodies fit together as if we were made from the same mold. He begins to trace his fingertip up and down my arm while I draw circles over his chest.

"Tell me something that no one else knows?" He asks, breaking the comfortable silence enveloping us.

"Ummm, I don't like avocado but guacamole is life."

He laughs and it vibrates through his chest. "That makes no sense."

"Guac has all the extras and it doesn't taste like green snot."

"Green snot? That's how you describe avocado?"

I nod against his chest. "Yep. Your turn, I wanna know something that no one else knows."

"That's an easy one. I'm crazy in love with this dark-haired, dark-eyed angel, who came into my life and turned it upside down and inside out."

Lifting my head, I stare down at him. "I already knew that so it doesn't count but for the record, the same goes for me. When I first met you, I thought you were an arrogant, conceited ass but it turns out, you were just fractured, like me. And together, we're helping each other glue ourselves back together."

"I'm not an arrogant, conceited ass, I'm more of a sexy, romantic race car driver."

"Modest much?" I tease. "But seriously, Marshall, you've healed me. I never thought I'd love again, not after *him*." I bite my bottom lip. "I … I want to try again."

"Are you sure, Dimples? I don't want you to do anything you aren't comfortable with."

"I'm sure." Lifting up, I half cover him and lower my lips to his. He wraps his arms around me and pulls me closer to him. We lie here kissing for what feels like hours. His cock hardens against my leg. "Can I try on top?" I ask him.

He nods. "You can drive and I'll follow your lead, Dimples."

"I … I've never been on top before. I … I don't know what to do." I feel so embarrassed admitting this. With *him* I was always on the bottom, faceup or facedown. It all depended on his mood and it was never loving. Fucking me was just a means to an end for *him*. I can count on one hand the number of times he made me come. That right there should have been a red flag but I was stupid and in love, well I thought I was in love. I now know, it wasn't love. It was a dictatorship. Marshall has shown me what true unconditional love is and I never want to let this feeling go.

"I'll guide you but it's just like riding a horse."

"I've never ridden a horse."

"Well, how about you climb on top of me and you do what makes you comfortable."

"What about you?"

"Trust me, I'll be fine."

"How so?" I question him.

"Dimples, babe, as soon as my cock slides inside of you, I'll be in heaven. Anytime I'm with you is heaven, therefore, I know that once my cock slips into your pussy, it will be fucking nirvana. Now, climb on top of me and have at it."

Marshall is like no one I've ever met before and I'm going to do everything I can to keep him. Closing my eyes, I take a deep breath and climb on top. Straddling his thighs, I stare down at him. His eyes are locked on mine and all I see is love and affection reflecting back up at me.

Lifting my hand, I wrap my fingers around his length and stroke. His eyes droop and he hisses. Opening his eyes again, he stares intently at me and I know I can do this.

"I'm ready," I whisper.

Removing my hand, I rest my palm on his abs and lift to my knees. Shuffling forward, his cock brushes my clit and my body trembles at the brief connection. Blinking rapidly, my chest rises and falls in sync with my eyelids.

"Breath, Dimples," he murmurs.

Nodding, I take a few deep breaths.

Breathe in.

Breathe out.

In through the nose.

Out through the mouth.

In and out I breathe and a calmness washes over me. I want this more than I need my next breath. Lifting myself up that little bit higher, I slide myself down his shaft. I'm soaked and he slips inside with ease.

When I'm fully seated, I lift myself up and slide back down. Up and down, I rock my hips and ride him.

"That's it, baby. Ride my cock," Marshall utters, lust written all over his beautiful face.

That feeling begins to develop low in my belly, I can't remember the last time I came from intercourse. "I'm close," I mewl.

Closing my eyes, I give myself over to the pleasure. Running my hands up my chest, I brush over my breasts and moan at the touch. I arch my back and increase my hip movements.

Marshall grips my sides in his hands. It startles me and I stop moving, he quickly pulls away but I shake my head. Lowering my hands, I grab his and place them back on my hips. His gaze finds mine and once again, our connection reignites.

Everything around me ceases to exist.

Marshall is the only thing I see.

Rocking back and forth, I focus on him and my pleasure.

Out of nowhere, my orgasm detonates and I scream through my release. Marshall grunts beneath me and he comes. His grip on my hip tightens as he explodes but unlike before, I'm no longer scared.

We both come back to reality and I stare down at him. He lifts his hand and cups my cheek. I lean into it. Breaking the silence, he utters three words I'll never tire of hearing. "I love you."

"And I love you."

Leaning down, I press my lips to his. He wraps his arms around me, holding me closer to him. He slips his tongue into my mouth and kisses me deeper.

"Thank you," I whisper, resting my head on his chest.

"Why?"

"For being you. For loving me and all my flaws. For—"

"What flaws?" he asks.

Lifting my head, I scrunch my eyebrows and give him an 'are you serious' look. "Wheels, I have a 747 filled with baggage. I'm an emotional wreck, I don't know if I'll ever be whole again."

"You have baggage, but guess what? We all do. As for being an emotional wreck, you're far from that. You're one of the strongest people I know. Your past was shit. I can't sugarcoat that BUT I can damn make sure that your future is bright, safe, and happy."

"Marshall, I'm the happiest I've ever been and that's because of you."

"No, you're happy because you're strong, independent and you're looking after yourself. Your happiness is all on you."

"Let's agree to disagree, Wheels, because I know without a doubt that you, Nancy, Tony, and Miles are the reasons I'm alive and happy. I will forever be grateful for that." I bite my bottom lip. "I … I want …"

"You want what?"

"I want to do it again." His face morphs into a grin and he nods. "Aaaand, I want you to be on top."

"Are you sure?" he questions.

Nodding, I bite my lip. "Yes, I'm sure. Make me and my body forget all about him."

"I will on one condition."

"Anything."

"As soon as you feel uncomfortable, you let me know. I don't ever want to hurt you."

"Promise."

Climbing off of him, I lie down beside him. We lie on our sides and face one another. He reaches up and brushes a tendril of hair behind my ear and cups my cheek. Leaning forward, he covers my mouth with his and kisses me. Closing my eyes, I give myself to him—heart, body, mind and soul.

Our kiss starts slow and soft but it quickly turns carnal and heated. I'm consumed by our lust when he rolls me to my back.

His upper body presses into mine but unlike before, I don't freak out. The fear that enveloped me earlier is nowhere in sight. All I feel is lust and need for this man.

Opening my legs in a silent invitation, I feel him smile against my lips as he slides between my thighs. Breaking our kiss, he lifts to his elbows and hovers above me. Rubbing his dick up and down my slit a few times, I moan in utter delight when he presses inside. He rocks his hips back and forth with his eyes locked on mine. When I was on top, I was in control and even though he's on top this time, I still feel in control and I know, he's not going to hurt me as we make love. Gazing lovingly at one another, our bodies and minds become one.

Lifting my hand up, I cup his cheek, rubbing my thumb along his jaw. He nuzzles into my hand. "Babe, you need to come because I don't know how much longer I can hold off."

He slips his hand between us and when the pad of his finger brushes over my sensitive clit, I explode. My pussy tightens around his cock and I come hard. His body stiffens and he too comes, groaning my name as he spills his seed inside me for the second time this evening.

My eyes widen and like he said, he quickly rolls off of me and climbs off the bed. He stares down at me. "I'm so sorry," he pants, "did I hurt you?"

Shaking my head, I sit up and shuffle to the edge of the bed toward him. "No, I just realized we did it twice … and didn't use protection."

His eyes widen as my words register. "Shit, E, I'm so sorry."

"You called me E."

"Well, that is one of your many names but, babe, I'm so sorry. I'm clean."

"I am too but I'm not worried about that."

"What if you get pregnant?"

"I'm on the pill but tomorrow I can get the morning-after pill to be on the safe side."

"If that's what you want."

"Isn't it what you want?" I question.

He shrugs. "I wouldn't mind having a baby with you. The timing isn't ideal but we'd make it work."

"You really are something else," I honestly tell him and I mean it. Marshall Kerr is unlike anyone I've ever come across before. He's sweet, funny, sexy and caring. He'd go to the ends of the Earth and back again for those he loves and I just so happen to be one of the lucky ones whom he loves.

He turns away from me and walks into the bathroom, I hear the faucet turn on and then he returns with a wet washcloth. "Lie down, babe," he commands.

Dropping back to the mattress I do as I'm told. He taps my thigh and I open. He cleans me up, this is another first for me. Once I'm clean, he returns to the bathroom, rinses the washcloth and comes back to bed.

He stands beside the mattress and stares down at me. Reaching my hand out to him, he takes it and links his fingers with mine. Gently pulling, he climbs back in and we snuggle together.

Like earlier, I rest my head on his chest and throw a leg over. My eyes become heavy and just as I drift off to sleep, I swear I hear him whisper something about watching my belly expand as I carry his child. Blissfully, I drift off to sleep in the arms of the man I love.

MARSHALL

Having Dimples by my side and on #TeamKerr has really helped me with my recovery these last few weeks. I was already onto a good thing with the new program—thank you, Doc Michels—but since she and I became an official couple, it's like a switch was flipped inside me and the old focused and determined Marshall reappeared.

It's amazing what a different mindset can do, both physically and mentally. I feel stronger, physically and mentally. It's like my mind has found its happy place and I think that happiness is due to Dimples.

She's one of the strongest people I know, especially with what's happened to her. When she told me everything about her past and what she's overcome, it made my accident seem like a drop in the ocean. Emotional scars run so much deeper than physical ones. She doesn't realize it but she helped me heal emotionally and physically to an extent. The physical healing is mostly due to Nancy and her sadistic work ethic.

Now that Dimples is officially mine, I'm going to make damn sure that she's looked after emotionally, physically and everything in between. If anyone deserves to get their happily ever after, it's her. I just so happen to be her knight in a shiny green race car. Move over Prince Charming, Marshall Kerr is here.

I'm on my way to one of the private rooms here to have a phone conference with Linc and the racing board about me returning to the track. We decided not to specify an exact date. We don't want to seem too confident but unofficially, we're hoping for next season. That way, I will have only missed one season which isn't too bad. Linc likes to remind me that if I had of followed orders straight after the accident, I'd probably be back out there by now.

I'm yet to get behind the wheel of my car, well, any car to be exact. We don't know if I'm going to have flashbacks of the accident and we need to keep this at the forefront of our minds. We need to take it slow—not my usually style—and be cautious. It'll be hard because I don't do life in the slow lane but I really want this, so I'll follow the rules … for once.

Hopefully we can prove to the board that I'm serious and ready to return to the track. I don't know what I'll do if they refuse, but I guess we'll cross that bridge if we come to it.

Rounding the corner, I feel her before I see her and when I look up, I see my girl exiting the kitchen. "Hey, Dimples."

"Wheels," she replies with a smile that lights up her face and makes my heart beat faster. I swear each time my gaze lands on her, she's prettier than the last time I saw her. We walk toward one another and stop in the middle of the corridor. "Where are you off to looking all suave?" Today I swapped out the gray sweats and workout attire, for dress slacks and a black button-down with the Schofield Racing logo on the left breast pocket.

"Phone conference with Linc and the board. Hoping to get the all clear to recommence racing."

"That's so great," she replies, but I don't think she means it. Her tone is high-pitched and now, she's looking at the floor and fidgeting with her hands. She looks up and smiles, but unlike moments ago, it doesn't reach her eyes. "Good luck with it all."

"Thanks." Leaning forward, she presses her lips to mine but this kiss doesn't have the usual Eloise and Marshall passion to it. "What was that for?"

"Luck," she nonchalantly responds with a shrug of her shoulders. Looking to the ground again, she refuses to make eye contact with me. "Not that you'll need it," she quietly tacks on. "The board will approve your return and then you'll be out of here."

Something is amiss, she seems flat and not herself. Stepping around me, she continues down the corridor without saying goodbye.

Turning around, I watch her walk away. Pressing my lips together, I watch until she turns the corner. Once she's out of sight, I shake my head and sigh. "What was that?" I mumble, spinning around I head toward the room allocated for me today.

Stepping into the room, I log onto the computer and bring up Zoom. Entering in the codes Linc emailed me, I wait for it to connect. He wanted to be here in person but I told him there's no need to do that, save the air miles and we can meet up somewhere amazing rather than the bumfuck of nowhere. Don't get me wrong, Brookvale is a beautiful little town but it's little and I don't do little. I need the hustle and bustle of the city. I can't wait to get back to Malibu, the smog and sunsets on my patio.

Zoom finally connects and I see Linc's smiling face. "How you doing?"

"Nervous as fuck," I honestly reply. "What if they say I can't return?"

"What if they do?" he throws back at me.

"Touché."

"You remember what we discussed?"

Nodding, I grin. "Yeah, yeah. Keep my mouth shut. Keep my attitude in check and most of all, don't fly off the handle otherwise I'll fuck it all up."

"Look at you, finally learning," he mocks like a proud father. A few seconds with him and the unease I felt begins to lift. Flipping him the bird he laughs. "There's the arrogant conceited ass I know."

A laugh breaks free. "That's how E describes me too."

"She's a wise woman," he replies and then broaches the one question that I've been too scared to ask. "Is she coming back with you when you get the all clear?"

"I haven't asked her yet."

"Why not?"

Shrugging my shoulders, I purse my lips. "What if she says no?"

"What if she—"

"—says yes?" I interrupt him, he nods and chuckles—asshole. "You and your fucking glass half full bullshit."

Before we can chat further about Dimples coming back to Cali with me, the racing board connects into our call. *This is it.*

ELOISE

Walking away from Marshall just now, a funny feeling washes over me and I don't like it. In the back of my mind, I always knew he'd leave but now that it's a possibility, I don't like it and I don't know how I feel about that. The thought of not seeing him every day hurts, but I don't know if I'm emotionally ready to immerse myself into his life. Into his public life.

Here we have the security of no one knowing but out in the real world, it'll be blown wide open, allowing *him* to find me. I'm not ready to face *him*. I don't think I ever will be but I can't hide forever, can I? Maybe I just need to pull off the Band-Aid as they say and face *him*. Confront *him* head-on, make *him* admit to what *he* did. Get *him* to apologize—ha, that will never happen—and then we can both move on. But I know *him*, *he* will never let me go and *he* will do whatever it takes for me to pay for running. Am I strong enough to face *him*? And will *he* manipulate me into staying? I know I'm stronger than I was back then but *he's* a manipulative, psychopathic prickface. *He* tricked me once and I'm one-million-percent positive, *he'd* try to do it again.

Pushing open the door to the staff room, it loudly bounces off the wall. "Easy there, Tiger," Tony jokes with me, until he notices the pissed-off expression on my face. "Who pissed in your Cheerios?"

"No one," I angrily growl at him.

"You sure about that? You sound like you want to rip someone to shreds." He pauses. "Do I need to get my knives?"

"No," even if letting Tony at *him* with his knives would make my life easier. "I just … I … umm, gah," I groan.

Leaning my head against my locker, my eyes well with tears. Slapping my palm against the metal, the door rattles. Turning my head, I look over to Tony. "He's going to leave and I'm going to miss him."

"So go with him," he urges me, as if it's that simple.

"I can't. I … what if … I just can't." The first tear falls and then an avalanche of them cascade down my cheeks. Tony wraps me in his arms and hugs me. "What if he doesn't ask me to go? What if he doesn't want me to go? What if *he* finds me? There are too many what-ifs," I cry into his shoulder.

"What if he asks? What if he, whoever he may be, doesn't find you? What if … what if …what if. You can't live with what-ifs."

"But—"

"Nope, no buts. If it's meant to be, it will be," he encourages me.

"But I want it to be," I tearfully sob into his chest.

"Then tell him," he commands, as if it's as easy as that. "Men sometimes need a neon flashing sign to help them determine exactly what they want. But, E, babe, that man loves you like you love my caramel slice. He wants you to go with him."

Shrugging my shoulders, I continue to cry into his chest. There are too many variables and I don't know the outcome. If I go to California with him, where would I live? Where would I work? What will happen when WtB plasters my face and name every-where? What happens when *he* arrives and not only turns my life upside down but Marshall's too? Wheels has worked too damn hard for me to ruin this for him. I can't do that to him, I just can't. I guess I have to put my happiness aside and let him go.

"If you love them, set them free," I mumble.

Lifting my head, I stare up at Tony, his eyes bore into me. "That's a stupid saying." Clearly he disagrees with my opinion. "I haven't seen you smile like you do when you're with him and vice versa. You two were meant to be and if you let him go, you'll be making a big mistake."

Tony squeezes my upper arm in a reassuring way and steps away, leaving me alone. I flinched when he gripped me and once again, I'm transported back to my previous hell. Is *he* going to hold me and my life hostage for the rest of time? Will I ever be free of you?

Leaning back, I slide down my locker and rest my head on my knees and sigh. Looks like I'm not as strong as I thought.

Fuck you, Duncan Montgomery.

Fuck you and your controlling hold over me and my life.

Fuck you.

MARSHALL

"We can't wait to see you back on the track, Marshall," the chairman of the board reiterates. *I'm back baby.*

"I can't wait to get back out there," I honestly respond, my face beaming with glee.

We all say our goodbyes and the Zoom call ends. Leaning back in my chair, I'm still grinning when my phone rings. Picking it up, I see it's Linc Face Timing. I swipe to answer and before I can say hello, he yells down the line, "Fuckin' told ya!" His face sporting a grin as big as mine.

"I don't need a told ya so but, Linc, thank you. I couldn't have done this without you."

"We're a team, Marsh. Always have been, always will be." He's right, from the moment I signed with Scofield this wasn't just about me. It was about every single person in the garage. Not only are we #TeamKerr, but we're also a family. I often wonder what would have happened had I signed with 777. Sure, Chance is a god on the track and his team is seamless, but mine is too … only better.

"So when do you think you'll be back in Cali?" Linc questions me.

"Ummm, ahh, I don't know. I need to check with Nancy before I lock anything in. I'd like to be back ASAP since that charity race is only a few weeks away but it all comes down to the medical clearance from here."

The board thought the annual charity race in California would be the perfect event for my return. And I have to say, returning to the track this season is so much better than we could have hoped for.

"Okay, sounds like a plan. You go see Nancy and keep me posted. We can't wait to have you back in the garage with us, Marsh. The place just isn't the same without you."

Hearing that I'm missed is pretty awesome. Linc could have brought in another driver while I was out but he didn't and that means everything to me. "I'll call you when I have news."

"Deal. Later." Before I can reply, Linc disconnects.

Standing up, I exit the room to search for Nancy. Looking at the time, I deduce she'll be in the weight room, so I head there.

Passing Dylan on the way, I notice he's not limping. "Looking good, kid," I praise him, slapping him on the back in an encouraging way.

"All going well, I'll be home soon."

"That's great to hear." I want to tell him the same for me, but I want to chat to Nance and Dimples before I tell anyone. He nods and keeps walking.

Finally I find Nancy. And like I thought, she's in the weight room, packing away some weights. "What can I do for you, Marshall?"

"The board has officially approved for me to return to racing," I share with her, helping her pack things away.

"That's great news. What's our time frame?"

"I'd like to be back in Cali ..." but I don't finish. I'm worried she's going to say it's too soon and I need to be here for another six months.

"Next week?" she suggests, shocking the shit out of me.

"Come again?" I ask. I'm not sure I heard her correctly.

"Marshall, you've been ready for weeks now. Your movement is back to normal and unless you're talking shit, you've said the pain is gone."

"I'm not lying," I assure her and for once, I'm not. Physically I feel like the old me but mentally and emotionally, I'm stronger than ever before.

"I know." She pauses. "Another reason I didn't say anything is that I didn't want you to get your hopes up if today didn't go well. You can do the rest of your therapy at home. I'm a call away if you need anything and I'll be happy to collaborate with your trainer back in Cali. Marshall, there's no reason for you to stay."

Yeah, there is, I think and Nancy being Nancy, she doesn't miss a thing. "You're gonna miss her, aren't you?"

"Yeah, I am. I didn't expect to fall in love with anyone while I was here and now that I have the opportunity to leave, I kinda don't want to." And then it hits me, she can come to Cali with me. "Do you think that if I … ummm … ahh, asked her to come back to Cali with me when I blow this joint, do you think she'd come?"

"Really?" She seems shocked that I'm asking this.

"Yep … do you think she'll come?"

She shrugs at me. "You can only ask." Well, that isn't encouraging and I'm starting to doubt if I should ask at all. Like I get it, we've only known each other for a little while, but Dimples and I have this connection that's worth fighting for. I know she feels it too, but there's that little issue of her douchebag ex.

Nancy senses my hesitation and walks over to me and squeezes my shoulder. "Look, Marshall, all you can do is ask."

It all seems so simple.

"Hey, Eloise, wanna come back to Cali with me?"

"Yep, sure, I'd love that."

"Sweet."

"Sweet."

If only it was that easy.

ELOISE

…one week later

Waking up wrapped in Marshall's arms—him big spoon, me littler spoon—is the best way to wake up. He doesn't get to stay over at my place too often since he's still a resident at LTRWC, therefore it makes the times he can, much more special.

Last week Marshall was given approval from the racing board to return to the track in an upcoming charity race, meaning that soon, he'll be leaving. I knew this day would come but now that it's looming, I hate it.

Never did I expect to meet someone while I was here, but Wheels rolled into my fractured heart and glued me back together. Piece by piece, he healed me and at the same time, made me fall in love with him. He's so patient with me. Caring, loving, and understanding. I have moments where I'm transported back in time to when I was with *him,* but Marshall always makes me feel better and doesn't make me feel like shit for ruining the moment.

Each time I freak out, I'm sure he's going to dump my sorry ass, but those moments only seem to bring us closer together. And with his departure looming, I don't know what it's going to mean for us. Not wanting to dwell on it, I put my head in the sand and enjoy each sacred moment I have with him.

"Morning, Dimples," he whispers against my ear.

"Morning," I reply.

Swiveling my hips, I feel his cock harden against my backside.

"If you keep that up," he huskily drawls, "I'm going to fuck you."

Sliding my hand between us, I grip his cock and stroke. Rolling over to face him, I grin. "Have at it, Wheels."

He rolls me to my back and slides between my thighs, running his cock up and down my slit. His cock presses at my entrance and with our eyes locked on one another, he thrusts his hips forward and presses into me. My eyes close in euphoria as I adjust to his girth. He pistons his hips back and forth.

In and out.

Faster and faster.

Together we tumble over the orgasmic cliff, moaning each other's names as we ride out our release. When we both return to Earth, he kisses me deeply. "That is by far, the best way to wake up."

"I agree, but you know what's better?"

"Doing that twice to wake up?"

"Fiend," I tease with a slap to his shoulder. "I was thinking waffles and maple syrup."

"I like your style, Ms. Masters. How about we get dressed and I take you out for brunch?"

"I'd love that."

Two orgasms and an hour and a half later, we walk hand in hand into Cass's Diner for brunch. Once we're seated, I look up and notice someone with a phone camera pointed in our direction. Lowering my head, I look intently at the menu.

"You okay, Dimples?"

"Mmmhmpf," I nonchalantly reply with a nod.

"Wanna try again, babe?"

"Camera," I murmur and flick my eyes in the direction of the camera wielding person. Marshall looks over his shoulder and when he spots the person, he growls low in his throat.

"Gimme a sec." He stands up and walks over to them. From where I'm sitting, I can't hear what they're saying but the guy plays with his phone. Then Marshall poses with the guy for a selfie and signs something before walking back over to me. "All sorted."

"How?" I question, confused as to how he could have fixed it so easily.

"I asked him to delete the one of you and then I offered a selfie with me."

"And he deleted it? Just like that?" I ask, shocked it was so simple.

"Yep, he's not a pap, therefore he can be reasoned with."

"How do you put up with that? I don't think I could handle living with that day in, day out."

"You get used to it," he offers with a shrug.

Staring at him, my mouth opens and closes a few times. "How?" I ask again.

He shrugs nonchalantly. "You just do. I honestly don't notice them anymore."

"But what about being on WtB and all that? The rumors? The lies?"

Again he shrugs. "I don't pay any attention to it, plus that's what I pay Jaxson for."

"You and I are from two very different worlds, Marshall."

"We don't have to be."

"How so?"

Before he can answer, the waitress arrives, halting our conversation. Leaving me wondering what he was going to ask. We place our order and then on the television in the corner, I see another image of Marshall and me. "...spotted again leaving the center where he has been since his career-shattering accident. Everyone is speculating if the rookie driver will ever race again."

Marshall laughs. "If only you knew Margie baby."

"She's like a rabid dog with a bone."

Margaret from WtB is relentless in trying to figure out who I am, but somehow Jaxson and Wheels have managed to keep my identity a secret. I'm not sure how much longer that will happen and I'm trying not to worry about it, but it's always there, lingering just under the surface of my mind.

"Ignore her, it's what I do."

"I wish I could just brush it off like you, but I can't. Not with my past looming in the background. Waiting to strike like the snake that *he* is."

"I will never let him hurt you."

"You can't protect me forever, Wheels."

"Watch me, Dimples. Watch me."

Opening my mouth, I go to refute that claim but again the waitress arrives and interrupts us. She drops off our breakfast and our conversation comes to a halt as we dig in. While I eat my waffles—which were exactly like I hoped—I process his words and I believe that he'd do what it takes to protect me, but can I put that responsibility on him?

ELOISE

After breakfast, we head back to the center and when we step through the front doors, Lincoln and Grayson are at the front desk chatting with Nancy and Linda.

"What are you guys doing here?" Marshall asks as we walk toward them, hand in hand.

"We're here to spring you out of this joint," Grayson informs us as when we reach them. Marshall drops my hand and the guys do the one-arm bro hug thing and then he comes back to me and pulls me into his side. "Dimples, I'd like you to officially meet Grayson and Linc."

"Dimples?" Grayson questions.

"E." I offer my hand to Grayson, just as Marshall blurts out my real name, "Eloise." My eyes widen at the use of my full name. "Just E is fine," I tell them.

"It's nice to finally meet you, E. I hear you're to thank for his recovery once he pulled his head out of his ass."

"I didn't do much. Nancy and Doc Michels are the ones you should be thanking."

"What about me?" Marshall cries, butthurt that he's not getting any of the recognition for his recovery.

"If you weren't such a whiney little bitch you'd have been out of here months ago and wouldn't have missed most of this season," Linc sasses.

"Yep," Grayson and Nancy both say at the same time.

"Is it pick on Marshall day?" He pouts, yes, the grown baby pouts.

"Ohh, poor baby, can the big bad race car driver not handle the truth?" Linc teases and we all laugh. Mine stops when he says, "Go pack your shit and we can get you out of here."

Marshall nods and takes my hand in his, dragging me toward his room. We step inside and he kicks the door closed behind him. He stares at me intently. I can feel his gaze deep in my soul.

"Come with me, E?"

One question. Four words and I don't know what to say.

My mouth opens and closes, I'm speechless. We've never discussed what will happen, I had hoped he'd want me to go but I'm safe here. Can I put my new life at jeopardy for a man? Sure, I love him with all my heart, but I thought I loved *him* too and we all know how that worked out for me.

"Please, Eloise," he begs. He uses my full name, therefore, I know he means business. He steps over to me and takes my hands in his. He squeezes in that sincere way I've come to love and he pleads with his eyes. "Please come back to Cali with me."

My mouth opens and closes but the fear wrapped around at the thought of leaving is suffocating me. "I ... I can't, Marshall. I want more than anything to say yes—"

"Then say yes."

"I ... I can't." Pulling my hands free, I shake my head. "I can't. There's too much at stake. I ...I, I'm sorry ." Stepping around him, I open the door and run down the corridor. Running through reception and past Nancy, Linda, Grayson, and Linc, I head toward the exit. Pushing the front doors open, I race out into the daylight.

My name is being yelled, but I ignore them. I put one foot in front of the other and I run. I run all the way to my place.

Racing up the stairs, I unlock the door, step inside and slam it closed behind me. Turning around, I lean back against the wood huffing and puffing. Sliding down the door, I land on my butt and begin to cry.

A guttural sob breaks free, I just pushed away the best thing to ever happen to me. He offered me a future and I let my fear take hold. Deep down I know Marshall isn't *him*. I know he'll never hurt me like *he* did. Wheels is offering me a future that doesn't involve me cowering in fear. He's offering me a future by his side as an equal. But instead of embracing the opportunity, I ran like a coward.

I'm starting to regret my decision. "Stupid, Eloise," I mumble. Folding myself into a ball, I cry over the dumb decision I just made.

After lying here for a while, I suddenly sit up right. "I want to go," I say to my empty apartment.

Standing up, I open my front door and race back to the center. I run faster than the wind, not stopping for anything or anyone. Flying through the front doors, I head toward Marshall's room but when I arrive … it's empty. The bed has been stripped bare. His few personal belongings are missing and there's a faint disinfectant smell lingering in the air.

"He's gone," I whisper.

My eyes well with tears as I look around the empty room. Hoping to see something to indicate he's still here but nothing materializes. It's empty and it confirms, he's really gone.

Falling to my knees, I cover my face with my hands and break down, I let out all my pent-up grief. Tears pour down my cheeks and I cry my broken little heart out. I just let the best thing to ever happen to me go due to the fear from my past.

A hand touches my shoulder, startling me. Looking up I see Tony staring down at me, concern and worry etched on his face. My mouth opens and closes but I don't know how to voice my heartache right now. It's my fault my heart is broken and now I'm all alone.

"E, babe, what happened?" he asks, breaking the silence, well, silence apart from my uncontrollable sobbing.

Swallowing deeply, I tearfully wail, "I let him go and he's gone. He's gone."

MARSHALL

"**I** *... I can't, Marshall. I want more than anything to say yes. I ... I can't.*"

Those fifteen words play on repeat in my mind as I pack up my room. I really thought she'd come with me or at least let us discuss what would happen, but instead she refused and then ran away. Guess that's what she does. She ran from that and now, she ran from me too.

My mood on the way back to Cali could be described as grumpy asshole with a side of surly. Sitting in the front passenger seat of Grayson's Rover, I mope as the miles passed by, taking me away from Dimples. With each mile we drove, my heart fractured at leaving her behind. I knew there was a chance that she wouldn't want to come, but there was also a part of me that hoped she would jump at the opportunity.

"…later this week we have track time booked," Linc informs me from the back.

"That soon?" I ask, finally paying attention.

"I'd have you out tomorrow—"

"Do it," I growl like the asshole I am.

"You don't want to settle in first?"

"Nope, this is what I've been aiming for. What I've been working toward. Go hard or go home, isn't that what they say?"

"That can be the team's new motto," he says.

"Mmmhmpf," I nonchalantly reply, then I add a stern, "just lock it in."

"Okay, I'll lock it in."

After telling Linc to lock in track time, I revert back into asshole mode. The rest of the trip goes by silently, well for me anyway. Meanwhile, Linc and Grayson chat but I couldn't tell you what they talked about.

Pulling up to my house and into the driveway, I smile for the first time since we left LTRWC … that is until I see a pap across the street and they snap my pic as I climb out of the car.

"Fuck off," I bellow at the paparazzi scum, my blood pressure rising because this just reaffirms *why* she didn't return with me. They are the bane of my existence. I'm used to them, but for her they could be dangerous to her safety and I get her hesitation to come back with me but at the same time, it cuts deeply.

A car pulls in next to us and when I see it's Mom and Dad, a wave of happiness washes through me. Not seeing them each week has been tough … but I had Dimples … and now, I don't.

"How's my boy doing?" Mom asks, enveloping me in a hug. Nonchalantly I shrug. "What's wrong?" she immediately questions. It's scary how well she knows me. Keri Kerr knows all my tics, I shouldn't be surprised that she knows something's up.

"Dimples didn't come back with me," I sadly state.

Mom looks at me. "Well, did you ask or demand?" A laugh escapes me, trust Mom to think it's my fault but when I think about her words, I guess I did kind of demand she come with me. I did put her on the spot, but I thought our love was enough.

"A little of both, I guess," I honestly tell her. "I thought she loved me, Mom."

"Marshall, that girl does love you. I don't know her story but I can tell she's fragile, yet strong. Give her time and then call her and see where it goes. You might be surprised at what happens."

"What if she doesn't answer or ever want to come here?"

"What if she does?" both Mom and Linc voice at the same time.

"Stop ganging up on me," I complain.

Mom says, "It's not ganging up when—"

I interrupt her, "—it comes from love."

"Let's take this inside," Dad interrupts, he nods to the side.

Looking to the street, I see more paps have arrived. Seems my return is going to be all over the news tonight ... and that's not going to help me with Dimples. *Fuck my life.*

Today is my first time back behind the wheel of my green machine since my accident. As soon as my ass slides into the driver's seat, a feeling of contentment washes over me, I feel like I'm home.

Being back on the track is everything, but I really wish Dimples was here with me. It's only been twenty-four hours since I left but I miss her like crazy. I know I need to give her time but patience is not my virtue.

After Linc and Grayson left last night, Mom and Dad stayed a little longer. Mom being Mom took me aside for a KK chat. Out on the back patio, overlooking the ocean, I gave Mom the Cliffs-Notes version of her story…

"…and that's how and why she ended up in Brookvale."

"That poor girl," Mom cries, wiping away a stray tear.

"Don't cry, Mom."

"How can I not? She's been through so much in her short life. Knowing all of that, you need to give her time, don't push her. Let her know you're here and that you're not going anywhere. She's never had that before. She was on her own for so long and then with a monster, it's all overwhelming for the poor girl," she pauses, "I think you should send her fl—"

"Flowers," I interrupt. "I was already thinking that. Your suggestion of flowers previously worked so maybe they'll work again."

"You have a good heart, Marshall Kerr, and I'm so proud of the man you've become."

"Thanks, Mom. I couldn't have done it without you and Dad."

"Yes, you could have. Now, go win back my daughter-in-law."

…The sound of Linc's voice through my headset snaps me back to the present. "You right, dude?"

"Yeah, just…" I don't finish because if I tell him my head is in Brookvale with Dimples, he'll pull me in quicker than a fat kid can inhale a Ho Ho.

"Just what?" he questions, his voice raised and laced with a hint of unease, just like I knew it would.

"Just taking it all in," I lie.

"You sure you want to do this?" he asks, for what feels like the millionth time since I arrived at the track.

"Yep, let's do this."

Taking a deep breath, I tighten my grip on the steering wheel and quietly mumble, "You can do this, Kerr."

Pressing my foot down on the accelerator, the engine revs and the vibration rumbles through my body. Instantly I'm transported to my happy place, I imagine this is what a junkie feels when the heroin hits their bloodstream. That euphoric feeling envelops you. Your body enters a subspace and there's no better sensation in the world. Easing my foot off the brake, the car moves forward slowly.

"Take it easy, Kerr," Linc warns through the headset. "This is just to get a feel of the car and track, it's been a while. No silly shit."

"I wouldn't do anything like that."

A rumble of laugher comes through the speakers.

"It's good to have you back."

"It's fuckin' good to be back," I assure him as I increase my speed.

It's all coming back to me, it's just like riding a bicycle. Muscle memory takes over and I'm just a passenger to what I'm doing. My mind drifts to Dimples and I really wish she was here. Shaking my head, I focus on the track, I can't be thinking about Dimples and how much I miss her … and her pussy.

"How's it feel?" Grayson asks.

"Like I'm home." And it's true. This is my home. My happy place … I just wish Dimples was here by my side, living in my home. My mind drifts to what it would be like if she was here. Her excitement at seeing me race. Being able to wake up next to her each and every day. To be able to have sex with her anytime I want. To bend her over and fuck her on my green machine. To—

"Marshall," Linc yells, snapping and getting my attention. "Get back to the garage, your head isn't in this."

"I'm fine," I snarl and to show him that I am, I push my foot down on the accelerator and floor it. The inertia pushes me back in my seat and everything around me blurs as I speed around the track.

I forget about Dimples.

I forget about the heartache.

I forget about everything.

I focus on the track.

I focus on becoming one with my car.

I focus on being Marshall Kerr, race car driver.

Around and around I go.

Lap after lap passes me by. Linc and Grayson are yelling at me, but I tune them out and focus on the pavement ahead of me.

Around and around I continue to drive.

Sweat pours out of me.

My heart erratically beats within my chest.

"Woo Hoo!" I scream within the car, not a care in the world that I'm currently driving recklessly. Ignoring the voices coming through my headset, I push my foot down flat and fly faster and faster around the track. I haven't felt an adrenaline rush like this in months and it feels good.

"Get the fuck back in here now, Kerr, or your ass is fired!" Linc bellows, the sound of his voice sparks something within and this time, I do as he demands. Easing off the accelerator, I slow down and pull into the garage.

Coming to a stop, I sit here, breathing rapidly. My heart racing in my chest. Gripping the steering wheel tightly. My body is tense and on edge. I don't know what happened out there, I was unable to stop myself from pushing my foot down. I've never been reckless like that before, but something overtook my body and I was helpless to stop it.

"What the fuck, man?" Grayson scolds me as he helps me out of the car.

Linc storms over and pushes on my chest, thrusting me back into the side of my car. "You're fucking done until I say so, Kerr. That was reckless and fucking irresponsible." He shakes his head. "I'm so disappointed in you right now."

Before I have a chance to reply, he pokes me in the chest and storms off. Kicking a trash can in anger on his way out.

Grayson hands me a bottle of water. "You really pissed him off." Nodding my thanks, I twist the cap off and chug it back. "What happened out there, man?" I shrug, not looking him in the eye. "This isn't you, Marsh. I think you need more time before you do this again."

"I'm fine," I snarl. "I just needed the adrenaline rush."

"So go skydiving or to the shooting range. You don't let loose on the racetrack in a two-million-dollar car."

"Whatever, man." Pushing off my car, I undo my race suit and head toward the bathroom to change back into my normal clothes.

Exiting the bathroom, all conversations in the garage halt. All eyes are on me. The tension is palpable. No one speaks a word as I walk across the garage and out to my car. Climbing into the driver's seat of my McLaren, I start the engine and floor it out of the parking lot, kicking up gravel, and not caring about the damage to the paint.

Once I hit the PCH, I put my foot down and drive. Recklessly I weave in and out of traffic. I'm driving dangerously but I do this for a living, I can handle the streets. I pass the turnoff to my house and I keep going. Eventually, I reach Point Mugu Naval Air Station, thirty miles north of my place in Malibu. Sighing in frustration, I turn around and head back to my house.

When I pull onto my street, I sigh in relief; there's not a pap in sight. The gate slides open and I park my car out front. Walking inside, I head out to the patio and flop onto a chair. Staring out at the ocean, a calmness washes over me. This is another happy place of mine but I feel out of sorts, I really wish Dimples was here. I need her like I need the next adrenalin rush of being out on the track. I've come to realize she's my anchor. Without her by my side, I'm drifting and I feel lost without her. How am I going to survive without her?

Pulling my phone out, I snap a photo of the sunset and send it to Dimples.

MARSHALL

picture of sunset

Wish you were here Xo

After sending the text to Dimples, I email the florist in Brookvale and order a bunch of flowers for her and hope that Mom is right. With time, she'll be here by my side but I'm worried I'll do something stupid, again, without her calming influence.

ELOISE

Marshall has only been gone for forty-eight hours and already I miss him like crazy. I cried myself to sleep that first night after Tony found me on the floor in his room. And I haven't stopped crying since.

I cry in the shower. I cry when I walked past his room. I cry as I watched the sunset.

I've been on autopilot, going about my day in a tear-filled haze. Looking up, I see Nancy walking toward me with a huge bouquet of teal chrysanthemums.

"Someone's a lucky girl," she singsongs—like she always did—and hands them to me.

My eyes well with tears as I look at the gorgeous array. Plucking out the card, I read and the tears flow.

Looking up at Nancy, I tearfully inform her, "I love him and miss him."

"So go to him?" she suggests, as if it's that easy. That simple.

"I can't, I already said I can't."

"You can and you will. I'll drive you."

"I can't ask you to do that."

"You're not asking, I'm offering. Now, go tell Linda and we can leave after my shift."

"I can't leave Linda in the lurch like that."

"Yes, you can," she voices from behind me. Startling me, I spin around to face my boss. "I knew when he left that you would too."

"How?"

"I have eyes, E, and you two love each other fiercely. No one and nothing will keep you apart."

"But what if I ruined us by saying no?"

"Well, there's only one way to find out."

Staring at her I wonder if it's that simple. Nothing in my life ever has been before, why should it be any different now?

"I don't know where he lives," I tell them.

"Well, lucky for you, I just happen to have a way to get that," Linda informs us. "I am the boss, after all."

My eyes widen. "Can't you get in trouble for that?"

"Only if this turns to shit, but my inner Vi Summers says this is going to have a happily ever after and the girl is going to get the guy. My romance loving heart knows it."

"I wish I was as confident as you."

"Trust me," Linda replies, reaching out she squeezes my shoulder.

"Why are we trusting you?" Tony questions, joining us.

"That when E turns up on Marshall's doorstep they'll get their happily ever after reunion."

"More like a boom-chicka-wow-wow reunion."

"Tony," I scoff and slap him on the arm.

"What? It's totally true. Blind Freddie can see you two are meant for each other."

"But—"

"Nope, no buts," Linda interrupts. "Head on home and pack. Someone—"

"—me!" Nancy shouts, waving her hands excitedly.

"Okay, Nancy will pick you up in the morning and then you can go get your man."

"I hope it's that simple." And I really mean that but with everything in my life, I'm not positive at all.

"Let's get you back to your place and packed up," Tony suggests.

"I need to finish my shift," I remind him.

"Nope, you don't," Linda refutes, shaking her head. She looks to me and has this look on her face. "You're fired."

My eyes widen and my heart drops. I've never been fired in my life, never. Until now. "Fired?" I whisper.

"Yeah, fired," she repeats with a smile. "E, you have been an amazing employee, but this was always temporary. Your life now, it's in Malibu, with that man. Now go, before you change your mind."

Pursing my lips, I grin, shake my head, and laugh. "There's no changing my mind. I need him like I need my next breath. I made a mistake letting him go and now I need to fix what I fractured."

"There's nothing to fix, not going by those flowers," Tony retorts, nodding to the flowers, "in your arms."

"You really think so?" I question, but as soon as those words pass through my lips, I know he's correct. You don't send flowers or write a message like that for someone you don't love.

"I know so. I'm going to miss you, E." He throws his arm around my shoulder, pulling me into his side and kissing the side of my head.

"And I'll miss you, too, Tony … and your knives."

We all laugh.

Looking between the three of them, I realize I'm going to miss them all, but I know with all my heart that I need to be in California with Wheels. As corny as it is, he completes me. I say this in my mind in a Tom Cruise from *Jerry Maguire* kind of way.

"You better keep in touch," I tell them.

"And you better keep in touch too. When you and that boy get married, I want a front-row seat."

"Let's see if he wants me first."

"I bet my left nut he'll take you back."

"I wish I was as confident as you, Tony." The thought that he doesn't scares me. I'm ninety-nine percent sure he feels what I feel but did me pushing him away, change how he feels.

"Everyone needs to have confidence and to believe in themselves, E. When they do that, they get what they want."

"Okay, I'll try. And please, don't mention your nuts to me again."

"Anything for you, now, let's get packing."

Four hours later, what few possessions I have are all packed into the back of Nancy's Jeep. The three of us are sitting on the floor in my empty apartment, eating pizza and drinking wine from paper cups. "I really am going to miss you guys."

"You better keep in touch," Nancy sniffles, reaching over to take my hand.

Nodding, I tear up. "I will. And you too," I inform Tony, taking his hand in mine. "You both mean the world to me. Along with Wheels, you guys helped heal me and I will forever be grateful for that."

"One day you will open up to me, E, and tell me all about the man who hurt you. Just remember, I have my knives and I know how to use them."

A laugh escapes me. "I'm sure you would but as I previously told you, orange really isn't your color and I can't have that on my conscience. Plus, I've come to realize me moving on and being happy is the best form of torture for *him*."

"But aren't you worried?" Nancy asks. She knows the full story so her question doesn't surprise me at all.

"I'm worried each and every day, but I can't let *him* dictate my life anymore. *He* doesn't get to win."

"You really are an exceptional woman, E."

"Says the exceptional woman," I look to Tony, "and you're pretty awesome too."

"I know," he states with a cocky grin and an air of grace that only Tony can portray.

I really am going to miss these two but I miss Marshall more. He's my future, I know that and it's time I started living, not hiding. I'm coming, Marshall Kerr … I just hope it's not too late for us.

MARSHALL

Eloise should have received my flowers yesterday and I still haven't heard from her. I thought she would have at least texted to say thank you, but nothing. With a coffee in hand, I head toward the patio but a knock at my front door stops me in my tracks. Clearly I didn't shut the gate last night when I got home. *So much for private property.* The paps have been relentless since I returned. Maybe it's time to set up a press conference, hopefully if I address them, they'll piss off and leave me alone. I'll get in touch with Jaxson later today.

Placing my mug on the countertop, I head to the front door and before I get there, they knock again. "I'm coming," I angrily shout but when I open the door, all that anger disappears. "Dimples."

"Hey, Wheels," she timidly replies.

We silently stare at one another. I rapidly blink because I'm sure I'm daydreaming and if I am, I never want to stop. Lifting my hand, I cup her cheek in my palm. She leans into it. "You're here. You're really here. I'm not dreaming."

"I'm really here," she quietly confirms. "Can I—"

"Yes," I eagerly express, not letting her finish. I'd say yes to anything she asks me right now. I knew I was missing her but seeing her in the flesh makes me realize just how much I did miss her.

"Really?" she questions.

"Really-really." Taking her hand in mine, I close my eyes and savor the connection. Opening them again, I smile when I see Nancy standing behind her. "Thanks for bringing me my girl."

"Anything for you guys," Nancy affirms, " but before you two get to the sexy schmexy reunion, can I use your bathroom? Then I can get back on the road and leave you alone."

"Of course, but are you sure you don't want to stay the night? It's a long drive."

"It's fine, I've got friends in San Clemente who I'd love to catch up with. Plus, I don't want to hinder the reunion between you two."

"Come in. Piss and then piss off," I tease her.

"So hospitable," she jokes as we walk into my place.

"Holy shit," Eloise says, as she takes in the view before her. "I can just about see all the way to Australia."

"Not quite but yeah, it's pretty stunning." Since I opened my door and saw her standing there, I haven't been able to take my eyes off of her. It's only been a few days but somehow she seems even more beautiful than I remember.

"Bathroom?" Nancy asks.

"Down the hall, first door on the left," I instruct her, with my eyes still locked on Dimples. She turns to face me and with the light shining behind her, she looks like an angel, glowing in the morning sunlight. "You really are beautiful." I step closer and ask the one question I'm scared to know the answer to, "What are you doing here?"

"I missed you. I've been miserable since you left and when I got your flowers yesterday, I knew I needed to be here. Linda fired me, then Nance and Tony helped me pack and Nancy drove me here today. I …"

"You what?" Stopping in front of her, I stare into her chocolate orbs.

"I was worried you'd turn me away."

"No way in hell, Dimples. I've missed you so, so much." Taking her hands in mine I squeeze. I've missed touching her and it reaffirms that she's actually here and I'm not dreaming. "I was on the track yester—"

"How was it?" she excitedly squeals. Her excitement warms my heart, she knows how much I wanted that.

"It was a shitshow. All I could think about was you not being here and I kinda did something reckless and Linc banned me from the track until I pull my head in."

"Marshall," she scolds.

"You called me Marshall."

"Well, when you do stupid and reckless things you don't get your nickname. What were you thinking?"

"I wasn't," I snap.

"Well, that was just fucking stupid. You better not ever do anything reckless again, Marshall Kerr, or so help me God."

"I am so fucking turned on right now with how feisty you are."

"Aaaaand, that's my cue to leave." Nancy rejoins us just as I said that, I totally forgot she was here. "I'll leave you two lovebirds alone and maybe before I leave tomorrow we can catch up for coffee or lunch?"

"I'd like that." Dimples walks over to her friend and embraces her. "Thank you, thank you for everything."

"Why does this feel like a goodbye?" Nancy sadly mumbles and I chuckle, this tough as nails woman is trying to hold back tears.

"Because you are leaving but it's not a forever thing, it's a see you soon thing."

"You better mean that."

Dimples smiles and nods. "Yep, totally. You can't get rid of me that easily, Nance. You know all my secrets and I'd hate to have to kill you."

"Pffft, you couldn't kill a fly, therefore I know I'm safe."

"Tony'd do it for me," she nonchalantly replies with a laugh.

"Yes, yes he would. I won't be surprised to see him on the news one day for slicing and dicing someone with his knives."

We all laugh at that because it's true. He's always threatening 'to get his knives' but in all honesty, I couldn't imagine him doing that. He's a big teddy bear underneath his burly exterior.

Dimples and I walk Nancy out and wave goodbye. We watch her drive away and then Dimples turns to face me. "I really did miss you, Wheels."

"I fucking missed you like I missed racing." Stepping to her, I slide my arms around her waist and pull her to me. "Now that you're here, I'm never letting you go." Leaning forward, I press my lips to hers and dip her back. My lips fused to hers in a searing all-consuming romantic kiss.

When I pull her upright, I see a pap across the road snapping away. Taking her hand in mine, I lace our fingers together and walk us inside where there will be no prying eyes … and I make sure to press the button and close the gate.

Dimples enters first and as soon as the door closes behind me, I pull on her hand, halting her. She turns to face me. We stare at each other for a few beats before she throws herself forward. Catching her, I tighten my arms around her waist. Lowering my hands, I grip her ass and lift her into my arms. She wraps her legs around me and I cover her mouth with mine.

Spinning around, I press her into the wood of my front door. I continue to assault her mouth with my tongue. My cock is harder than steel and I'm thankful I'm in sweats. She grinds herself again my dick and I groan into her mouth.

"I need to fuck you," I whisper against her lips.

"I need that too," she whispers back.

Sliding her hand between us, she pushes my sweats down, freeing my cock. She squeezes my shaft and I hiss. She pulls her panties to the side and tries to guide my cock but it's hard—pun intended—to do one-handed. Pressing her farther into the door, I remove one hand, shift my grip and take over. Guiding it to her slit, the head slides between her lips and we both moan at the contact. Thrusting forward, I sink balls deep inside of her. "Fuck, babe, you feel like heaven."

"Mmmhmpf," she confirms against my lips.

Pulling back, I look down and watch my cock slides in and out of her. Lifting my gaze, I stare into her eyes as we fuck against the door. "I'm gonna come, Dimples," I groan.

"I'm close," she pants.

Slipping her hand between us, she presses on her clit. Her breathing quickens and I know she's close. I increase my thrusts and then I feel it. Her walls clench my dick, her body stiffens and then she screams my name as her climaxes unleashes. The sound sets me off and I come inside of her with a grunt of my own.

"I love you, Dimples," I pant.

"I love you too, Wheels, and I'm sorry."

"Why are you sorry?"

"For not coming when you asked. If I'd done that you wouldn't be banned from the track."

"Now that you're here, I won't be banned anymore."

"You sure about that?"

"Yep, now let's go have a shower and then we can think about going out on a date." She nods and bites her lip and I can tell something's eating at her. "What's wrong?"

"Now that I'm here, it'll be easier for us to be seen. That means *he's* going to know where I am. Are … are you sure you want me and all that it entails?"

"Yep, he doesn't scare me," I matter of factly tell her. "I want the world to know that Eloise Masters, my Dimples, is mine and I love her to the moon and back."

"But—" I press my finger to her lips.

"But nothing, Dimples. I love you. The end. Period. Together, we'll deal with him. And you never know, maybe he's forgotten all about you and has moved on. He won't give a rat's ass that you're with me." But even as I say that, I know there's no ounce of truth to the statement. I only lost Dimples for a few days, this fucker has been without her for months. Eloise is not someone you easily get over and therefore I know this isn't going to be smooth sailing. But that's an issue for future Marshall. Future Marshall will come up with a game plan, present Marshall, he's going to take his girl out on a proper date.

ELOISE

My date tonight with Marshall was not what I expected. I was expecting a flashy restaurant with a gazillion paps out front waiting to snap our pic. Instead, we drove to the Santa Monica Pier and paid homage to our previous dates. We ate burgers from Pier Burger and then we rode the Pacific Wheel. And at the very top, we kissed under the stars.

It was the most amazing date ever and it made me fall even more in love with him.

We've just gotten home and his phone is continually beeping and ringing. As soon as the ringing stops, it starts again but he keeps ignoring it.

He throws his phone onto the side table, once again ignoring the incessant ringing, and begins to undress. "Don't you think you better get that?" I ask.

He shrugs and continues to strip down to his boxer briefs. "I'll deal with it in the morning, right now, I want to make love to my woman and then drift off to sleep wrapped in her arms."

SWOON!

"I think I just fell more in love with you," I confess.

He pulls his briefs off and kneels on his side of the bed gloriously naked … and I fall in love with him and his body all over again. He raises his eyebrows suggestively and I quickly remove my clothes. Once naked, I rest my knee on the edge of the bed and shuffle toward him. He mimics my motions and we meet in the middle of the mattress.

Leaning forward, he nuzzles my neck and whispers, "I fall deeper in love with you each and every day, Eloise Masters, and I will do so until my dying breath."

Holy ovaries, Batman, they just exploded, much like my heart right now. This man keeps getting swoonier and swoonier. I'm so glad I decided to come here because I love feeling like this. I never want this euphoria to disappear.

He nibbles on my neck and his phone rings again. "Wheels, you really need to answer that," leaning up, I huskily whisper, "Deal with it and then I'm going to suck your cock until you come in my mouth and then we're going to fuck All. Night. Long."

"Did you just Lionel Ritchie me?"

"Yes, yes I did but I mean it, I'm going to fuck you all night long." I sing the last three words Lionel Ritchie style and voice is aloud, does something to me and now, I cannot wait.

"Promise to fuck me, All. Night. Long.?"

Nodding, I lean around him and grab his phone from the nightstand. Handing it to him, I flop onto my back and ogle him as I circle my nipple. He really is a fine specimen, I'm a lucky, lucky woman.

It stops ringing before he can answer but like before, it immediately starts ringing again.

He lies down next to me and I slide my hand toward his cock because like him, it's beautiful and I can't help myself. He answers with a strained, "Evening, Jaxson." Not wanting to be left out, he reaches over and cups my boob. Massaging my plump mound, I have to bite my tongue to hold back my moans.

"What?" he growls sitting upright,.. "When?" I have no clue what's going on but he's pissed off. "Send me the link." He nods and listens intently. "Okay, meet you at the office first thing in the morning." I'm only getting one side of this conversation but regardless, I don't like it. "Night, Jaxson, and thanks for everything."

He hangs up and drops his phone to the bed. He runs his hands through his hair, he's agitated and on edge.

"Marshall," I hesitantly murmur his name, "what's going on?" Sitting up next to him, I hug his arm. His body is tense and that feeling of unease building within intensifies. "Marshall?" I ask again.

"That was Jaxson."

"I guessed that."

He utters five words that freeze me to my core. "They know who you are." Sharply I intake a deep breath and hold it, and then he continues with the blows. "Duncan the douchecanoe is speaking with that bitch, Margaret, from WtB. It's … It's not good, babe."

"How so?" I ask.

"It'll be easier if I just play this." He picks up his phone and clicks on the link Jaxson texted him.

Staring at the screen, I see Margaret in the WtB office, or wherever the hell they film their shit. "Marshall Kerr was spotted in Santa Monica this evening with his mystery lady, who we can now confirm is Eloise Masters, former fiancée of renowned businessman, Duncan Montgomery, from Collinsville, Florida. The two split earlier this year and it seems the nobody is now shacking up with the playboy racer.

"Our investigations reveal Ms. Masters is an orphan and she likes to hook rich men. We spoke with her ex, Duncan, earlier and he revealed to us that she was just using him. She loves the rich and carefree lifestyle and when she got all that she needed from him, she abruptly left. He's been searching for her since she disappeared, but she's covered her tracks well. He had no idea where she was or if she was even alive.

"Is Marshall her next victim? We'll continue to investigate this gold digger and keep you informed." She stares intently at the camera. "Marshall, you might wanna lock away the fine China now she's living with you."

"That's not true," I cry, a lone tear slipping down my cheek.

"I know and I'll do everything in my power to keep you safe. We'll meet with Jaxson in the morning and he'll come up with a game plan for us." I nod but I don't know how I feel. One minute I was high on life and now, now I'm scared for my life … and for Marshall's.

"Maybe I should just go," I suggest. "Leave before this gets worse for you."

"Not a chance in hell, Dimples," he rebuffs, "we will get through this together."

"I can't ask that of you."

"You're not asking, I'm offering. As I keep saying, I'll do anything to keep you safe, Dimples."

"But what about you? What if he comes here? What if—"

"Let him," Marshall interrupts. "I'm not afraid of him. Anyone who hurts a woman, especially the one he supposedly loves, doesn't deserve to live."

"What about the bad publicity? You're trying to get back on the track, this won't be helping that."

"Dimples, you mean more to me. Yes, I love racing, but I'm IN love with you." He places emphasis on the word 'in.' "You protect what you love and I will do just that. Mom would have my ass if I didn't."

His phone rings again and the words 'Momma Bear' appear on the screen. "I better get this or she WILL kick my ass." I nod and he answers, "Hey, Momma Bear."

I can hear Keri chatting loudly, Marshall pulls the phone away from his ear. "Mom, she's here next to me, let me put you on speaker."

"Hi, Mrs. Kerr," I say when he clicks the speaker button.

"It's Keri," she states matter-of-factly. "I just saw that horrible woman on the television and her report, not that I'd call it a report. I want you to know we don't think of you like that and we will protect you. You protect those you love and my son loves you unconditionally, therefore, Ryan and I love you unconditionally."

My eyes well with tears, this is what having a loving and caring family must be like. "I … I don't know what to say. I've been on my own for so long. I … I, just, thank you." The first tear falls and an avalanche follow, cascading down my cheeks.

"Don't cry, babe." He pulls me into his side and places a kiss on my temple. That one simple gesture means the world to me.

"These are happy tears," I tearfully mumble, wiping at my tear stained cheeks. "Even though this is all turning to shit, I'm not alone but what if my past affects you all?"

"Then we deal with it together," Ryan informs us, he and Keri must be on speaker too.

"I can't ask that of you."

"You aren't," the three of them say in unison.

This causes me to laugh thought my tears. "Thank you."

"No thanks needed," Keri replies, "you make Marshall happy and as parents that's all we've ever wanted. Continue to make him happy and that'll be enough. Now, Eloise, what can we do to help you?"

"I don't know." And that's the truth, I don't know what to do.

"Mom, we're meeting with Jaxson in the morning. As soon as we have a game plan, I'll let you and Dad know."

"We'll come over for lunch tomorrow." She doesn't ask, she tells us she's coming for lunch tomorrow.

Marshall nods and smiles. "Sounds great, Mom. If we aren't back when you get here, let yourselves in. We shouldn't be too far behind you."

We say our goodbyes and Marshall hangs up, tossing his phone back onto the side table.

"Are you sure you're okay with this?" I ask.

"Yep, I am. I love you and I want you to be safe." He pulls me into his side and we snuggle in bed together "How dangerous do you think he is?"

"Against me, very. Against you and everyone else, I have no idea."

"Well, we'll just have to stick together because you and me, we make a dynamite team. Together we can take him and anyone who comes our way, better watch out."

Nodding, I don't say anything because I'm not sure I agree. Duncan Montgomery is an unhinged man. I was the first person to defy him, I just hope my escape doesn't affect Marshall and his return to the track.

MARSHALL

We've just left Life's Too Sports LA office and I'd hedge a bet and say that Jaxson didn't sleep a wink last night. Luckily for me, he's in LA at the moment and we can meet face-to-face. As soon as we walked in, it was go-go-go. He had a plan of action laid out and was ready to roll. He really is the best and I'm glad to have him on my team … even if he refuses to refer to us as #TeamKerr, party pooper.

We all agreed that silence on Duncan's claims is the best course of action because very few people know the truth. Apart from Eloise's word, it's a case of he said/she said. There's no proof of the abuse and it may come across as deflection. We've decided I need to up my social media presence. We'll start showing more of Dimples and me as a couple, proving we're in love and that she's not the gold digger Duncan is making her out to be. He assures us, it will slowly fade away if we show the world how loved up we are and keep doing the low-key things. She was hesitant at first and I totally get that, but Jaxson can be quite convincing when he needs to be.

We, well, I agreed to do a press conference at the track as soon as my official return to the track date is announced. To do that, I needed to speak to Linc but he's still pissed at me. After he gave me a lecture and I promised to be safe, he came on board.

With Dimples here by my side, I'm in the right headspace. With her love and support, I can do anything I set my mind to.

With a solid plan in place, we all say our goodbyes and Dimples and I head home to have lunch with mom and dad. Driving up my street, I groan, when I see paps everywhere.

"Wow, I can't believe this is entertaining to them. Who cares about us?" She reaches over and rests her hand on my knee.

"Babe, I don't get the fascination either," I tell her as I pull into my driveway. "Maybe they just want to gaze upon all my sexiness."

"Nah," she shakes her head and playfully adds, "it's definitely not that."

"Guess we will never know."

"Guess not," she replies as I turn off the engine.

Thankfully the ones here don't seem to be aggressive as the ones who were at LTS when we left. These guys step aside and allow us to pull into my driveway safely.

"Do you think we should do what Jaxson suggested and play nice with them?" Dimples asks hesitantly.

"Do you want to play nice?"

"I'd rather not have to deal with this at all, but it is what it is."

"You really are something, Dimples." Leaning across the center console, I slide my hand behind her head and kiss her. The sound of cameras clicking pulls us apart and it gives me an idea. "Fancy giving them a shot that will hopefully appease them?"

"For you, Wheels, I'll do anything."

Climbing out, we meet up at the back of the car and walk toward them. They all begin shouting but I raise my hand. "If we give you a few photos, will you guys go away? My parents will be here soon and as much as I know you love my mom, I'd like to visit with them in peace."

They all nod in agreement. Dimples and I pose and then say our goodbyes. The paps leave with their 'money' shots and we head inside. Placing her bag on the entry table, she sighs. "That was simple."

"It's not always like that. Some of them can be relentless blood-hounds but I've found over the years, if you give them something, they generally leave you alone."

"Are you sure you want me and my baggage overshadowing your return?"

"I want you by my side, Dimples. End of story." I pull her into my arms. "Plus, once I get back on the track, my amazingness will be all they focus on and no offense, but it'll be like 'Eloise who?' to them."

"Cocky much?" she teases.

"You love my cock."

"Ugh, I don't want to hear about my son's cock," Mom protests as she enters through the side entrance.

"Oh My God," Eloise voices in embarrassment, lowering her head into my chest to hide from my parents.

"Mom. Dad," I offer in greeting.

Eloise lifts her head and spins to face my parents. "Hello, Mr. and Mrs. Kerr."

"What have I told you?" Mom scolds her.

"Sorry. Hello, Ryan and Keri."

"Much better, now come here and let me give you a mom hug. Then while the boys heat up the grill, I want you to tell me your story. I need to know everything so I can protect my family."

"I don't need protecting," Dimples matter-of-factly states, "I have Marshall."

"And Marshall has us, therefore, you also have us."

"You may as well grab a bottle of wine, get comfy and tell her, Dimples. She won't give up 'til she has all the answers. You think Margaret is a rabid dog, Keri Kerr is a pit bull."

I can see my girl is uncomfortable, but I can also see that she wants to open up to Mom. All Eloise wants is a family and a normal life. I will do everything in my power to give that to her. If anyone deserves it, it's her.

Dad and I leave Mom and Dimples in the living room to chat. He and I head into the kitchen and grab what we need. I fill two glasses with wine and hand them to Mom and Dimples.

Placing a kiss on her head, I follow Dad out to the patio, just as she begins telling Mom about her dad dying and her mom leaving. Looking back at her before I step outside, I know the next part will be hard for her but she's in good hands with mom.

While I light the grill, Dad pops the top off two beers. And hands one to me. "You love her wholeheartedly, don't you, Son?"

Looking inside, I see Mom and Dimples engrossed in their conversation. The two most important women in my life are together and they already love one another. "Yeah, Dad, I do. She's it for me."

"This past of hers, you're not worried about it? The possibility there's truth to the rumors."

"Not at all, she's not a gold digger," I reaffirm.

"But—"

"Dad," I interrupt, my anger rising at him thinking this about the woman I love. Turning from the grill, I stare at him. "He abused her, Dad. Physically and emotionally. He caused her to lose their baby. If she hadn't run, who knows if she'd even still be alive."

"I'm sorry, Marshall, I didn't know."

"No one does. She suffered alone. For years. And then he took her baby from her. She's the strongest person I know and I'm never letting her go. I'll protect her with everything I have now that she's mine."

Glancing inside again, this time I see Mom has Dimples in her arms. The two of them are crying, it hurts seeing her so upset but as the days pass and with each new person she lets in, she gets stronger. That man better watch out because if he ever shows his face around here, I won't be held accountable for what I do. No one hurts the woman I love, no one.

ELOISE

Marshall is at the track practicing, his comeback race is next week in the annual charity race and after that, he will officially race in the last few rounds of the current season.

Right now, it's all go-go-go for #TeamKerr. To say I'm nervous would be an understatement. I'm nervous for Wheels out on the track and I'm nervous *he* is going to pop up out of nowhere and cause mayhem. I was sure I'd have heard from *him* by now, especially after his appearance on WtB but it's been radio silent on the Duncan front. Maybe he's realized that I've moved on and he'll let me go but that's not his style. I know him, he will bide his time until he's ready to strike like the snake he is.

Most of my days are spent at the track with Marshall. Watching him fly around and around is exhilarating but at the same time it scares the absolute shit out of me. He's going so fast, what if he crashes, again?

I've wanted to ask that question many times but I'm scared to voice it aloud in case the universe takes it as a challenge.

Today, I stayed home and I've decided I want to make a special dinner for Marshall tonight, I'm going to recreate our first dinner date at my place. Climbing into the car Marshall arranged for me, I head to the grocery store. Parking in the lot of the market, I switch off the engine and grab my bag.

When I step out of the car, I turn around and come face-to-face with the devil himself, "Duncan," I utter.

"Eloise," he thunders in greeting. Just hearing my name pass his lips causes the color to drain from my face and goosebumps to prickle my skin.

My mouth goes dry.

My heart races as panic and fear course through my veins.

My body is frozen.

Standing here, I stare at a menacing and foreboding Duncan Montgomery.

"You ready to come home yet?" he calmly asks. His even monotone is unnerving and scarier than if he was screaming and shouting and losing his shit.

"Wwwwwwhat?" I stammer.

"Your little adventure is over, Eloise. It's time to come home and be by my side again. People are talking and you know how I feel about negative publicity."

"People are talking because *you* are talking," I snap, shocking myself at the outburst.

"You will come with me," he roars, taking a step closer. Stepping back, I press myself into the side of my car. My moment of bravery fading as the fear I used to feel slams back into me.

"I'm n-n-n-not going anywhere with you," I tell him. "M-m-m-m-my life is h-h-h-here." My voice waivers, submissive and meek Eloise is back.

"No," he bellows, "your life is by my side as my bitch. Ever since I took you from that slum you called home, you became mine. I've been looking for you since you left. You hid well, until you were plastered all over WtB with that pindicked weasel. I was hoping when he discovered you're nothing but a gold-digging whore, he'd kick your ass to the curb and you'd come crawling back. However, it seems your cunt has cast a magic spell on him, I might just have to do something about that."

At the mention of hurting Marshall, something inside of me snaps and a fierceness I didn't know I could have before *him* slams into me. Through clenches teeth, I snarl. "You leave him alone."

"Come back with me and he'll be left alone. You have three days to make your decision. If you call me to pick you up before the deadline, your punishment will be less severe."

Without waiting for me to reply, he turns on his heel and walks over to a waiting car. Miles climbs out and my eyes widen when I see my friend. Subtly he shakes his head and opens the back door for Duncan. Once Duncan is inside the car, Miles smiles and mouths, "I'm fine."

It's like he knew what I was going to ask before I even knew. Knowing he's okay is a relief but I want nothing more than to get him away from Duncan. Before he climbs into the driver's seat, he lifts his hand and mimics calling. He points to himself and then me, indicating he'll call me when he can.

Nodding, I watch them drive away. And then I remember, he doesn't have my new number. I call Linda and after filling her in on what just happened, I ask her to pass my number onto Miles. She assures me she will and wishes me luck.

Closing my eyes, I take a deep breath. "How am I going to fix this?" I mumble as I walk toward the market.

On autopilot, I walk around the store. Throwing this and that into my cart. Before I know it, I'm back at Marshall's place. I have no recollection of leaving the market, let alone driving here. That was reckless and dangerous of me. Unloading the groceries, I walk inside and unpack them.

My hands are shaking but I realize I need to nip this in the bud. I'm not going anywhere and he cannot make me. Leaving the groceries on the counter, I grab my phone, I walk out onto the patio. Leaning on the railing, I stare out at the ocean before me. There's blue water for as far as the eye can see. Never in my wildest dreams did I think I'd get to wake up to a view like this or be hopelessly in love like I am. I feel like I'm living in a fairy tale but I know first-hand that fairy tales are bullshit. Well I used to think that until my knight in a shiny green race car wheeled into me and knocked me on my ass, literally and figuratively.

Marshall Kerr bowled me over and began to fix my fractured heart. But as with everything in my life, it's not smooth sailing. No, that's too much to ask. Marshall's and my relationship has been exposed and *he* found me. *He* knows where I am and who I'm with and *he's* threatening to destroy my happiness. I knew this would happen, the fame associated in being with someone like Marshall threw me into the spotlight but surprisingly, I'm fine being in the spotlight. I'm coping and happier than ever. I'm not the meek woman I once was. I have a backbone now and if *he* thinks I'm going to walk away from the best thing to ever happen to me, *he* has another thing coming.

Waking my phone, I bring up his number and press call. He picks up immediately, "Eloise. I knew you'd call. I take it you want me to come and get you?"

"I … I …"

"I what, Eloise? You know I don't like waiting," he snarls, like the impatient asshole he is.

His reaction confirms that I've made the right decision. Taking a deep breath, I inform him exactly how I feel. "You can go fuck yourself sideways with a rusty fork, Dunc. I'm not coming back. Ever."

"Excuse me," he hisses. "What did you just say?"

"You heard me, Dunc," I defiantly reply, once again using the nickname that he hates.

"You don't speak to me like that."

"I just did," I rebuff, my heart rapidly racing in my chest. I've never spoken to him, or anyone, like this before, but a surge of energy hits and right now I feel like I can conquer anything. It's liberating to finally stand up to him. "You don't control me anymore, Duncan. I control me now. I make my own decisions and I've decided, I'm not coming back. You and I are done. Dead. Dusted. Kaput."

"We'll see about that, you little bitch," he snarls, his tone filled with venom. I quiver at the thought of what he's going to do if he ever gets his hands on me but Marshall vowed to keep me safe but I now know that *I* can keep me safe too. "No one tells me no, Eloise. No-fucking-one. You just made a grave mistake, my dear. I'm Duncan Montgomery and I always win." Always needing the last word, he hangs up.

"Not this time," I quietly murmur.

Dropping down onto the lounger, I let out a breath just as the front door to Marshall's beachfront condo opens. "Dimples, babe, I'm home," Marshall yells out.

At the sound of voice, I know that everything will be fine.

"Out here," I shout, my voice isn't as strong as usual but after standing up to *him* just now, I'm wiped and exhausted.

He steps out onto the patio and when his gaze lands on me, he knows something is amiss. He races over and pulls me into his arms. "What's happened?"

"Duncan," I tell him. My eyes welling with tears as I crash after the adrenalin high of telling Duncan to go fuck himself. "I … I saw him earlier. He gave me an ultimatum and a deadline but I won't go." I shake my head, causing the first tear to fall. "I can't go back, so I called him. I … I told him to go fuck himself with a rusty fork sideways."

"You did?"

"Yep." I nod. "He said it was a mistake and now, now I—" I can't finish, I'm hysterically crying now. Tears pour down my cheeks. Marshall wraps his arms around me tighter and as if he's magical, I instantly relax. "I can't lose you," I blubber into his chest. "I can't lose you."

"You won't lose me, Dimples. You and me, remember?"

"I remember but what if …" I can't finish that sentence. The thought of losing Marshall or something happening to him, it's unbearable to think about.

Sitting on the lounger, we wrap our arms around one another and hold on tight. Just being in his arms relaxes me and I know we'll be fine … but as usual, I was wrong.

MARSHALL

When I arrived home last week and found Dimples out on the patio in a state, I thought she was leaving me. Just turns out, Duncan, her asshole ex was once again being an asshole.

That night, once she drifted off to sleep, I looked into security for her when I'm not around and for someone to watch Duncan. I don't trust that he won't try something again. He's not the type of person to give up easily and losing someone like Eloise, that must be killing him. I only lost her for two days and that was hard enough.

Eloise has been by my side twenty-four seven since her encounter with him. The guys give me flack for it but I don't care. Her safety is worth all the jabs and taunts. Having her at the track has been fantastic. She's become my lucky charm because each time she's here, I race amazingly.

Let's hope the same happens tomorrow. Finally, my return race is here and to say I'm nervous is an understatement. I know it's just a charity race, but I need to prove to everyone, and myself, that I can do this.

We've finished practice for the day and everyone's gone, it's just Dimples and me in the garage. This is an unofficial ritual with the team. The night before a race, everyone leaves, leaving me alone in the garage with my car. I have my moment where I mentally prepare for the race tomorrow and then I lock up the green machine and head home. Tonight is no different, except for the fact Dimples is here with me.

"Do you need me to wait at the car so you can have your moment, or whatever you do the night before a race?"

"Nope," I tell her shaking my head. "I want you here and I want to start a new tradition."

"Ohh yeah," she drawls, "and what tradition might that be?" She runs her fingertip up and down my chest. She's staring at me with a 'I need you to fuck me' look in her eyes. Looks like we're both on the same page with this new tradition.

Leaning down, I suck on her earlobe and whisper, "I want to fuck you over the hood of my car before we leave."

"Really?" She steps back, breathing deeply. Her cheeks are flushed and her eyes have dilated. She's turned on at the thought of me bending her over the green machine and having my wicked way with her.

"Yep."

"Weeeelll," she draws out the word, backing away from me. She's wearing a black-and-white spotted sundress that accentuates her tits. I've wanted to fuck her all afternoon, it was hard—pun intended—to concentrate. My gaze kept drifting over to her. She stops and runs her fingertip across the top of her breasts and down her stomach. She plays with the hemline of her dress. The hunger in her gaze has every nerve ending in my body zinging to life. "It just so happens that I've lost my panties." She raises her eyebrows at me, lighting the fuse within. I'm ready to detonate and we're still fully clothed.

Walking backward to my car, she spins around and lifts her dress up. Exposing her naked delectable ass. "Oops," she purrs, bending over, she rests her forearms on the hood. Hungrily she looks at me over her shoulder and beckons me forward with her index finger.

My feet start moving toward her. Pushing my pants and briefs down, I step out of them, freeing my cock, which is already rock fucking hard. Seeing her bent over my car like this is the hottest sight ever. "Fuck, Dimples," I moan as I take in the view before me. This vision will be seared into my brain for all eternity.

"That's the plan." She winks.

Sassy minx. Stopping behind her, I run my palm over her ass cheek and down between her thighs. She moans. "Fuck, babe, you're soaked."

"I've been thinking about this all afternoon," she shares with me, wriggling her ass at me.

Gripping her hip with one hand, I grab my cock and line it up at her entrance. My dick easily slides inside her and we both moan at the intrusion. "This is going to be quick but when we get home, I'm going to take my time."

"Shut up and fuck me, Wheels."

She doesn't need to tell me twice.

Holding on to her hips, I piston mine back and forth. My dick sliding in and out or her wet pussy. Her pleasurable moans echo around the garage. This is something I've always wanted to do but something always held me back and I'm glad I waited. This is the hottest sex of my life and I've had some hot sex before.

Leaning against her back, I slide one of my hands around into the top of her dress and caress her tits.

"Yes. Yes. Yes," she pants.

"I'm close," she hisses when I pinch her nipple.

Her pussy tightens around me and then she comes. Screaming my name as her orgasm erupts. The sound of her carnal wails set me off and I too, explode. Her walls clench my cock as she milks every last drop from me.

Pulling out of her, I lift her up, spin her around and slam my lips to hers for an all-encompassing kiss. "Fuck, I love you, Dimples."

"I love you too, Wheels. Now, take me home and make love to me."

What my woman wants, my woman gets.

Later that evening, I blissfully drift off to sleep happy and content with Dimples in my arms. Even if I don't win tomorrow,

I'm still a winner because I have the woman I love by my side and there's nothing better than that.

MARSHALL

"Two laps to go," Linc informs, "Randall is hot on your ass but he's getting sloppy. I think you're getting to him."

Marcus Randall my nemesis.

My mortal enemy on and off the track.

He's been on the top since my accident and is set to win this season, but I'm back and next season, he's going to have to get used to second position; again.

"I've got this," I confidently reply.

It's not cocky, it's the truth. I was born to race and my comeback today proves that. My lucky charm, Dimples is up in the team box with Mom and Dad and after today, I'm never letting her go. She's mine to protect and love.

When I think about her ex threatening her, I see red. Hearing how she stood up to him made me so proud. She's no damsel in distress, she's a mother-fucking-fighter. She's *my* mother-fucking-fighter.

"Last lap," Linc states, excitement in his voice because in my current position, this race is mine.

"Bring it home, Marsh," Grayson states, like he always used to at this part of a race.

"Roger that."

Pressing my foot down, my lead increases. The finish line and my spot on top of the podium are in reach. Before I know it, that checkered flag comes down, indicating I'm the winner.

I just won my return race.

"I'm back!" I shout into my car, slamming my hand on the steering wheel.

"Great work, dude," Grayson comments, his voice filled with elation.

"I knew you had it in you," Linc adds, "come on back and we can celebrate."

Pulling my car into pit lane there are people everywhere. Grayson helps me out and before I take off my helmet, we do the bro hug slapping each other on the back. Removing my helmet, I'm grinning. I missed this and when I look into the garage and see Dimples with Mom, and Dad, my grin widens.

Our gaze connects and we both start walking, well, running toward each other. She jumps into my arms and I catch her. "Congrats, Wheels," she gleefully cheers. Spinning us around, I press my lips to hers for my victory kiss—my new favorite kind of kiss.

I've never shared a win with anyone like this before and this, kissing her in pit lane with the excitement of my win around us, makes this moment that much more special.

Breaking the kiss, I place her back on her feet and lace our fingers together. Looking up, I see Randall walking toward us. "Great race, Kerr." He offers me his hand. "It's good to have you back."

"Thanks, man, it's good to be back."

"I can't wait to kick your ass out there," he razzes, but his eyes are locked on Dimples in my arms. He smirks and steps in front of her. "How you doin', baby cakes?" My blood boils at his blatant flirting with my girl, that is until I hear her reply.

"Fantastic now that my man beat your ass," she pauses and then adds, "baby cakes," before gently tapping his cheek.

"Buuuuuurn," Grayson roars. Everyone, well, everyone but Marcus, laughs.

"Fuck you all," Marcus scoffs, muttering something about always being second fiddle as he storms off in a huff.

Turning to my girl, I shake my head in awe. "Babe, that was fucking classic."

She shrugs. "It kinda was, wasn't it?"

"Fuck, I love you," I tell her. I can't wait to get home and show her exactly how much I do.

"I love you too." We stare at one another and even though we're surrounded by people, they all fade into the background and all I see is Dimples. "Wheels, that was incredible. I've never watched a race live before and I'm so glad I popped my racing cherry with you."

"Happy to have popped your racing cherry."

"Why does this all sound kinky and dirty?"

"Because you have a dirty mind," I tease her.

"Says the dirty-minded one."

"You love it."

"Yeah," she nods, "I kinda do. So, what happens next?"

"There's the podium and presentation where we hand over the funds raised to the charity. Then the guys and I debrief. Usually there's a press conference and after that, we party 'til the wee hours of the morning."

"Ohh," she says, looking deflated.

"Why the long face?"

"I was hoping it would be just us."

"I can tell them all to fuck off and th—"

"No," she refutes, shaking her head, "it's fine."

"We won't make it a late one, how about that?" She nods. "And tomorrow, it will just be me and you. Deal?"

"Deal." She bites her lip.

"Fuck, I love it when you do that."

"And I fucking love you in this." She slides her fingertip down my chest.

"You just swore."

"That's how much I love it." She steps closer to me, wrapping her arms around my neck. "I keep thinking about what we did in the garage last night. I hope we can do it again … and soon."

"Fuck, babe," I groan, "you can't say shit like that to me now." She nonchalantly shrugs. "Ohh, you will pay for that later."

"I hope so. Now, go claim your win."

"With pleasure," I assure her. Tugging her to me, I dip her backward and kiss the life out of her. Pulling her upright, I grin. "Claimed."

"I meant the race win."

"I know, but I just had to claim those delectable lips of yours."

"You're a fiend."

"Says the fiend who wants me to bend her over the hood of my car … again."

"Okay, that's TMI," Grayson complains, shaking his head next to us.

"You're just jealous you don't have a woman as fine as mine."

"Fuck off, asshole." He flips me the bird and both Dimples and I laugh. "We need to get you up on that podium."

"Okay, let's do it."

Lacing my fingers with Dimples, we make our way over for the presentation. It takes us an eternity to make it there because people keep stopping to congratulate me and reminisce about previous races and my accident.

It's still raw talking about it, especially when I think about Joe not making it. That easily could have been me so I decide to dedicate this win to Joe, it feels right to do that.

Standing on top of the podium in the number one position is like coming home after being away. It's everything I remember it to be but with Dimples by my side, it's so much more.

Looking out over the crowd, I smile and take it all in. The pit lizards are jumping and screaming. Pressing out their tits, hoping to snag my attention. The old me would be all over that but I don't need them anymore, not when I have the most amazing woman in the world by my side. I'm on a massive high right now and nothing can bring me down.

ELOISE

...eight weeks later

Marshall is at the top of his game. He keeps winning race after race, only losing to Marcus once. There's no sign of his injury and he's happier than I've ever seen him.

WtB no longer seems to be interested in Marshall and me. It's like now they know who I am, it's no more fun. Duncan has been quiet too, but I'm still wary and cautious in regard to him. He doesn't like to lose and me standing up to him how I did, I just know it'll blow back on us one of these days.

I don't know when. I don't know where but I know with Marshall on my team, I can face anything.

We're flying to Chicago later today and to say I'm anxious would be an understatement. Everyone on the team is on edge, Chicago is where Marshall crashed. It's where his life shattered. I think it's playing in the back of his mind too because he's not as vocal and excited for this race.

"You okay, babe?" I ask as we take our seats in first class.

"Yep," he replies and his one word answer confirms everything.

"Wanna try again without lying this time?"

"How do you do that?" he asks me, turning to face me in his seat.

"Do what?"

"Know me so well."

"Probably because right now, I'm thinking the same things you are. This track is where it happened. Where your life changed. If it's playing on my mind, it must be on a loop in yours."

"It's scary how well you know me," he voices. Reaching over he takes my hand in his. "If I'm to be honest, I'm shit-fucking-scared for this race."

"If you weren't, I'd be worried. All you can do is do your best." I pause. "Okay, let's break the weekend down. We have Linc's gala tonight, where we can dance and drink and chillax. Then tomorrow, you practice." I lower my voice, lean in, and whisper, "If you think it'll help, you can fuck me over the hood of your car anytime you want." My words shock him so I continue, "Then we'll have a quiet dinner with the team. Then you'll kick Marcus's ass on the track. Then we celebrate—"

"Can the celebration be naked? Just me and you?"

"Is there any other way to celebrate?" I say, raising my eyebrows suggestively.

He leans over and beckons me to him. "Think we can practice celebrating?"

"I'm not having sex with you in the plane bathroom."

"You're no fun," he pouts. He actually pouts. "Well, how about some handsy fun under the covers?"

Looking around the cabin, I nod. "But not until we're in the air."

"I don't think I can wait that long, babe."

"You're insatiable."

"Only for you, baby, only for you. Can you at least give me a little kiss to tide me over?"

"Won't that just make the situation harder?"

"I thought you liked it hard."

"Marshall," I scold and slap his arm.

From across the aisle, Grayson sasses, "Ohhhhhhh she called you Marshall." Then he singsongs, "Ohh oh, you're in trouble."

Marshall flips him the bird and I laugh. The hostess walks past and I call out, "Excuse me, can I grab a blanket, please?"

Winking at Marshall, I settle back and stare out the window, watching as the plane rolls out to the runway for takeoff and for my handsy fun under the covers to begin.

Once we're at cruising altitude, the hostess returns with my blanket and quicker than the speed of light, Marshall flicks it out and covers us both. "Eager much?" I tease.

"Well, we're in the air now, therefore, it's handsy fun under the covers time." Lifting the armrest between us, I turn on my side and snuggle back into him. He lifts his arm and places it over my chest, cupping my breast in his palm, gently massaging it. My eyes droop closed and my body comes alive. It's not even skin on skin contact but somehow Marshall manages to make my body thrum from just a simple touch … or fondle.

A small moan escapes. "Shhhh," he whispers into my ear. "I'm going to make you come now and you're going to keep quiet."

"Mmmhmpf," I reply, trying to hold back another moan. His hand under the blanket is between my thighs and he's rubbing me through my panties. "Please," I whimper.

"I love it when you beg."

"Marsha—" Before I get to finish his name, he pulls my panties to the side and pushes his fingers inside.

"Fuck, baby, you're soaked." He thrusts his digits in and out. Closing my eyes, I concentrate on the pleasure building low in my belly. He presses on my clit and my eyes pop wide open and I come. Clenching on his fingers, I bite my lip and quietly ride out my release.

He leans into me and covers my mouth with his. "I love you, Dimples. Thank you for taking my mind off everything."

"I love you too, Wheels." With my eyes locked on his, I reach back and cup his cock through his jeans. "If you free him, I'll take your mind off everything some more."

His hand slides under the blanket and awkwardly, with one hand, he frees his cock. Wrapping my hand around his shaft, I begin to stroke. He hisses, biting down on his lip to contain his sounds. Throwing his words from before back at him, I quietly say, "Shhhh, I'm going to make you come and you're going to keep quiet."

"Brat," he growls through clenched teeth as I continue to flick my wrist and jerk him off. With a grunt, he comes, spilling his seed all over my hand and the blanket. Pulling my hand out, I lick the top of my hand with my eyes locked on his.

"Your ass is mine as soon as we get to the hotel room."

"I look forward to it," I sassily reply. Wiping my hand on the blanket, I unclip my seat belt and shimmy past him to wash up in the bathroom.

Returning to my seat, I sit back down and notice the blanket is missing. Not thinking anything more, I grab my Kindle and begin to read when from across the aisle, Grayson squeals like a girl and snarls, "Ugh, Marshall, you dirty fucking prick." Seems while I was in the bathroom, Marshall handed him our cum-covered blanket since he was cold. Grayson balls up the blanket and throws it back to us.

Marshall and I laugh, as he jumps up and storms to the bathroom to clean up.

After a bumpy descent and landing, we're finally in Chicago. I power up my phone while we wait for our luggage and my phone pings with a text. Pulling it out of my pocket, I don't recognize the number. Opening the message, my eyes widen as I read.

UNKNOWN

Peek-a-Boo, I see you

Glancing around baggage claim, I can't see anyone but the hairs on the back of my neck stand on end. I quickly delete the message without replying and slip my phone into my bag. Sliding my arm around Marshall's waist, I snuggle into his side.

"You okay?"

"Yep, couldn't be better," I lie and hope he believes me. He pulls away to grab our luggage off the conveyor belt. With our bags in tow, we head out to the waiting cars and make our way to the hotel.

Just as we arrive, my phone pings with another text, followed by three more notifications. Climbing out of the car, I pull out my phone. Again, I don't recognize the number but I can guess whom it's from.

UNKNOWN

Ring-a-ring-the-rosie

A pocket full of posies

Ashes. Ashes

YOU fall down

It feels like a threat this time.

Looking up from my phone, I freeze. Across the driveway I see *him*. Our eyes lock and the way *he's* leering at me gives me the heebie-jeebies but I refuse to let *him* affect me in any way.

Closing my eyes, I take a deep breath and when I open them again, *he's* gone. I search for *him* but *he's* vanished, maybe I imagined seeing *him*.

My phone pings again and when I read the latest text, I know I *did* see him.

UNKNOWN

You are mine, now and forever.

"You okay, Dimples? You look like you've seen a ghost," Marshall questions, stopping next to me and pulling me into his side.

Nodding I smile at him, hoping I can fake my way through this. "Just a little tired," I reassure him, I can't let him know I saw *him*. He's already got enough going on without me adding to his plate.

Lacing my fingers with his, I suggest, "Maybe an afternoon nap is what I need."

"A naked afternoon nap?"

With four words, all my anxieties disappear. "Maybe." Tugging on his hand, I pull him into the hotel so we can check into our penthouse suite and have a naked afternoon nap.

MARSHALL

After a naked afternoon nap, Dimples and I get ready for Linc's gala. This annual gala for Scofield Racing is always a good time and as much as I hate wearing a monkey suit, I can't fucking wait to see Dimples all dressed up. Don't get me wrong, I love it when she's naked but dressed to the nines, fuck me sideways, she's stunning.

The view from up here overlooking Lake Michigan is beautiful. Add in the light reflecting on the water from tonight's full moon and it's breathtaking. The hairs on the back of my neck prickle and when I spin around, my mouth drops open. The view I was just looking at was breathtaking but seeing Dimples just now, I have no words. "Fuck me, Dimples, you're gorgeous."

"You look mighty fine too, Mr. Kerr."

Eating up the distance between us, I slide my hands around her waist and stare into her eyes. "I can't wait to peel this off you later." I slide my fingertip under the spaghetti strap and down across the top of her breasts. Pulling the material out for a peek, I confirm, "No bra?" She nods. "Panties?" She shrugs. Grazing my palms down her side, I grab the material in my hand and bunch it up. Sliding my hand up her thigh, much to my disappointment I feel silky material. "I can't wait to remove these with my teeth later."

Rubbing my finger up and down her slit, she leans her head on my chest and quietly mewls as I continue to stroke her. Removing my hand, she lifts her head and glares at me.

"Time to go," I inform her, placing a kiss on the tip of her nose.

"You're a teasing asshole," she admonishes me.

"You love me."

"I'm starting to question that," she sasses.

"I promise to make it up to you when we get back."

"I'll hold you to that."

"Shall we?" I offer her my arm.

"We shall," she agrees with a nod. Sliding her hand through the gap, she smiles and that little lip lift, hits me right in the chest.

We make our way downstairs, across the lobby and into the waiting car. Every head turns to watch us. All the men are jealous of the beauty on my arm and I have to say, it feels good to know she's mine and not theirs.

We pull up at The Geraghty and I climb out first. Turning around, I offer my hand to Dimples and help her out of the car. Camera flashes go off all around us. Reporters shout my name and the fans squeal when they see me.

Dimples clenches my hand tightly in hers. Pulling her to me, I kiss her head and drag her up the red carpet. Normally I'd stop and chat to at least one reporter but I know Dimples hates this so we make a beeline for the doors.

Once inside, I feel her let out the breath she was holding. "Do you ever get used to that?"

I shrug. "It comes with the territory. I just don't let it bother me anymore."

"I wish I could be like that."

"One day, babe, one day. Let's get a drink and then I'd like to dance with you."

"You dance?"

"For you, I'd do anything," and I mean it. I'd go to the ends of the Earth and back for her.

We make our way to the bar and while in line, Darby and Chance join us. Chance offers me his hand. "Good to see you up and about."

"It's good to be up and about," I honestly tell him. Pulling Dimples closer to me, I introduce her. "Dimples, this is Chance Daniels and his lovely wife, Darby. Chance, Darby, this is Dimples."

She offers her hand to Chance. "Or you can just call me Eloise."

"It's a pleasure to meet you and you can call me DD, all my friends do." Darby smiles and flicks her gaze between the two of us. "So you're the one who tamed the wild playboy."

"I … umm … ahh—"

"I'm teasing, but it's nice to meet you. Why don't we let these two chat shop and you and I can get to know one another?" Darby takes the two champagnes Chance is holding and hands one to Dimples. They link arms and Darby pulls her away from me.

"She really is something," Chance remarks.

Nodding, I agree, "Yep."

"I was referring to my wife."

Looking to him, I wink. "I know."

"Don't make me put you back in that chair," Chance teases.

"That's never going to happen," I fire back. "Been there. Done that. Got the T-shirt. I'm all good now."

Chance laughs. "Seems the break was good for you, you're at the top of your game right now."

"Thanks, man. Some guy told me there was a difference between focus and being focused, turns out, he was right." And I mean every word.

"He does sound amazing," he gloats, "but it's great to see you at the top of your game. You are an excellent driver and I cannot wait to see you smash it."

To hear praise like that coming from my hero, it's pretty awesome. I'm on a high right now, but it comes crashing down when someone from behind me growls, "Marshall-fucking-Kerr."

Spinning around I come face-to-face with the last person I expected to see here tonight. "Duncan," I grit through clenched teeth.

"Where's the little whore? I was hoping for a happy reunion," he sneers.

"Stay the fuck away from her," I snarl, my fists clenching by my side.

"Or what? Her cunt isn't that good. A playboy like you can get good pussy just by smiling. How about you return her to me and then you can go back to your cunty ways?"

Stepping forward, Chance stops me by pressing his arm across my chest. "I don't know who you are, but I think you need to leave."

"Fuck you, asshole. You fucking her too?" he spits at Chance and that's when I smell it, he's drunk. Linc catches my eye and a few moments later, security arrives.

"It's time to leave," the burly security guy commands, grabbing Duncan by the arm but he shoves the guard off of him.

"Fuck you," Duncan shouts, garnering the attention of those around us. "I have every right to be here."

"And as the organizer, I have every right to ask you to leave," Linc states, coming over to join us. "Now, before you make an even bigger ass of yourself, I suggest you leave."

"She's mine, just you remember that." He looks over the growing crowd, searching for Dimples. "Eloise, you bitch!" he yells into the room. "You will come home with me. You are mine, now and forever. You will regret the day you ran and hid from me."

I'm seeing red at his threats, no one threatens my woman, no one. Stepping forward, I cock my arm back and slam my fist into his face. Arms grab me from behind, stopping me from swinging at him again. Looking over my shoulder, I see Grayson and Chance holding me back. "He's not worth it, Marshall," Grayson whispers into my ear, just as Duncan yells, "That fucker hit me, I'm pressing charges!"

Chance steps in between us. "Pressing charges for you being drunk and falling over?"

"He hit me," Duncan cries.

"I didn't see anyone hit you." Chance looks around the crowd. "Anyone see someone hit this man?"

A chorus of no and headshakes come from the crowd.

"Fuck you all!" Duncan bellows. He steps toward me and gets in my face. "I hope you crash and burn tomorrow." Shoving me in the chest, I stumble backward and before I can retaliate, he turns and storms away. Muttering ineligible words to himself and shoving people out of the way. I'm searching for Eloise but I can't see her. The crowd parts and a wave of relief crashes into me when I see her standing next to Darby by the exit. The feeling plummets when I see Duncan stop in front of them. Her face pales, she's as white as a ghost and looks ready to collapse.

My feet begin moving and I make my way over to them.

"See you soon," Duncan snickers. "And remember, Eloise, always find you. You are mine, now and forever." He leans forward and kisses her cheek. If possible, her face turns whiter and she stumbles on her feet. If it wasn't for Darby by her side, she'd be on the floor right now.

Duncan steps around her and saunters out of the ballroom.

Reaching them, I pull her into my embrace, kissing the top of her head softly. Her body is shaking with fear. Pulling back, I grip her cheeks in my palms. Her eyes lift to mine but they are vacant and dazed. "Are you okay, baby?"

She tearfully nods and then shakes her head as she tried to swallow down a sob. Closing her eyes, she inhales deeply and then sadly whispers, "Yes. No. I don't know."

Something behind me garners her attention. Lifting her head, she pulls away from my embrace, steps around me, and walks away. My heart drops at her pulling away but when I turn around, I see her walking toward Lincoln.

Quickly, I follow.

"I'm so sorry I ruined your event." Her voice is so timid and I hate seeing her like this.

"Don't worry about that, are you okay?" he asks her, griping her upper arms tenderly, but she flinches at the touch. Linc instantly removes his hands and raises them up defensively. He asks again, "Are you okay, Eloise?"

She shrugs. Stepping behind her, I rest my hands on her hips. She looks at me over her shoulder. "Can you take me back to the hotel, please?"

"Of course." I look to Linc.

He nods. "It's fine go. We'll catch up tomorrow."

"Thanks, Linc."

Sliding my arm around her shoulder, I pull her into my side and we head toward the exit. Before we reach the entrance to the ball-room, Grayson tugs on my arm, halting us.

"Let me make sure the cocksucker is gone before you go out there. Who knows what you'd do if you see him again."

"I'd knock the fucker out," I growl through clenched teeth. Eloise sucks in a breath at my words and I know that's not what she needs. "Yeah, good idea, thanks, man," I tell him and slap him on the back as he walks away.

Turning my attention back to Dimples, I pull her into my chest and wrap my arms tightly around her. She's shaking like a leaf. "He can't hurt you, babe," I whisper into her hair. "I won't let that happen."

"I knew this would happen," she cries into my chest. "He hates to lose and now I've put you and everyone in harm's way. I … I need to get out of here."

"We're going back to the hotel, we'll be safe there."

"No," she shakes her head, "I mean leave, leave."

"Not a chance in hell," I insist, my tone harsher than I intend. "Look at me." She keeps her head down. "Look. At. Me," I demand, enunciating each word, and thankfully this time, she lifts her gaze to mine. "You're not going anywhere without me. You and I are a team—"

"I—"

"There's no I in team, Dimples. Me and you will fight him together."

"And me," Grayson interjects, joining us. "It's safe to head back to the hotel and tomorrow, we'll come up with a game plan to keep you safe."

"No!" she shouts. "I can't do this to you guys."

"It's already happening, Dimples, and I'm not going anywhere."

"Same goes for me," Grayson reaffirms. "I'll see you both in the morning." He walks away, leaving us alone.

"Let's get back to the hotel and then we can talk about this," I tell her.

"I just want to sleep and then tomorrow, I guess I'll figure out my next move."

"We'll figure it out." I place emphasis on the we'll because there is no way in hell I'm letting her deal with this on her own. Dimples and I are a team and teams work together.

Lacing my fingers with hers, we exit The Geraghty and climb into the waiting car. It takes us back to the hotel and by the time we arrive, she's asleep. Scooping her up into my arms, I carry her into the hotel and up to our suite.

Placing her down on the bed, I remove her dress and tuck her under the covers. Removing my suit, I climb in behind her. She whimpers in her sleep and it breaks my heart seeing her like this.

Pulling her into me, she calms down and drifts back to sleep.

Lying here, I watch over her while she sleeps. This woman means the world to me and tomorrow when we chat, I need her to realize that she belongs by my side. I'm not going anywhere and neither is she. Together we will fight this prick and I refuse to let him take her down.

ELOISE

Waking the next morning, I feel like shit. My head hurts. My body is tense from being on edge because my sleep was plagued with nightmares of Duncan attacking me. I also dreamt of Marshall crashing in tomorrow's race because his mind was on me and not the track.

"Morning," my sexy as sin man coos from the doorway.

Sitting up, resting against the headboard, I sleepily mumble, "Morning." I sigh and as I breathe in, I smell coffee. Looking to the side table, I see a hot steaming mug sitting there. "Thank you," I tell him as I lift the mug and inhale. Blowing, I take a sip and sigh in delight as the caffeine goodness infuses my soul.

"How you feeling?" he asks me, I hate the distance between us. Outstretching my arm, I call him over with my hand. Hesitantly he walks over and sits on the end of the bed, out of reach. I pat the mattress next to me.

He climbs up next to me and gets comfy. I place my mug back on the nightstand and snuggle into his side, throwing a leg over and draping my arm across his stomach. "I'm sorry I ruined last night."

"You didn't ruin anything," he replies, running his palm up and down my arm.

"But Duncan did," I pause. "He's not going to give up." Looking up at him, I tell him exactly how I feel. "Wheels, I'm scared."

"I won't let him hurt you." He holds me tighter and places a kiss on my temple. "You mean the world to me."

"You mean the world to me too," I blubber into his chest. "Now that I've found you, I don't want to lose you. I can't lose you. But I'm petrified he's going to take you from me. He took my baby, what if he takes you too?"

"He can try but I promise you, he'll lose. I protect what's mine and you are mine, Eloise Masters."

"Caveman much?"

"If it means you're safe then loincloth me up, baby."

"I wouldn't mind seeing you in a loincloth," I tell him with a chuckle.

"I'll see what I can arrange but for now, we need to meet with Linc."

"Why?" I ask, my heart beating furiously in my chest. My mind running rampant with different scenarios playing out before me.

"He needs to know why last night happened."

"So you're not getting fired?"

"Nope." He shakes his head, then looks serious. "Well, I don't think I am."

"Is he always going to be there waiting in the wings to ruin my life?"

"Nope," he matter-of-factly declares.

"How can you be so sure?"

"Because people like him always get what's coming to them. Mark my words, he'll fall from grace sooner or later and then everyone will know what kind of person he truly is."

"I hope so." I just hope he doesn't take Wheels and me down with him.

"…and that's the story of how I ended up at LTWRC and in Brookvale."

"Fuck me," Grayson utters. Leaning forward, he rests his elbows on his knees and runs his fingers across his scalp, bunching his hair in his fist, pulling and shaking his head in disbelief at my story.

Lincoln, on the other hand, is silent. Staring into space. Finally he looks over to me. "I … I have no words, Eloise. I'm so sorry that happened to you. What can we do?"

"So you're not firing Marshall?"

"Fuck no, why would I do that?" His face scrunched in confusion at my preposterous suggestion.

"Because Duncan ruined your gala last night."

"Exactly, Duncan did that. Not you. Not Marshall … him. Besides, Marshall is the best racer out there, I want him on my team."

"Really?"

"Really, really. Your ex doesn't determine who I hire. I determine whom I hire."

"I … I don't know what to say. Thank you, I guess."

"Nothing to thank me for. Now, do you know how to protect yourself?"

I nod. "Yeah, I took self-defense lessons when I first left."

"Good." He pauses. "Do you know how to fire a gun?"

My eyes widen.

"No fucking way!" Marshall shouts. "No guns."

"What if I want a gun?" I ask him.

He looks to me. "No guns," he reiterates.

"You're no fun," I playfully reply. "But yeah, I agree, no guns. Knowing my luck, I'd shoot myself … or the cat."

"When did you get a cat?" Greyson asks and I can't help but laugh.

"Okay, I think we all agree with the no gun option," Linc confirms. He stands up and walks over to me. He squats down and takes my hands in his, squeezing. "You are one of us now, Eloise. When you're a part of #TeamKerr, we stick together. You hurt. We hurt. Now, honestly, how are you?"

"Honestly?" I repeat. He nods. "Honestly, I'm scared shitless. I knew being with Marshall would expose me but he and I agreed it was a risk we were willing to take because we love one another so much. I just never expected for it to flow on to those closest to him too."

"It's simple, really, we stick together. No one is to be alone, especially you." Linc nods toward me.

"I can't ask you guys to do that."

"You aren't asking, we're offering."

"What about a bodyguard?" Marshall suggests. "I had someone arranged to watch you when I couldn't. I haven't seen a need to need him yet as we've been together twenty-four seven but I think it's time."

"Pussy-whipped," Grayson sasses under his breath with a smirk. Marshall reaches over and smacks him in the arm. "Ouch, you fucker," Grayson whines, rubbing his arm.

"As I was saying, before Grayson rudely interrupted, I'll arrange the bodyguard for you."

"I can't afford a bodyguard."

"But I can," Marshall states, as if he's offering to buy me a coffee.

"No, no bodyguard. I'll be fine. As Grayson said, we stick together."

The three of them bicker like children for the next twenty minutes on what's the best course of action. Sitting back, I watch them intently. They're going round and round in circles as to the best way to protect me. Eventually, I burst out laughing. Full-on belly snort laughing. They all stop and stare at me.

"You okay, Dimples?"

"I … you … you guys are just funny."

"Sexy funny, right?" Grayson flirts with me and from beside me, Marshall growls.

"Yeah, sure, whatever, Grayson. But seriously, don't fret over this. If he wants to get to me, he will. No matter what plan we come up with. He'll do what he wants, plans be damned." Standing up, I take a deep breath. "I'm going to put on my running shoes and go down to the gym. I'm going to get the endorphins pumping and clear my head. You three are going to head to the track for the last practice before tomorrow's race. While you guys are playing race car drivers, I'm going to cook dinner for all of us and tonight we will have a Team Kerr dinner here. We'll have a quiet night before an early bedtime and then tomorrow, Marshall is going to kick ass on the track. Plus, I cannot in good conscience stay in a penthouse suite like this and not cook a meal in that amazeballs kitchen."

Marshall tries to say something but I raise my hand to silence him. "Nope, no arguing. HE will not have control over me and my life. Now, get to the track. No arguments."

Walking into the bedroom, I pull on my workout gear and my shoes. When I return, it's just Marshall in the living area. "Where are Lincoln and Grayson?"

"Gone to get ready. I'm meeting them downstairs in ten." He walks over and wraps his arms around my waist. "You sure you're okay? I can stay."

"I'm fine, really. I need life to continue as normal but I'll be careful. Promise. Duncan will not attack me in public—"

"He did last night," Marshall retorts.

"Just trust me, please?"

"I trust you, it's him I don't."

"Thank you for caring but I'm a big girl, Wheels. Now, get to the track, kick ass in practice and after dinner you can fuck me over the dining table. It's not the green machine but we need to keep the tradition going, even if we improvise of the item we fuck on."

Stepping over to him, I trace my fingertip down his chest before cupping and squeezing his junk. "A squeeze for good luck," I purr, pressing a quick kiss to his lips.

"You're so going to pay for that when I get back," he huskily murmurs. My insides quiver at the thought of what's to come later. I've never had such a visceral reaction to a man like this before but then again, I've never met a man like Marshall Kerr before. He loves with his whole heart and I'm the lucky one on the receiving end of his love.

"I look forward to it." Placing another quick kiss on his lips, I turn and make my way down to the gym. Before exiting the suite, I look over my shoulder. "Knock 'em dead, Wheels." Blowing him a kiss, I step out and close the door behind me.

Heading to the elevator, I push the call button and wait. Even though Duncan has reappeared, I feel strong and confident. I know I can face him if it comes to that but I know him, he doesn't want to tarnish his name so he won't try anything again … I hope.

After a strenuous workout, I head back upstairs. I'm a hot sweaty mess but I feel invigorated and my mind has been reset. Getting those endorphins moving was the best thing for my psyche.

Entering the suite, I flick on the television just as my phone pings with a text. Grabbing a bottle of water from the refrigerator, I walk back to the sofa and collapse onto it.

Picking up my phone, I freeze when I see the text is from *him*. Yesterday, I had the foresight to save his number. A lump forms in the back of my throat as I stare at the message icon. Clicking on it, I read.

PRICKFACE

> You looked gorgeous in the gym just now. I can't
> wait 'til you're back home and by my side.

> Remember, you are mine, now and forever.

Dropping my phone, I stare down at it. Why is this happening to me? I must have done something extremely terrible in a past life. I need Marshall and as if the universe is against me and trying to put bad juju into the world, it's a sports report about Marshall and the race tomorrow.

"Tomorrow will mark Kerr's return to Chicago. The last time he was here it didn't end well for him. Kerr, Marcus Randall and Joe Johnstone crashed with Joe Johnstone losing his life. All eyes will be on Kerr's green #3 car tomorrow. Since returning to the competition, Kerr has only lost one race. Will his lucky streak continue? Or will Chicago once again eat him alive?"

I can't tell him about this threat from Duncan, he needs his head in the game. I'll tell him after the race. If I just hang with the guys and Marshall's family, I'll be safe. *He* can't get me if I'm never alone. *You're alone right now, Eloise,* my inner voice bitchily snarls.

A knock at the door garners my attention. I freeze thinking it's *him* and then I hear, Keri's voice, "Eloise, darling, it's Keri."

"Coming," I shout. Taking a deep breath I swing the door open to greet Keri and Ryan.

"Hey," I offer in greeting, my voice giving away that something's wrong and Keri's mom radar immediately kicks in.

"You okay, Eloise?" she asks, stepping into the suite, kissing my cheek as she passes, Ryan doing the same.

"Yeah," I respond with a smile. "Think I overdid it on the elliptical machine just now." Closing the door, I follow them to the living area of the suite. "It's great you're here actually," I tell her, "I'm going to cook dinner for everyone tonight and I was hoping you could help me."

"I'd love to help," Keri eagerly agrees.

"Great, let me shower and then we can get started."

Leaving her and Ryan, I enter the master bedroom and close the door behind me. This is what I need, to be around people and to keep busy. I just need to get through the race tomorrow and then Marshall and I can come up with a game plan to deal with *him* once and for all.

MARSHALL

Practice today went well, really fucking well. Not once did I freeze out on the track, I thought for sure there'd be some sort of PTSD kind of freak-out considering what happened the last time I was here but nothing. The only thing that would have made the session perfect, would have been bending Dimples over the hood of my green machine and fucking her. At least I can do that later this evening like she suggested after everyone leaves.

When I arrive back at the hotel, Dad is watching television and Mom and Dimples are in the penthouse kitchen together, giggling and cooking up a storm. By the smell of things, she's making my favorite chicken dish. "Is that pesto chicken I smell?" I ask, closing the door behind me.

"It sure is, Wheels."

"I so fucking love you."

"Marshall," Mom scolds me for swearing and my woman teases, "You only love me for my pesto chicken."

She walks, no saunters, over to me, swaying her delectable hips side to side and wiping her hands on a tea towel. When she's in reaching distance, I slide my hand around her waist and pull her into me. "I love you for more than that," I tell her, placing a kiss on her cheek. I quietly whisper, "I love fucking you more than your pesto chicken."

Her cheeks darken and she whispers, "Later," and head nods toward the dining table. My mind goes to a dirty place of feasting on her on top of the table before climbing over her and fucking her senseless. My cock twitches and she winks at me before returning to the kitchen.

"Just grabbing a shower," I inform everyone and I head into the master suite … to rub one out in the shower because my little minx of a girlfriend got me wound up just now and if I'm to sit through dinner with my parents and team, I need to let off some of the built up tension in my nether region.

A few moments later, the door to the shower opens and I'm greeted with a naked Eloise. "Umm, babe, my parents are out there."

She shakes her head and seductively grins. "Nope, I sent them out to get garlic bread and more wine."

"Fuck, I love you," I tell her as I pull her to me and press my lips to hers. She breaks the kiss and drops to her knees. With her eyes on mine, she wraps her mouth around my cock and sucks. "Fuck, I love you," I repeat as she continues to suck me off.

Pulling my dick from her mouth, she looks confused. "As much as that is fucking amazing, I need inside your pussy." Offering her my hand, she places her palm in mine and I pull her up. She throws her arms around my neck and I walk us backward, pressing her into the tiled wall.

With my eyes locked on hers, I glide my hands down her side, slip them under her ass and lift her up. Wrapping her legs around my waist, my cock pushes against her slit.

"Please," she pants, pressing her lips to mine.

Lifting her a little higher, I line my cock up at her entrance and ease inside. We both hiss as she slides down to the hilt. With our eyes on one another, I lift her up and down my shaft. It's slow but fast and ohh so fucking perfect.

Her head drops back and her body stiffens, she's about to come and there is no sight more beautiful. "Eyes on me as you come," I growl.

Lifting her head, she looks deep into my eyes and together we come.

"You are my everything, Wheels," she murmurs, as the last of her release ebbs away. "I love you."

"You are my everything too, Dimples."

Letting her down, we quietly wash ourselves, watching each other as we soap up. "If you keep looking at me like that, I'm going to fuck you again."

"Later, once everyone is gone we can."

Stepping to me, she places a quick kiss on my lips and steps out of the shower. Through the steamed-up glass, I watch her dry off and re-dress.

By the time I'm changed and enter the living area, everyone is here. Everyone has a glass of wine in hand and I have water, the night before a race I refrain from alcohol. Linc used to ban sex too but since Dimples that rule has become moot.

She's quiet tonight, actually everyone is. I think it's because of the track we're at, this is where it all changed. The closer we get to the start of the race, the more my mind races—pun intended.

"We need more wine," Dad states after dinner.

"I'll go, none of you will get served since you're all three sheets to the wind."

No one comments on my dig which surprises me. Grabbing my wallet, I kiss Dimples on the cheek and head out to get more wine.

There's a liquor store across the road so I don't have too far to go. On my way back, someone steps out from the bushes and stops me in my tracks. Looking up, I'm shocked to see Duncan.

"She's not yours," he spits at me.

"She's no one's," I retort. "Eloise is her own person."

"She's mine you fucking prick," he snarls. "She'll be back in my bed before you know it. Mark my words. Once a cunt, always a cunt. Just you watch, she'll come running back to me."

"And why do you think that?"

"Because I always get what I want. I had her once and I'll have her again."

"You really are an egotistical prick."

"Takes a prick to know a prick," he throws back at me.

"Whatever." Stepping around him, I go to leave but he reaches out and grabs my arm. "Enjoy the little time you have with her."

Reefing my arm free, I watch as he walks away. He turns to face me. "Enjoy the ride tomorrow." And with his hands, he mimics an explosion and murmurs, "BOOM!"

Standing here, I watch him walk away but his last comment plays on my mind, *Enjoy the ride tomorrow. BOOM!* He wouldn't sabotage me, would he?

"There you are," Dimples exclaims with a smile, joining me on the sidewalk. "We thought you'd gotten lost."

"Not lost, just taking my time." I look behind me to make sure Duncan's gone, and thankfully he is.

"You okay?"

"Yeah, just a little anxious about tomorrow." And by a little, I now mean a fuckton after my run in with Duncan.

"You've got this, babe."

Staring at the woman who has become my everything, I realize she's right. I do have this, I need to take a page from her book and not let this fucker get in my head … famous last words.

MARSHALL

Waking this morning with a naked Dimples in my arms immediately put me in a good mood. The wake-up blow job followed by more naked snuggles increased that happiness, but it all came crashing down with a knock at the suite's door.

Slipping out of bed, I place a kiss on my sleeping angel's temple and answer, it's the concierge with an envelope with my name.

"Good morning, Mr. Kerr. This was just dropped off for you."

"Thanks," I reply, taking the envelope from him.

Closing the door, I open it and pull out the sheet of paper. One word is written in black marker.

A feeling of unease washes over me as I stare at the menacing piece of paper in my hands.

"Who was that?" Eloise asks, stepping into the living area.

"No one," I lie. "Coffee?" I ask, changing the topic and slipping the piece of paper into my pocket.

"Coffee for me. Smoothie for you," she declares, walking into the kitchen swaying her ass side to side. Taking a seat at the counter, I watch her sashay around the kitchen. Her silk robe barely covers her butt, giving me the slightest and most perfect view of her naked ass. My cock likes the idea that she's naked underneath, or is she wearing a G-string?

"Are you naked underneath that?" I ask, leaning forward a little to get a better look at her delectable ass.

"Maybe." She shrugs and bends down to grab the blender from the lower cabinet and halle-fucking-lu-jah, I'm met with a view of her bare ass.

"Babe, really? You know I don't have time to fuck you this morning."

"Not even a quickie?" she throws over her shoulder, sliding the silky material up her thigh. My cock is rock fucking hard now.

"Linc will fucking kill me if—"

"Too fucking right Linc will," the cockblocker himself says, letting himself into the suite.

"How the fuck did you get a key?"

"Eloise."

Looking to her, she shrugs. "Smoothie?" she deflects. Picking up the knife, she begins to chop up fresh fruit from the bowl on the countertop.

"Please," he replies, taking a seat next to me.

"I'll make the smoothies," I offer, standing up and walking around the counter. Taking the knife from her, I lean into her and whisper. "You, Dimples, need to put some clothes on."

"First time you've ever said that to me," she teases, popping a strawberry into her mouth.

"It's a shock for me too, babe, but no one," I glare over at Linc, "no one gets to see your bits except me."

"You're such a spoilsport," Linc huffs, while at the same time, Dimples cheekily adds, "I thought friends showed friends their bits?"

"I like that plan," Linc teases.

"Don't make me kill you," I threaten, pointing the knife in my hand at him before I go back to chopping the fruit. "You. Clothes. Now," I growl to Dimples. "You," I point the knife in Linc's direction, "don't fucking move and keep your eyes on me."

They both laugh, but thankfully, they both do as they're told. I really don't have time to clean up a murder before my race today. This interaction just now, took my mind off the piece of paper and foreboding note currently burning a hole in my pocket.

Before I know it, it's time to head to the track. Eloise is going to head over with Mom and Dad later this morning. I hate leaving her alone but she promises me that she'll stay in the room until it's time to head to the track. I trust she'll do that, she takes her safety just as seriously as I do. I just don't trust that the fucker won't try something when he knows I'll be preoccupied with prerace prep.

Kissing her goodbye, I hug her tighter than usual and hold on for longer. Pulling away, I follow Linc out of the suite and we head downstairs to meet Grayson.

As soon as we step out into the sunlight, I'm accosted with paps and reporters throwing questions at me. Camera flashes flash, blinding me and lighting up the already bright day.

"Marshall, are you worried about crashing again?"

"Are you nervous about today's race?"

"Is Eloise getting back with Duncan Montgomery?"

That last question stops me in my tracks. "Excuse me?" I growl. "She will never go back to that fucking asshole. Over my dead fucking body she will."

"Care to elaborate?" the reporter asks.

"No, he doesn't," Linc growls, "we need to get to the track."

He drags me through the crowd and into the car, Grayson is already behind the wheel and ready to pull away.

"You know you don't encourage them," Linc snaps. "Ignore. Ignore. Ignore. Have you learned nothing from Jaxson over the years when it comes to personal shit?"

"Sorry," I bite back, "but that fucker is in my head right now."

"Well, get him out," Linc berates. "You need your A game today, Marshall. All eyes will be on you today, waiting to see how you go. Yesterday went well but it was only you out there. Today there will be others and you need to focus."

"But—"

"No fucking buts," Linc growls, "don't make me pull you from the race. If I for one second think your head's not in it, you're out."

"Fine," I snap at him, crossing my arms like a petulant child. "I'll behave and I'll get my head in the right frame of mind before the race."

"Good," he hisses and then silence fills the car, except for Metallica singing about fuel burning quietly in the background.

Linc is right, I need to focus but I have so much shit whirling through my head right now it hard. The crash. Eloise. Duncan. Eloise and Duncan together. Eloise leaving me. Duncan killing Eloise. The note. I need to get my head in the game, otherwise I'm fucked and not in the good naked sexy way.

It's too bad I didn't listen to Marshall from this morning because I was off my game from the moment I arrived at the track. The note was weighing heavily on my mind and even though I checked the car, twice, for tampering, it did nothing to ease my anxieties.

As soon as I pulled onto the grid, I was fucked. From the get-go, I drove like shit and each lap progressively got worse. Hell, ten-year-old me could have driven better than I did today. My head was all over the place and it showed in my racing because I lost and I didn't just slightly lose, I was fucking annihilated out there. How I didn't end up in the wall is beyond me, guess someone was watching over me out there today.

I'm in a foul mood. Snapping and growling at everyone. I'm being a right royal asshole, not even a hug or kiss from Dimples eases my shithouse disposition. The gem that she is, she tells everyone I need a night alone and no surprises, everyone happily, and eagerly, agrees to not have to spend time with me.

We return to the hotel and she drags me into our suite, not letting anyone talk to me. She's like my own sexy as hell bodyguard. We enter the suite and it's just the two of us.

Walking over to the window, I stare out at the lake and sigh in frustration. Dimples walks over and wraps her arms around me from behind. "What can I do to make this better?" she asks, placing a kiss on my back, trying to relax me.

"Nothing," I snap in anger. "I lost. End of fucking story." I smack my palms against the window in frustration.

She pulls away from me and immediately I feel her loss. "There's always next time." She tries to calm me down but I'm too worked up. Resting her hand on my shoulder, she squeezes in a way that normally would have my skin buzzing and my cock springing to life, but right now, all I feel is anger at my annihilation out there today.

"No!" I scream. Grabbing her hand, I throw it off me. "I fucking lost, Dimples. I don't lose but I lost because *he* got into my head. *He* fucked me up and I lost because of him!" I shout at her.

"What do you mean he got into your head?" she quizzes and her question, innocent as it is, pisses me the fuck off.

"As if you don't fucking know," I spit at her.

Turning away from her, I kick the ottoman in anger and it flies across the room. Hitting the wall with a thud.

Eloise shrieks and when I look back at her, she's cowering and trying to hide herself behind the sofa. Straight away, I feel like a dick for my outburst. "Shit," I grumble, running my hands through my hair. I'm about to apologize for being an asshole, but what she does next completely shocks me—she stands up for herself.

Standing to full height, she steps around the sofa and stalks over to me. She pokes me in the chest and berates me. She calls me out on my childish behavior. My little spitfire stands up for herself and shows me exactly how strong she is.

We bicker back and forth but all I can focus on is pressing her into the floor-to-ceiling windows and fucking her from behind. Her tenacity and seeing her so feisty has my cock tenting in my pants. But even I know now isn't the time for sex, though I cannot stop the vision in my mind playing out.

Her words snap my attention from fucking to focusing. "… when I come back up here, if your head's no longer up your ass, we can go out for a nice dinner." *Shit*, I have no fucking clue what she just said to me but the fact she's leaving, isn't a good sign.

Before I can reply, she walks out of our suite, slamming the door behind her. Leaving me to feel like a complete and utter jerk for taking my loss out on her. *I'm such an asshole.*

ELOISE

When he kicks the ottoman, I scream in fright and I'm taken back to the mansion and my time with *him*. I watch Marshall transform before my eyes but as quickly as the anger appears, it dissipates. I know he feels like an ass and so he should, but I made a promise to myself that I'd never let a man treat me like a piece of shit ever again.

This surge of adrenaline spikes through my body. I stand up from my hiding place behind the sofa and stalk over to him. Lifting my hand, I poke him in the chest and I tell him exactly how I feel. "Don't you dare use me as a punching bag," I spit at him, anger pouring through my veins.

"I never laid a hand on you," he defensively retorts, his tone even, quiet and laced with hurt.

"Emotionally," I snap. "No man will ever, E-V-E-R use me as an emotional or physical punching bag again. I know you're hurting and angry right now, but it's not my fault you came in last." He growls at the mention of his loss. "It's just a race and there's another one around the corner. Cut yourself some slack. This time last year you were in a wheelchair, actually right this second you were unconscious in the ER. No one thought you'd ever race again, not even you. So the fact that you are makes you a winner already."

"But—"

"No buts, Marshall, it's a massive achievement. Focus on that and tomorrow, come up with a new game plan with the team.

Then after the next race, you'll be up on that podium again. You can't win all the time, no one is that perfect. Now, I'm going down to the bar. I'm ordering a big-ass margarita and when I come back up here, if your head's no longer up your ass and you've cooled down, we can go out for a nice dinner."

Straightening up, I walk toward the door, my heart racing for standing up for myself. A part of me is waiting for the shove or punch for speaking out of line to come, but it doesn't. The door clicks closed behind me and I let out the breath I didn't realize I was holding.

With my head held high, I walk over to the elevators. As I wait for the car, I remember that Marshall isn't *him*. He'd never hurt me like that. He's just disappointed right now and frustrated. And I get that, I do but I refuse to let him take it out on me. Never again will I allow anyone to have power like that over me.

Walking into the bistro, I head to the bar. Taking a seat, I order my margarita and while I'm waiting, someone sits next to me. Looking over, I smile when I see it's DD. Before we can say anything the barman places my big-ass margarita in front of me and I smile at the deliciousness before me.

"Ohh, I'll have what she's having," she tells the barman. He nods and goes about making her drink. "Wanna talk about it?"

"How did you know?" I question.

"Marshall reminds me so much of Chance when he was younger."

"A pretentious conceited ass?" Taking a sip of my drink, I watch as DD laughs.

"Close, I gave Chance the nickname PEN—presumptions, egotistical neanderthal—when we first met, but underneath the PENness is the man I fell in love with and I wouldn't change a thing."

"I know what you mean. I love Wheels with all my heart but sometimes I just want to smother him with a pillow," I confide to her.

"That," she points to me, "that right there, is the definition of true unconditional love."

We both fall silent and I process her words. My phone pings with a text, breaking the silence that's fallen between the two of us. Expecting it to be an apology from Marshall, I unlock without looking at the screen, but when I read the text, my eyes widen.

PRICKFACE

Your tits look phenomenal in that top. Can't wait to fuck them

ELOISE

Leave me alone.

PRICKFACE

Remember, you are mine, now and forever.

You WILL be leaving Chicago with me.

…and I always get what I want

"Are you okay, Eloise? You look like you've just seen a ghost."

"No, no, I'm fine. Just a little light-headed. That drink is strong," I lie. I need to get out of here and away from Darby. If he's here, I can't put her in harm's way. Grabbing my glass, I chug back what's left. "Thanks for the chat, DD, but I think I need to get back to Marshall."

Without waiting for a reply, I stand up and race away from her.

Walking to the elevators, I see there's a huge lineup. I can't wait, I need to get out of here. I need Marshall. I need him to make me feel safe. I just need him. Spotting the sign for the emergency stairwell, I head down the corridor toward it.

Pushing the door open, I enter. These places always give me the heebie-jeebies and when the door slams closed behind me, I jump in fright. Shaking my head, I start walking.

I'm five flights up when I begin to regret my decision, especially since we're on the nineteenth floor. Taking a deep breath, I continue up.

"Well, well, what do we have here?" Turning around, I look down and see Duncan standing on the landing below me. I was so in my head, I didn't hear anyone else enter the stairwell.

My eyes widen in fear as I stare into the evil eyes of the devil himself. He begins to walk toward me. I shuffle backward, my back hitting the wall. I should turn and run but fear has frozen my limbs.

He comes to a stop in front of me. I can feel his breath on my face. Anger radiates from his body.

"L-l-l-leave m-m-m-e a-a-a-alllone," I stutter.

"Never!" he grunts, "you are mine, Eloise."

"No, I'm not," I timidly state.

SLAP "Yes, you are."

It's been a while so I didn't see the hit coming. My cheek begins to burn and tingle, a sensation I haven't felt in a very long time. But this time, rather than cowering in fear it lights that fuse inside of me and gives me the courage I need to once again stand up for myself.

"Fuck you, Duncan," I throw at him. "You never loved me. You loved the idea of me but you never loved me."

"And racer boy does?" he taunts.

"Yes, he loves me, flaws and all."

"And there's a fuckton of them, sweet cheeks. You'd be nothing without me, nothing. It's time you came home and paid me back."

"I'd rather be dead than leave with you."

"That can be arranged." **SLAP** "After all, you do have a habit of falling down stairs."

Memories of that day come flooding back to me. My breath hitches in the back of my throat and my hand instinctively goes to my belly. Glaring at him, through clenched teeth, I snarl, "I fucking hate you."

"Hate fucks are always the best fucks. Whadda ya say? A quick hate fuck here for old times' sake?

"I'm not fucking you ever again and there's no way in fucking hell that I'm going anywhere with you."

WHACK The punch comes out of nowhere. My head flies to the side and immediately I taste copper in my mouth. Covering my jaw, I look back to the man I once loved and see nothing but a monster. How I was ever in love with him, I will never know.

"You are my fucking fiancée and you are coming with me. Don't fucking make me angry, Eloise."

"I'm not your fucking fiancée," I spit through gritted teeth. "You don't do to the one you love all the things you did to me."

"What did I fucking do?" he yells, his voice echoing in the stair-well. Closing my eyes I cower, but that was a mistake because he lashes out while I'm not paying attention.

SLAP

My head flies to the left. "I gave you a roof over your head."

SLAP

My head flies to the right. "I fed you."

SLAP

My head flies to the left again. "I fucked you."

SLAP

My head flies to the right again. "I gave you a child for fuck's sake."

SLAP

SLAP

SLAP

My head flips back and forth as the hits continue.

Through my tears, I stare at him, his anger is palpable. No matter what I say or do, I'm going to die. I feel it in my bones. So I go for it. "You took that child from me," I cry, hitting him in the chest with my finger. "And as much as I mourn the loss of my son or daughter, I'm fucking grateful because they don't have to grow up with you as their father."

My words piss him off.

He roughly grabs my upper arms and begins to slam me repeatedly into the wall, my head colliding with the cement. My vision begins to blur and there's a ringing in my ears. He's yelling but I have no clue what he's saying because everything is muffled.

Another surge of energy unleashes and reaching out in anger, I strike and scratch at his face. Raising his fist, he punches me in the stomach and I double. He pulls me up by my hair so I look into his evil eyes.

"Fuck you," I mumble but it comes out a jumbled mess.

"With fucking pleasure." He pulls on my arm and drags me down the stairs. I'm tripping and falling all over the place. Each time I fall, he pulls me back up and continues to drag me down the stairs.

My arm feels like it's going to pop out of my shoulder socket.

Why? Why didn't I just wait for the elevator.

Reaching the last floor, he pauses, opens the door and cautiously looks out. Seeing no one, he drags me out onto a landing that leads down to the basement level of the hotel. "Help," I scream, but my pleas only earn me another punch to the guts.

Reaching out, I grip onto the railing to hold myself up. Gripping my shoulders, he spins me around and glares at me. I've never seen anger on his face like this before. He's angry like when Bruce Banner turns into the Hulk.

Pulling myself free, I duck under his arm and make a run for the door we just came through but I don't get far. He reaches out and grabs me by the hair. He tugs me by my strands, the follicles on my scalp burn. My back collides with his chest. Gripping my upper arms, he spins me around to face him.

His heated breath fans over my face and I see nothing but rage in his eyes. They are glossed over and I know there's no way to reason with him.

He begins to walk me backward and a sinister smirk appears on his face. Suddenly he stops and he slams his lips to mine and kisses me. He shoves his tongue into my mouth and I bite down. Pulling back, he hisses, "you bitch," then in a tone I have never heard before, he singsongs, "Ta-ta."

Shoving me backwards, I teeter on the edge at the top of the stairs and the kicks out his leg. His foot collides with my stomach and I begin to free-fall. My arms flail about as I tumble backward, flipping and flopping down the stairs. From above me, I hear *him* laughing maniacally.

My head collides with a thud on the ground.

My last thought before darkness engulfs me is of Marshall and the unconditional, unwavering, heartfelt love we have for one another.

MARSHALL

The door slams closed behind Eloise with a bang. Shaking my head, I collapse onto the sofa and lean back. Staring at the ceiling, I berate myself for taking the race loss out on her. It was just a race, I lost my fucking shit over a car race.

Walking into the bedroom, I strip off and climb into the shower. The hot water beats down on my muscles, instantly relaxing me. Dropping my head to the cold tiles, I mumble, "I'm so sorry, Dimples."

With a sigh, I soap up and wash myself. Climbing out, I dress in jeans and a black Henley. I know she said she wants to be alone, but I need her to know I'm not *him*. I need her to know that I just had a bad day and I love her unconditionally.

Pulling on my shoes, I head down to the bar.

The elevator takes forever to arrive and finally, I'm on my way down. Walking into the bistro, I immediately spot Darby and Chance at the bar. Walking over I stop next to them. "Hey, have you guys seen Eloise?"

"She left to go find you," Darby informs me.

"Ohh," I reply. "We must have passed each other in the elevators."

Darby shakes her head. "No, she left like ten, maybe fifteen, minutes ago. She got a text, finished her drink and left."

"Who was the text from?"

She shrugs. "Whatever was in it caused her to turn white. She blamed it on the margarita and I didn't think anything of it because they are strong. But now that you're here, it's giving me the chills." She pauses. "Would it have anything to do with the man from the gala?"

"I fucking hope not. I'm going to go back up to the suite and see if she's there. If she comes back, tell her to call me."

They nod and I race through the bar and head back up to the suite. The elevators take forever to arrive and even when I climb in, it feels like an eternity before I reach our floor.

"Dimples, you here?" I yell, as I push the door open but I know she's not here. I can't feel her. "Where are you, baby?" I whisper to myself just as there's a knock at the door.

Turning around, I open it, "Dimples?" I call out as I swing it open.

"What did you do?" Mom asks by way of greeting when she enters the suite. Shaking my head, a laugh escapes me, it's scary how well my mother knows me.

"What makes you think I did something?"

She gives me the 'really' look and cups my cheek. "I know you, Marshall Kerr. You were in a mood after the race and I can only guess how you were acting because I've been on the receiving end when you lose. You act like a toddler who lost a balloon at the fair and is pouting because mommy won't buy you another one."

"I wouldn't go that far, but I said some things that were out of line."

"At least you can admit when you're being stupid. I bet she's at the bar—"

"She was but Darby said she left a while ago and now I don't know where she is."

"Maybe she went for a walk to clear her head and to give you time to pull your head out of your ass." I chuckle. "What's so funny?"

"She said that when she returns after her margarita, if my head is no longer up my ass, then we can go out for a nice dinner."

"Well, let's go find her and we can all go out for dinner as a family."

Family, I love that.

Nodding at Mom, we exit the suite and head back downstairs. We all enter the bistro but still, no Eloise. Returning to the lobby, I look around while Mom checks the ladies' restrooms. I stop midstep when I see Duncan, storming through the lobby. He looks disheveled and his face is bleeding. He looks my way. Our eyes meet. He winks and continues across and lobby and exits the building. "Fucking asshole," I mumble under my breath.

Pulling out my phone, I dial Dimples but it rings until her voicemail picks up. This isn't like her, I know she's mad at me, but Darby said she was coming back to me. "Where are you, Dimples?" I whisper, dialing her again.

"Anything?" I ask Mom as she walks over to me.

"No, it was empty."

"Where could she be?" I question, running my hands through my hair in frustration. We split up again and when we regroup in the lobby ten minutes later, there's still no sign of her. Dad has now joined us.

Behind Mom, I see an ambulance pull up and I watch. A member of staff meets them on the door and then the paramedics follow behind the hotel staff. A feeling of unease washes over me.

"We need to follow them," I tell them. They both nod and we head down the same corridor, only to be stopped by security half way down.

"What's going on?" I ask him.

"Nothing to worry about, sir. If you can please clear the area, that'll be great."

"But—"

"Come on, Son, let them do their job," Dad instructs and he drags me back to the lobby, but we stand where we have a direct view of the corridor. I pace back and forth, waiting and worrying. I just know it's her.

The security guy from before enters the lobby and he clears a path. The paramedics come into view and they are pushing a gurney with someone on it. When I get a clear view of the patient, my eyes widen and my heart stops, the love of my life is on the gurney.

"Dimples!" I cry out.

Racing forward, I push past the security guy and over to her side. I take her hand in mine. "Dimples, baby. I'm here." I kiss her hand. "I'm here baby, I'm here." Looking to the paramedic, I ask, "What happened?"

"And you are?" a police officer asks from beside the paramedic.

"Marshall Kerr, her boyfriend."

"We need to ask you a few questions," he sternly states.

"Is she okay?" I ask the paramedic again, ignoring the officer.

"She's taken a tumble and it looks like she was assaulted."

My eyes widen and well with tears, I failed her. I can feel the heated gaze of the officer boring into me and from the look she's giving, she thinks I did this. Then I remember seeing Duncan waltz through the lobby not long ago. "That fucking asshole," I growl.

"Who are you referring to? Do you know who did this?" the officer throws the questions at me in succession.

"I'm pretty sure it was her ex, Duncan Montgomery."

"Why do you think it was him?"

"I saw him leave a few moments ago, he looked disheveled, was bleeding and had a sinister look on his smarmy face."

"Do you know where we can find him?"

"No, and you better hope you find him first. He comes near her ever again and I won't be held accountable for what I do to that prickface."

"Did you just threaten him?"

"Yep."

"You do realize you're talking to a police officer right now?"

"And do you realize that asshole used to beat and rape this woman and it appears he just beat her up again. Wouldn't you do anything to protect the one you love?"

"Well, yes," she replies, her tone softening for the first time.

"Then I rest my case."

"We need to get her to the hospital," the paramedic interrupts us.

"I'm going with you."

"We still have questions, Mr. Kerr."

"And you can ask them at the hospital. I'm going with her. I'm not letting her wake up alone and scared. I promised her I wouldn't let him get to her and I failed her. This is all my fault."

"Marshall," Mom pipes up from behind me, "this is not your fault."

"It is," I state matter-of-factly.

Looking to the paramedic, I urge, "Let's go."

Without saying a word, we make our way through the lobby and out to the waiting ambulance. Once Dimples has been loaded, I climb into the back with her. I hold her hand and pray like hell she'll be okay. I need her to be okay because I cannot live without this woman.

My heart is fracturing right now and this time. If she doesn't make it, I don't know if it will ever be repaired.

ELOISE

My body is numb yet fuzzy. Everything is muffled, as if I'm underwater.

I feel like I'm floating, it's an odd sensation.

I'm trying to open my eyes but I can't. It like a lead brick is holding them down.

Something squeezes my hand. Faintly I hear a "please wake up baby" and then there's a pressure on my temple … a kiss, someone just kissed me.

A whooshing sound appears out of nowhere and a bright light explodes before my eyes. As quickly as it appears it disappears and darkness drifts in like an early morning fog. My vision darkens again and I let the blackness engulf me.

There's a never-ending beeping and it's grating through my head, causing it to throb. My body aches and there's still that foggy feeling but it's not as strong as when I woke up before.

That pressure on my hand is still there and like before, it doesn't hurt, it's oddly comforting.

Finally I manage to crack my eyes open but I quickly close them. The room is really bright, the lights above burning my retinas. Carefully I open them again and I let my eyes adjust to the light. The room comes into focus, my eyes dart around the room and I realize I'm in a hospital bed.

The pressure on my hand is from someone holding it. They're holding on tight and I find myself smiling at the gesture. Looking down, I see a head of fluffy dirty blond hair resting on the mattress. Their shoulders are moving up and down and I realize they're crying. And then I hear them tearfully mumble, "I'm so sorry I let you down, Dimples. Please wake up, baby. I can't live without you. I need you by my side. I'm better when you're around."

"Marshall," I croak, but it's rough and quiet. He doesn't hear me.

He hugs my hand tighter and lifts it up, placing a gentle kiss on my knuckles. Then he lets out a guttural cry that pierces my brain and heart.

"Marshall," I whisper again, but he's too emotional and lost in his head to hear me.

With all my might, I squeeze his hand. That garners his attention and he lifts his head toward me. He blinks rapidly and mutely stares at me staring back at him. Offering him a smile, his eyes widen when he finally registers that I'm awake. The smile of all smiles graces his tearstained face. "Dimples," he softly whispers, and hearing the brokenness in his voice cuts me deep. "You're awake."

"Water," I rasp.

Letting go of my hand, he pours me a glass and holds the straw to my lips. I take a sip. The coolness of the liquid feels like heaven but all too soon, he pulls the cup away and places is down.

Taking my hand in his again, he brings it to his lips and kisses it again. "I'm so sorry, Dimples," he tearfully repeats. Pulling my hand free, I wipe away the tears on his cheek. "I promised to keep you safe and I didn't. I let you down."

"You didn't let me down, Wheels—" He tries to interrupt me but I give him a look that has him zipping up. He kisses my hand again, it's like he needs the contact and will die without it. "You've saved me in more ways than I can ever voice. You saved me the day you wheeled into me at the center. I just didn't know it then." Taking a deep breath, I continue, "You showed me how to live. You've shown me unconditional, all-consuming, fairy tale love and I will forever be grateful for that. But you know what?"

"What?"

"You love me, fractures and all."

MARSHALL

"**I** do love you fractures and all, just as you love me fractures and all. But, Dimples, he hurt you … again, and this time it was because of me."

She pulls her hand from mine and my heart breaks, then she cups my cheek and stares intently at me. "No," she protests, "it was because he's a psychopath. Regardless of where I was, he was always going to find me and get to me. But you know what?"

"What?"

"When I needed you, you appeared and rescued me. You, Marshall Kerr, you saved me."

"You're my everything, Dimples. Everything." Cupping her cheek like she's cupping mine, I stare deep into her chocolate brown orbs. "You are the best thing to come from my accident, Dimples. If I hadn't ended up in Brookvale, we never would have met."

"I think we were always meant to meet, Marshall."

"How so?"

"A love like we have is inevitable. Somehow, somewhere, our paths would have crossed." She stares at me intently and I can feel the love behind each word she utters and I know that everything is going to be fine.

"That's very poetic of you, Dimples."

"It's the truth. I love you so much, Marshall. I thank the heavens every day for sending you to me." She brushes a tendril of hair off her face and winces. "Ugh, I must look like a hot mess right now."

"You're beautiful, just the way you are," I assure her.

"Did you just Bruno Mars me?"

A chuckle slips out when I realize I inadvertently did. "I could have Meredith Brookesed you."

She thinks about the song, then her eyes widen and she shakes her head. She thinks for a bit and then smiles in that cheeky way I love. "Well, I'd just have to Denis Leary you back."

"Fuck, I love you, Dimples. And FYI, that one is a Marshall Kerr original." Silently I think, *one of these days I'll be Bruno Marsing her again but this time it will be with "Marry You." She's my forever and I'm never letting her go.*

"You're such a dork," she teases. It's so good to see her getting back to her chirpy fun self, seeing her lying there unconscious is not something I want to have to go through ever again.

"Yeah, but I'm your dork."

"Yes, yes, you are. Now when can I get out of here?"

A voice from the doorway interrupts, "Not for a day or two." The doctor attached to the voice enters the room. "I'm Dr. Kelly, how are you feeling, Ms. Masters?"

"Eloise, please call me Eloise." He nods. "I feel pretty good, considering," she advises him and then her eyes widen and she snaps her gaze back to me. "Where's Duncan?"

"Sitting in a jail cell," I tell her. My voice filled with anger, that man deserves to be pummeled like he did to dimples. Jail time is an easy punishment if you ask me.

"Really?"

"Yep, the security cameras caught everything. From the moment he followed you in the stairwell, to what happened in there and in the basement and again when he walked away, leaving you for dead. He's lucky they picked him up because if I had of gotten my hands on him, it would have been me sitting in a jail cell."

"Orange really isn't your color, babe."

"Green is more your color," Dr. Kelly admits with a chuckle. "It's great to see you back on the track. After you were admitted last year, I had my doubts you ever would." I look quizzically at him. "I was the doctor who first treated you after your accident last year."

Standing up, I walk over to him and outstretch my hand to him. "I owe you a thank-you. I was told that the first doctor to treat me did an outstanding job. I'm sorry I didn't seek you out sooner to pass on my thanks."

"No thanks necessary, it's my job."

"Well, either way, I thank you and knowing that you're the one looking after Dimples, I know she's in good hands."

"Speaking of, can you step out so I can check on my patient?"

"He can stay," Dimples assures him.

"Very well." Dr. Kelly nods. "How are you feeling?"

"Like I was pushed down a set of stairs."

"Too soon, babe, too soon."

"Well, how else do I describe it?"

"It hurts here and you point to said hurt area."

"I think I have a good idea on the hurt. Now on a scale of one to ten?"

"About a seven right now."

"I'll prescribe some painkillers for you. You were quite lucky to just walk away with a few cracked ribs and a bump on the head, but I can see a history of—"

"Abuse," I interrupt him, the word comes out harsher than I intended but whenever I think about what that fucker did to her, my blood boils. "That fucker used to abuse Dimples, but thankfully he can never hurt her again."

Dr. Kelly nods and looks to Dimples, and rather than pity, he looks at her with admiration. "Glad to see you got away, relatively unscathed."

"Not sure unscathed is the right word but yes, I did get away. Are there any medical ramifications I need to be concerned about?"

"Not that I can see. You're one of the lucky ones, Eloise."

"I wouldn't call it lucky," I snarl.

"Wheels, I am lucky. Lucky I escaped. Lucky I survived. Lucky I met you. See, lucky."

"I think I agree with her, Marshall." I notice that once again, he gets a goofy grin when he mentions my name.

"What's with the goofy look every time you say my name?"

He laughs. "One of my twins is named Marshall. It's weird treating, well, interacting with an adult Marshall, you remind me of him in more ways than just your name."

"He sounds like a cool kid."

"Cool. Rambunctious. Energetic. He and his brother sure keep my wife and me on our toes."

"He sounds like me as a kid, must go with the name."

"Hopefully, he grows up to be as determined and focused as you are."

"With you as his dad, I'm sure he will be."

A knock on the door interrupts us. "Sorry to barge in." A nurse pops her head in. "But, Dr. Kelly, your sister-in-law is in emergency and she's demanding you, or Dr. Knight, treat her friend. We've assured her that Dr. Cruz is capable but—"

"But Baylor is being Baylor. I'll be right there." He looks back to Dimples. "We'll keep you overnight for observation and tomorrow, if all goes well tonight, you can be discharged."

"Thanks, Dr. Kelly."

The doctor leaves and I walk back over to the bed. She taps the mattress and shuffles over. Climbing in next to her, she snuggles into my side. "Is it really over? He can no longer hurt me?" she timidly asks.

"He's going away for a long time, a very long time. I'll make damn sure of it. I won't ever let him get to you again." I place a kiss on her temple as we lay here and snuggle.

A knock at the door startles us both. "Come in," I yell.

The door opens and the officers from the hotel enter the room. "Ms. Masters, I'm Officer Stickler and this is my partner, Officer Chibbs. Are you up to giving your statement of events from the incident at the hotel?"

She swallows deeply. I take her hand in mine and squeeze. "you can do this," I whisper.

Nodding, she takes a deep breath. "Yeah, I am." Then she proceeds to tell them her version of what happened after she left Darby in the bar. I hate that she was down there because I was being an asshole. And hearing her account makes it all the more real.

"It's all my fault," I admit again after the officers leave.

"No, it's not."

"Yes, it is. If I hadn't of acted like a dick, you wouldn't have been alone and he wouldn't have been able to get you."

"If he hadn't gotten me then, he eventually would have. Duncan doesn't like losing and he wasn't going to stop until I was his again ... or dead."

"I'm never letting you out of my sight," I tell her, placing a kiss on her temple and pulling her closer to my side.

"I think I like the sound of that," she replies through a yawn.

"Someone's sleepy."

"Don't know why when I've been asleep for the last two days ... even if it feels like only a few hours ago I was telling you to pull your head out of your ass."

"My head is well and truly out of my ass now but me being an ass head aside, unconscious and sleeping aren't really the same thing."

She shrugs. "Tomato. Tomahto."

Shuffling down, she rests her head on my chest and hugs me. A few moments later, she's sound asleep. I lie here with her in my arms and watch her sleep. When I saw her on that stretcher, I thought I was going to lose her, but as usual, she showed me just how strong she really is.

Dr. Kelly is right, she is lucky.

That prickface could have killed her and I don't know how I would've coped if that had occurred.

A knock at the door garners my attention. "Come in," I whisper-shout.

The door opens and a tall, stylishly dressed lady walks in. "Hi, I'm Agent Rebecca Barber, I was hoping to have a word with Ms. Masters about her ex, Duncan Montgomery."

"She's just drifted off to sleep," I inform the agent. Carefully, I slide off the bed. Dimples doesn't stir, thankfully. I nod to the door and the agent and I step out into the hallway. "Can I help you with anything?"

"Duncan Montgomery was found dead in his cell earlier this afternoon."

"Good riddance to the fucker," I blurt out. "What happened?"

"It looks like suicide. Mr. Montgomery was being investigated—"

"For what?" I ask her.

"I'm not at liberty to discuss the case. I can tell you, they were going to make an arrest later this week. However, with what went down with Ms. Masters, they brought forward their timeline. They didn't want to take the chance he'd run to avoid the charges in relation to the assault."

"So rather than face up to what he'd done, he took the coward's way out?"

"That is correct. He left a note blaming Ms. Masters for ruining his life."

"That fucker," I hiss just as a guttural scream comes from inside Eloise's room.

ELOISE

The stairwell is dark but I can clearly see the scene before me. Duncan has Marshall pressed against the wall. Marshall's face is covered in blood. He throws him to the ground but Marshall doesn't move.

"Marshall," I cry out. The sound of my voice causes Duncan look at me. There's pure evil in his gaze. He kicks Marshall in the stomach and still, he doesn't move. "You're nothing but a two-bit whore," he spits at me. "And now, he's going to pay for your deceit."

Duncan pulls a gun from behind his back. He points it at Marshall and fires…

…I wake from the nightmare screaming.

Sweat covers my skin. My heart's racing. My body is stiff and rigid with fear. Looking around, I don't see Marshall. Where is he? The panic within increases at the thought of him not being here. The door to my room opens and there in the doorway he stands. "Marshall," I cry.

He races over and envelops me in a hug. Wrapping my arms around him, I begin to sob. "You're … you're okay," I cry into his chest. "He … he shot you."

"Who shot me?" he questions, rubbing my back. My body begins to relax with each soothing rub of his touch.

"Dddddd-Duncan," I blubber. "You were in the stairwell with us and … and he shot you."

"It was just a nightmare, babe. He can never hurt you again."

"What if he gets out? He'll come after me and hurt you. I can't lose you, Marshall, I just can't." I continue to cry into his chest, the thought of Marshall not being here is too unbearable to fathom.

"He can't hurt you ever again," Marshall states.

"How can you be so sure?"

"Because he's dead," he replies matter-of-factly.

Pushing him back, I stare at him open-mouthed and in shock. "Come again?"

"Detective Barber just told me he's dead."

"What?" How? What?" I stammer.

"He committed suicide earlier today," Marshall tells me but his words don't make any sense.

"All because he attacked me?"

"Partly that, but I think it's because he was under investigation by the feds and they arrested him for that too."

"Holy shit." My mouth drops open in shock. "So he really can't hurt you or me anymore?"

"Nope," he states, shaking his head from side to side.

"The Duncan chapter is over?" I question, not quite believing it. "Like really, really over?"

"Yep."

My eyes well with tears and I begin to cry again. Whereas my tears before were in fear, these are in relief and happiness. "I never thought I'd be free of him. I always thought I'd be looking over my shoulder, waiting for the prickface to strike again."

"You're free."

"I'm glad he's dead," I honestly voice and then I scoff. "I'm a bad person for thinking that."

"You are the least bad person I know, babe. He reaped what he sowed."

"What do I do now?"

"Whatever your heart desires." He pauses. "But I think the detective still needs to speak to you."

Nodding, I whisper, "Okay."

He climbs off the bed and returns with the detective. She asks questions. I answer what I can. I don't know anything about his business so I'm not much help. Once again, I have to retell the story about our relationship and the abuse but knowing he's no longer alive, it's easier to tell my side.

Knowing he can no longer hurt me, or those I love, is a massive relief.

The detective leaves and a few moments later, there's another knock at my door. Looking up, I smile when I see Miles standing in the doorway. "Miles," I cry out to greet him. I try to climb out of bed to say hello but I wince in pain.

"Eloise, look after yourself, dear."

"You sound like, Marshall," I complain.

"Babe, you were just attacked and knocked unconscious, I'm allowed to be worried and fuss over you."

"You should listen to him," Miles agrees.

"Why are you two ganging up on me?" I whine.

"It's not ganging up when it comes from love," Marshall responds with a smirk. Miles nods in agreement as he walks over to the bed.

Reaching out, I take his hand in mine and squeeze. "How are you?" I ask him.

"I should be asking you that. If I had known he was going to do that, I never would have stayed out in the car. I failed you again, Eloise."

"No, Miles," I say, shaking my head. "This is not on you, it's all on him. You know what he was like, he hated to lose. No matter what you, or you," I look to Marshall beside me, "tried to do, he was going to get me one way or another."

"But—"

"No buts," I interrupt Miles and the look on his face hurts just as much as the hits from *him* did. "It's done and he can't hurt me anymore."

"What if he gets out?"

Shaking my head, I tell him. "He's dead, Miles."

"Come again?"

"He killed himself this morning."

"Gutless bastard," Miles scoffs and then he laughs. "Guess I'm out of a job now."

"Miles," I cry.

He raises his hand. "It's fine. I think it's time I retired. I'm too old to work for another asshole like him."

"You're a spring chicken," I tease.

"If by spring you mean old, then yes, I'm a spring chicken." He pauses. "I hear California is a nice place to retire."

My eyes widen. "You're going to move there?"

"Not there, there, it's too busy for me but I hear Palm Springs is quite nice."

"Really?" I ask again, my voice a few octaves higher.

"Well, I need to be close by for when you two make me an honorary granddad."

"Whoa," I say, holding my hand up in a stop motion. "Getting a bit ahead of yourself there."

"Poppy Miles, I like it," Marshall jokes

"Are you two crazy? I'm not even pregnant and we're not married."

"Never say never," Marshall informs us, and at the thought of marrying him and having his child, my belly fills with excited butterflies. Their wings flapping with joy.

"You two need to stop ganging up on me ... I'm not sure I want you two hanging out together."

"Tough," Miles states. "I kinda like racer boy. He's good for you."

"And I kinda like Miles too, he's pretty awesome ... for an old guy," Marshall teases.

"Ease up on the old or I'll take back my praise."

"No take-backs."

"Oh My God, you two are like children."

"You love us," Marshall nonchalantly informs us.

"Lucky for you two that is true." A yawn breaks free and I cover my mouth. "Sorry."

"I better let you rest," Miles tells me, and I become sad at the thought of him leaving. "I'll pop back tomorrow and see you." And those seven words ease my concerns.

"I'd like that, and, Miles?"

"Yes, dear?"

"Thank you for ... just thank you."

"You're welcome." He leans down and presses a kiss to my temple. "I'll see you tomorrow."

He leaves and I find myself grinning. I didn't realize how much I missed him and now that *Prickface* is gone, Miles and I can be friends.

After a toilet break, Marshall and I lie in bed together and talk about the future. I haven't looked to the future in so long, I was always just trying to survive until the next day but then I met a man who was fractured, just like me, and together we helped repair the cracks.

Marshall is the glue I needed and with him by my side, I know I can survive any new cracks that may appear. I'm fractured no more.

EPILOGUE

MARSHALL

…four years later

Standing on the podium, I raise the trophy above my head … for the fourth time, and like always, the crowd goes wild. Looking over to the side, I see Dimples with Mom, Dad, Grayson and Linc. The joy on her face mimics mine. Not only did I just win the series championship, again, but today, after my win, my beautiful, amazing wife told me she's pregnant. That news was even better than winning the championship.

And yeah, I said wife. Dimples and I got married while in Australia during the off-season earlier this year.

Grayson, Dimples and I were down under catching up with Saxon. It had been a few years since we'd seen him in person and a trip to Australia was the perfect excuse to see our third amigo, plus Australia is a gorgeous country. Apart from the fact that anything that moves can kill you and all the dangerous animals.

One night while on the Gold Coast, Saxon started ribbing me about slapping a ring on her finger. I turned to Dimples, took her hand in mine and as I gazed into her chocolate brown eyes, I knew I wanted to marry her. So finally, I Bruno Marsed her and I said, I wanna "Marry You." Without missing a beat, she said yes and we were officially engaged.

That night, the four of us celebrated our engagement with waaaaay too many beers and while in our drunken state, Grayson suggested we should do it while in Australia.

So we did.

We found a minister to officiate and we got hitched on the beach later that week, just the four of us. Technically it's not real as we didn't sign any papers, but semantics. As soon as we returned to the States, we went to the county courthouse and we made it official, but we will always call the day we had our ceremony in Oz as the day we got married.

Dimples and I are a powerhouse team. She took over my PR from Jaxson, and together we're going to take over the world. Margaret from WtB is still a thorn in our side, but there's nothing Dimples and I can't handle together.

As I stand here on the podium, I gaze at my wife and grin. I can't wait to see her belly swell as our baby grows inside her. If it's a little girl—God help me—but I hope she's as tenacious and strong as her mommy. And if it's a little boy, I want him to be courageous and adventurous like me.

Dimples came into my life when not only was my hip fractured but my soul too. She put me back together piece by piece, repairing the fractures, inside and out. She's my everything and I cannot wait to grow old with her and our family.

THE END!!!!

PLAYLIST

Falling - Harry Styles
Forever - Lewis Capaldi
Whatever It Takes - Imagine Dragons
Clocks - Coldplay
Cars - Fear Factory
Lay Me Down - Sam Smith, John Legend
Without Me - Halsey
Sad Song - We the Kings feat. Elena Coats
Grenade - Bruno Mars
Paradise - Coldplay
Danger Zone - Kenny Loggins
Enter Sandman - Metallica
Fuel - Metallica
Careless Whisper - Seether
Smooth Criminal - Alien Ant Farm
Tainted Love - Marilyn Manson
Sweet Dreams - Marilyn Manson
Lonely - Noah Cyrus
Sign of the Times - Harry Styles
Another Brick in the Wall - Korn
Hallelujah - Theory of a Deadman
Numb - Linken Park
Life is Beautiful - Sixx:A.M.
Torn to Pieces - Pop Evil
Everything - Lifehouse

Waves - Dean Lewis
Stereo Hearts - Gym Class Heroes feat. Adam Levine
Rise - Jonas Blue
Hold On - Chord Overstreet
All Night Long (All Night Long) - Lionel Ritchie
Bruises - Lewis Capaldi
Comfortably Numb - Pink Floyd
Bad Day - Daniel Powter
Let You Down - NF
Just the Way You Are - Bruno Mars
Bitch - Meredith Brooks
Asshole - Denis Leary
Marry You - Bruno Mars
Piece by Piece - Kelly Clarkson

This playlist can be found on Spotify.

ALSO BY DL GALLIE

STAND ALONES

Antecedent

Doc Steel

Oops

Off the Books

Deck…the Balls

Secrets and Sunrises

Always in the Cards

The Christmas Ornament

Before the Ashes

After the Ashes

Love Me Like You Do

Never Let Me Go

Seven Nights

Seven Kisses

PUCKING NOVELS

I Pucking Hate That I Love You
A Pucking Good Christmas
I Pucking Hate That You Love Me
I Pucking That To Love You
It's Pucking Fake

...and a few pucking more

FALLING NOVELS

These men make it hard not to fall for them

Falling for Dr. Kelly
Falling for Dr. Knight
Falling for Agent Cox
Falling for Agent Cruz

Falling: The Complete Collection

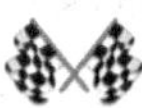

LORDS OF CRESTWOOD PREP

Co-write with Tara Lee

Thatcher
Reign
Hendrix
Saint

ABOUT THE AUTHOR

DL Gallie is from Queensland, Australia, but she's lived in many different places all over the world, including the UK and Canada. She currently resides in Central Queensland with her husband and two munchkins. She and her husband have been together since she was sixteen, and although they drive each other crazy at times, she couldn't imagine her life without him.

Shortly after her son was born, DL began reading again. With encouragement from her husband, she picked up the pen and started writing, and now the voices in her head won't shut up.

DL enjoys listening to music, drinking white wine in the summer, red wine in the winter, and beer all year round. She's also never been known to turn down a cocktail, especially a margarita.

FACEBOOK ~ INSTAGRAM ~ BOOKBUB

GOODREADS ~ WEBSITE

dana@dlgallieauthor.com